I am William McGuire

and other unexpected stories

Author of:

Hound - a mystery
(Small Beer Press)

Slepyng Hound to Wake - a mystery
(Small Beer Press)

The knight's tale - a story of the future

The Dark Heart of Night: a novel

John Finn - a mystery

A Republic of Books:
the novel and a play with handy footnotes

I am William McGuire and other unexpected stories

Biedermeier: identity, both mistaken and true

I imagine my salvation: a Menckenesque

A Young Man From Mars: the future retold

I am William McGuire

and other unexpected stories

by Vincent McCaffrey

Avenue Victor Hugo Books

Lee, New Hampshire

I am William McGuire
and other unexpected stories

* * *

isbn 978-0-9897903-6-9 (paperback)

An eBook edition is available of
I am William McGuire
isbn : 978-0-9897903-0-7 (eBook)

* * *

As always, the typos are my own speciality and are in no way the fault of those friends who helped to get the manuscript in shape. And once again, special thanks goes to Pamela Siska for saving me from many a presumptive error, and Cord Blomquist for helping me bring together the various technical elements.

Dedicated respectfully to those
who have passed this way before,
and now to their children.

Contents

*

I am William McGuire

The adventures of a Neanderthal in the 21st Century

by B. McGuire

The true story of William McGuire, an innocent in an age of cynicism, and a stranger in a strange land, who must find his own way in *Homo sapiens* society, as told by himself.

1.

I am William McGuire. I would say, 'Call me Bill,' in the vein of Mr. Melville and his Ishmael, but it would make a worse joke of all this from the start. It is enough that my life has already been made into a farce.

I am going to tell some things you should not know. Private matters really. But I am going to tell you what I can of these things because they are already a part of what many might think they know, and most of that is untrue. Simply, this is the story of what has actually happened. It's a history that is not so complicated, in the end. And this is an effort to unmake that joke.

Please forgive the gaps. My notes have never been kept faithfully. What I offer here are those parts I think relevant. But to appreciate what I want to tell you now, I believe you should learn all of what follows, just as I did. There is at least some order to that process. I make no pretense of being a reporter.

My father, as it were, is Edward H. McGuire, a Professor of Microbiology at Harvard University, Emeritus. My mother, Mary Eleanor Rice, was for many years a Professor of Linguistics at MIT. Myself? I am nothing of the sort. I did graduate from Boston University with a degree in history, but only just barely and after seven years. I dropped out twice along the way. You may have seen something about me in the news on a few occasions before. But none of that matters now.

A little more than a year ago, I received a call from my mother. It was early in the morning and I work late so I was groggy. She wanted to see me. Her tone was grave. I didn't argue. She had been in remission from breast cancer for two years, but that was after two previous bouts, and I had a sense of what she wanted to say.

She was never over-weight, even in her prime, but she looked so horribly thin when she opened the door. I suppose that recognition was on my face. She pursed her lips just a little, in a ghost of the expressions of disapproval she used to direct at me nearly every day. She was wearing a long cream-white robe that revealed the knobs of her shoulder bones and a blue scarf that, without the familiar coal-black hair beneath, made her head look very small. She had been slightly stooped for years, due to osteoporosis I think, from her first cancer treatments. I bent and kissed her on the cheek, but she didn't really move to offer the usual feigned kiss in return. Either she was already too weary to make the effort, or her mind was on what she was going to talk to me about. She always had that kind of focus. Everything else around her became secondary to what was on her brain.

She might have been brilliant. I don't know. I don't really understand the work she did in linguistics. The semiotics as much as the semantics. She has her name on a couple of texts concerning the evolutionary fertilization of biolinguistics by the algorithms of computer languages. Artificial languages seem pointless to me when we cannot communicate in the languages we have. No matter, I suppose.

She stepped aside like I was a visiting repairman and pointed to the couch.

It was a very nice apartment by some standards. Bright. Mostly off-white. Like such extra care facilities always are. Just the one bedroom, living room and kitchen. Her favorite photographs by Maurice Salvo were on the wall. Enlarged in black and white, they made the room feel even colder than it actually was. Most of her books were already gone. Given away. Only the one shelf behind her desk gave hint of what work had occupied her life.

She had never been one for small talk. She started right in even before she sat in the chair by her desk.

She spoke slowly, almost carefully, "I wanted to tell you something."

"Is it about your health?"

"Two things, actually . . . No, I think you know about my health. That's a foregone conclusion, isn't it? . . . No, it's about you. Things you should know about."

Always a bad host, she would have forgotten to offer me something to drink in any case, but she was licking her lips, so I spoke up.

"Can I get you something? Anything?"

3

"No . . . Yes. There is a glass of mineral water on the counter. You can get me that. There isn't much else, I'm afraid. I've been ordering from the service lately. I don't have the energy to cook. No! As a matter of fact, there's half a bottle of scotch I bought the last time I found out I was in remission. There's that, if you'd like it."

I brought her the water. She was never one to drink beer in any case, so I didn't look in the fridge and I poured myself a couple ounces of scotch in a wine glass—the only glass I saw in the cupboard—and sat down again on the couch.

"So, tell me what I should know about myself."

A flinch of an eyebrow. "Everything."

I said, "We can agree on that, at least. But I haven't been doing so well with that project on my own."

"It may not be your fault."

"Maybe. But I'm not one for the blame game. You and Father gave me a lot of advantages in life. I chose my own road. I have to live with it."

She pursed her lips. The criticism implied in my words was ignored.

"I mean that you might have issues you do not understand."

Now, at that instant, my thinking stopped cold. Over the years, there has always been some undercurrent of matters they would not speak to me about. I had formed my own ideas long before, of course.

Some of my first memories were of a small room at MIT, no more than a booth, with no one else and no sound, just the lights and the large colorful buttons, and my mother's voice coming from somewhere I couldn't see. I hated it. I know it was MIT because I remember the walk to the building along the river, holding Mother's hand.

By the time I was fourteen, I was sure I was adopted.

About that same time, I managed to find a copy of my birth certificate. I think it was in Mother's personal file in her closet. My mother had given birth to me by cesarean section at Brigham's Hospital. There was no doubt about that. And my father's name was listed right there on the proper line following hers. But things had been said in strange ways that always seemed to carry another load of mischief, if you know what I mean. Especially when my parents argued.

After they divorced, all that stopped and I had not really thought about it for years.

There were other matters to concern me then. But you have to understand. I was taller than my father by the time I was fourteen. I was twice his weight by the time I was in college. I am not particularly fat. I try to stay in shape. I work at it. If nothing else, out of self-preservation. After I won the wrestling championship my freshman year at BU, there seemed to be something of a sport around town in finding fellows to challenge me. Big guys just make easy targets.

Simply put, I don't look like either of my parents.

I suppose she was probably watching my face. She stopped and looked at me with what passes for pity in her own way. The way she would look at a hungry dog, really. She might take away a totally incorrect conclusion, but she is a good observer. That is the scientist in her, I suppose. After jamming up altogether, my own thoughts were suddenly racing. I knew just then that I was going to learn about the one thing that had always lurked at the back of my mind. Why was I different?

She sighed. That weariness of sound was her habit long before she became ill. "Maybe three things, then. The first is that I am dying. The medical review board has denied my request for additional treatment for the cancer."

What should be said? "I'm sorry. Knowing you, I'm sure you've tried everything you can."

She was shaking her head, as if to say this was not the matter of importance. "Yes. I believe so. Secondly, you should know that you are not my child. Not actually."

I did not say anything to that. I think I just released my own lungful of breath—a lifetime of breath held back, waiting.

"You see, it was just an experiment, to start. You have to understand. Twenty-eight years ago, your father and I were having an affair. He was already a full professor at Harvard then, and married. I hadn't gotten tenure yet at MIT. It was your father's idea that we should try an experiment and I was foolish enough to go along." She paused. I supposed to reflect on the event. "I believe his wife had already refused. He denied that, so it must be true . . . In any case, I agreed to become a surrogate—to carry a child that your father—more your step-father, actually—had essentially invented in his lab."

She had run right to the point. No elaboration. No niceties or detail that might have taken the edges off. No. Not my mother. Right to the point.

"I was an experiment."

"Essentially. Your father knew what he was doing. For him it was not an experiment. It was just a procedure. The experiment was in the result. He thought that would come later."

"But, why?"

"Just to see."

"To play with a human life?"

"It was science. We just wanted to know."

"And you are telling me this now? You're dying, and this is your confession? That you've played with a human life? With my life?"

6

"Well, . . . More than one. We aborted the first. I got cold feet . . . I've always had cold feet, you know. It's especially terrible now . . . But we tried again. Edward was so passionate about it. You have to understand. And I was in love. And curious too. He agreed to get a divorce and marry me if I would agree to have the child. So you were actually a love child! Don't you see?"

The subject of love seemed totally inappropriate to me just then.

"Actually, I don't. If it wasn't for Aunt Jane, I might never have known what love was."

That got her out of her own planned course. She reacted abruptly then. "Hah! Jane Dunne. That stupid woman! She was hired to care for you. Just a nanny! It's always bothered me that you call her 'Aunt.' She didn't really care about you. It was a paycheck. That and the fact that your father wanted to get her in bed, at least once, I believe."

I don't think he ever accomplished that. I am thankful that Jane held him off as long as she did. He would have fired her for good as soon as he accomplished his goal. That's the way Father is. Jane had been my real mother, from the time I was two until I was fourteen.

"You're wrong about that. But then, it looks like you were wrong about a lot of things."

"No! We were right! Your father was right. The experiment worked! We proved that it could be done! Successfully. You were born a healthy baby. You are a healthy intelligent human being!"

What do you say to such blindness?

"That's not science. It is done every day. The old fashioned way. A million times a day, all over the world."

"But in your case, it is."

"Why."

"Because . . . Because you are not of the same sub-species as everyone else."

This was not what I expected, even in the few moments after realizing what they had done. I cannot even tell you what thought was in my brain at the instant she said 'sub-species.' Whatever it was, it was blown away.

"What are you talking about?"

"Your DNA."

"What about my DNA?"

"You're *Neanderthalensis*."

I can hear my voice now. Like it was something overheard in another room. My own mind was that far away.

"Neanderthal?"

"Yes."

What could I have said? I probably didn't breathe for over a minute. It's scary how I can sometimes forget to breathe. She shook her head, shrugged the knobs on those thin shoulders, and shook her head again. She waited for me to say something. And I did finally speak.

"Why didn't you ever tell me before? Didn't you ever think something like this would matter to me? Didn't you tell anyone else? Ever?"

"No! Not unless your father did. Maybe he told one of his young women in the biology department that he was giving hands-on lessons to."

No other question seemed more important.

"But why?"

"Because it was the challenge of the moment. Someone was going to do it first. Why not us?"

"No. I meant why did you keep it a secret?"

"Because it was illegal. Don't you understand? There were laws against such things. There still are. It would have ruined both of our careers if it was ever known."

"Then why do it?"

"It was just the timing. You see, it was not actually illegal when we started. Just discouraged. And your father couldn't believe they would stop him once it was done. He wanted to be the first. He wanted that feather in his bonnet. But come down to it, it was a matter of federal funding for the University. They would have cut off the entire biology department. Hundreds of millions of dollars."

"And now?"

She shrugged again.

"Now it doesn't matter."

"To you. It doesn't matter to you. It's still all about you. And Father. Still! The ethics of what you did doesn't matter to you even today!"

She squinted at me in pained patience, the way she always did to students too slow on the uptake.

"It's not the same now. The labs are so poorly operated at Harvard that they couldn't even attempt it now. It's all proforma. The government tells us what they want to hear and we provide the evidence. There is no excellence anymore. But then —Then! There was still competition! There was a lab in Zurich that was already working with a similar concept. And another at the University of Amsterdam. The Dutch had most of the body of the child found frozen in that glacier in the Caucasus. It was in the papers then. Your father had already purchased viable material from another find—from the Russians, he said. And we never really knew what the Chinese were doing, but I believe it was with something they uncovered in Tibet." She shrugged. "Whatever it was, it didn't come to anything." She shook her head again as if all of that should be obvious. "Then there was the team at the University of Leeds. Rumor had it they finally brought a fetus to term. So you see, when we started, it was a whole new field . . . And then the politics changed. Overnight! The U.N. got involved. There were stories in the papers with an 'artist's conception of the face of the frozen child.' Congress attached a measure to an appropriation bill. And just like that, it was against the law. All that work was suddenly forbidden . . .Your father couldn't just throw it away. It was years of research. He was working on some way around it, but that never happened. So we did it in secret. It was our secret." A smile flinched at her wan cheeks. "I remember we were sitting on the stone wall down at the Charles River late one night. We'd been drinking wine. We were both giggling and fooling around. Your father was talking about winning the Nobel Prize. And I said, what about me? What do I get? He said, 'You get to be the mother of the Nobel Prize!' Well, I jumped right up to object to that, but I slipped and fell in. I almost drowned. Your father jumped in to save me—to save his experiment, actually, but he was useless. An MIT security guard pulled me out. I was in the hospital when they told me that I was pregnant. I didn't even know . . . So we married. And we kept or experiment a secret. Surely, the politics would change again, we thought. Then we heard that the Dutch government had destroyed the fetus at UVA. That would have happened to us, you understand. You would never have been born!"

That was a thought that had some merit.

2.

If he could, my father would have killed me.

He keeps an office at the old Natural History building on the Harvard campus, but he hasn't taught a course in years. I called first to make sure he was there. He wasn't interested in talking about Mother, but I told him there was something he would want to know. He said if I got there before noon, he would take me to lunch in the faculty dining room. They do not serve alcoholic beverages, but a free lunch is always in order, even without a beer. Besides that, a public place seemed perfect for the occasion. He likes to raise his voice, but he's very conscious of what other people think.

He looked as fit as ever. He keeps his hair shorter now that it's gray. He hasn't played handball since his Achilles went, but he rides a bike and swims.

He started his usual patter over the salad bar.

"What are you doing now, Billy?"

"I'm a bouncer."

"A what?"

"I'm a bouncer at a nightclub. It pays the bills."

The disdain barely flickered in one eyebrow.

"You know, I was hoping for more from you. What about all those history courses."

"They helped. They taught me that I don't want to have anything to do with teaching history. It's all a bloody mess."

I filled my plate with a bit more protein, mostly steak and potatoes, and sat down. I couldn't manage any small talk. I went right to the facts that I knew. Always the good poker player, Father took my initial declarations concerning what Mother had said as if I were talking about the weather.

With his chin extended over a mixed fruit salad to close the space between us, he told me "She's lying, Billy. She's always had a problem with the truth."

I showed him the letter he gave her twenty-nine years ago when she agreed to go forward with the 'experiment.' Actually, I showed him a copy, because he did exactly what I thought he would do. He tried to destroy the evidence by wadding it up in the palm of his hand. And then he smiled.

He has always been a charming fellow, if you did not know him.

He took a bite of the fruit salad and said, "If I could, I would have smothered you twenty-eight years ago. Your mother stopped me. You owe her that much."

I admitted another thought, "I'm indebted to both of you, really. I don't regret being alive, even if things aren't the way I want them to be. But what you did was wrong."

He ignored my judgment with another mouthful of fruit and spoke before he'd swallowed.

"I looked for that damned letter a hundred times. I wonder where she hid it?"

"She told me to tell you. It was in the frame behind your degree from Stanford."

"Damn! I should have thought of that. She was the one who had it framed."

Another admission came to mind. "And I don't even know why I'm here now. You're the one person I should never want to lay eyes on again."

"Hemph! Just the perversity of human nature, my boy. You want to see the defendant grovel. But that's not likely, now is it? You know me better than that . . . Is she going to die soon?"

"Yes."

"Well, at least that'll be over with."

"You have no pity." It was not actually a question but a statement. He took it the other way.

"Pity? She's lived a very comfortable life. Pity? What for? I was a ticket to a permanent position at MIT. She got it. Now she's dying and she wants to stick it to me, one last time."

"You are a very cold man."

"No. Practical. My real regret is that I had one chance at fame and immortality. But it passed me by."

"And it never occurred to you to think about me, did it?"

"You? You weren't even supposed to exist. You were an ancient accident. And then, an experiment. It worked. And then suddenly the plan fell apart. Some stupid self-serving idiot politician got himself elected by making what we were doing against the law."

"Aren't you concerned at all about the right or wrong of what you did?"

"Science is not about right and wrong. Science is about knowledge. To make knowledge illegal, that's wrong."

"My life means nothing?".

"That you exist. Yes. But you as a person? No. No more than the few billion other chunks of blood and bone-filled flesh walking around out there . . . Don't look so shocked. You're old enough to know better. You of all people should know better now. We are the species that has only dominated the earth for a mere thirty-thousand years or so. What about your ancestors? The Neanderthal were here for two hundred thousand! Where are they now? Barely a notch on the

13

anthropologic scale. Where is their god? Where are their cares and worries? What of the million moments of final horror in their lives as they were devoured by some creature of the night? What does it mean that you exist? Except for the knowledge that it can be done—nothing!"

I didn't have a lot to say after that. At least I managed to eat my free lunch as he attempted to explain himself.

It is easy to see my father as the villain in all this. He is, after all, responsible for what he did. But I have often believed he should be judged as part of his time and place.

Historically speaking, you cannot go back and fairly convict anyone by standards which were not theirs to begin with. This is not a matter of subjective values. On the contrary, it is the opposite. The values of today are not correct just because they are ours. They must stand on their own. And though I believe it's correct to harshly judge the Roman slave owner, it is not with the sharper edge I would use against the plantation owner in the South of a hundred and fifty years ago. My father caused all of these things that concern me here to happen. But it was certainly within the academic pay-to-play milieu of his moment. He was not alone in his actions. My mother was certainly his accomplice. And, as you will see, there were others.

In 2020, my father was still a young man, but already beyond that period of brilliance that burns so brightly for some in their first years. As his obligations at the university grew, absorbing more and more of his time, he would have been looking for that project which would set him apart. *Homo Neanderthalensis* must have seemed like ripe fruit to an eager hand.

As easily as he tells lies to himself or others, you would have to see his face at the moment of the telling to understand how persuasive he can be.

I said, "I'm just a clone then."

"No!" His face went wild first with irritation at my statement and then with the enthusiasm over what he had done, "I know this is not your field, but try to understand. A clone is just a copy. A copy of a really big file, but just an exact duplicate copy of the DNA of whatever you've got. You are not a copy of anything! You are a recreation of something that might have been. The Swiss—they tried the copy-thing until they were blue in the face. They had some fellow who'd fallen into a crack up in the Alps. Every clone was a failure. Why? Because it's not clock-making. It is life that you're making! Every clone they made was a damned cuckoo clock. Why? Because all life dies. All viable life must die. Your mother is dying. I'll die—We must! It's the recreation that matters. You can't just copy. And after we're dead and no longer able to recreate ourselves cell by cell, our DNA disintegrates over time. The x-rays alone will accomplish that. The Swiss kept trying to repair the damage. A needle in a thousand haystacks multiplied ten thousand times! Before they'd clean up one, another occurred. But if you recreate, that's the key. And you need material from a woman to start with. An X and a Y. An X alone won't do. This is not parthenogenesis! This is fertilization. Not the old fashioned way, I'll grant you, but not far from it! I found the way to remake all the parts from the tissue of that unfortunate boy and bring them together in the womb of a living woman. Your mother. We did it on a computer first, and then, we did it!"

"You are God . . ."

"No. Now don't get carried away. I'm pretty good, but God I'm not."

He was that serious. He could not hear the sarcasm in my voice.

He ate for a moment, grunting his private thoughts at his salad, then looked up. "No. As far as I'm concerned, the experiment is still on-going. I've been keeping notes, you understand. When my race is run, all of it will be in the hands of people who can see to it that it's published. I may not get the glory while I'm alive, but I'll get it in the end. I can at least rest assured of that. And there are things still to be learned." His voice dropped dramatically. "Why do you really think we didn't smother you a long time ago? There are things to learn. We have already established that the *Homo neanderthalensis* mind is as good as the *Homo sapiens*. Maybe better. But one example offers insufficient data to draw any larger conclusion than that you as an individual are capable. And, to my mind, I'm certain you are physically superior. But are there dark secrets still lurking in your genes?" He chewed at a leaf of lettuce too large for his mouth. "For instance, will you be dying a little earlier? There is a theory that your life span is half that of *sapiens*. That might even have been your disadvantage in the contest thirty-thousand years ago. And can you reproduce? That's a question I would love to know the answer to. You've got the juice, but will it do what it's supposed to." He smiled in the way he often did when referring to women. "You know, there is a female . . . Yes. The Dutch. Those tricky Dutchmen. They said they had aborted the fetus they brought to term. That was a lie. I have made inquiries. I've kept my ears open. And I can tell you. I'm certain of it. And maybe another at the University at Chengdu. Maybe . . ."

I got up. I shouldn't have. I should have stayed and heard more of what he knew. He was too happy spilling his secrets to someone he did not have to worry about. But the disgust had risen as a gorge in my throat and I had to stand.

He said, "Sit down, Billy. You're smart enough to handle all this. Don't play games with me."

"Life is not a game."

"Maybe. Maybe not. Look at history. The same damned thing over and over. You'd think we'd learn. But no. Just like baseball. If we get a hit one time out of three, we think we are winners."

"That's not the history I read. The history I read was the struggle to get out from under the whims of people like you."

"Ha! That's a selective reading, to be sure. But however you read it, you are a part of history now. Whether you like it or not."

"I think not. I think now my job in life may be to avoid history altogether."

"That's not in the cards, my boy. I've already seen to that. You exist. Even if you jump in the Charles River today, like your mother once did, by the way, you have existed."

"There are cleaner places to swim."

"What are you going to do now?"

"I don't know."

"You could be famous, you know"

"No, I don't."

"When my study is finally released, I suppose the authorities will want to see you."

"And make me a lab rat in some government basement. That's not going to happen."

Just the thought of that was enough to spoil my dreams.

3.

Aunt Jane is an odd duck. It's her own description of herself, and it fits.

She came over here from England when she was nineteen or so. She'd failed whatever test was required to attend the university she wanted. Her dream was to be the twenty-first century Jane Austen. She thought her chances might be better over here.

Following in the footsteps of her namesake, she never married. She had her boyfriends, of course. I even met a few when I was younger and they would come by the house to pick her up for a date. But she was determined in her ambition.

It was Jane who got me to write. Everyday. When I was no more than three years old, every morning she would sit down and write and I would sit down beside her and pretend I was doing the same. As a consequence, of course, I went in a wholly different direction than the one my parents wanted for me. I was reading very well by the time I was five. My father thought I was going to be a prodigy. They were testing me about once a week at the MIT labs back then. He got me into a local private school for 'gifted children.' But I was already difficult to handle. Jane was the only one who had any real control over me. The private school expelled me within a year. He tried another. Having enjoyed the experience of success I had with the first, I was gone from the second school within three months.

When I started public school again, Jane said, "Do what they say. Go along. It will be easier for you, and them, and you can get home sooner and play."

And that became my philosophy. Go along with it, and get it over with.

Of course, play for Jane meant books. I had learned to read French by the time I was seven. And then German.

At that point my mother stepped in. She was positive she could make a difference. I was indeed a prodigy! The problem was with the subjects my father wanted me to waste my time on. Forget about math! I was a natural linguist! I was packed off to a school in Vermont that specialized in languages. At least for another three months. And then I was back again.

The math was easy. As Father said more than once, "I was one of those fellows who could do the math in my head." And it was the same for the languages. But by themselves, they were boring. Awkward. Inconsistent and pointless, or rule-bound and predictable. It was what you could do with the languages that fascinated me. The fun was in the writing and in getting as close as I could to the sense of things that was in my head.

I said that to my father once. I said, "What is water to you? H2O. A chemical equation. Somehow that excites you. I don't see it. But water! Water may be the most fascinating thing on the earth! It's hard and soft, salty and sweet. How do you describe the difference of color and smell and taste of the water mid-ocean? That's not the 'wine-dark sea,' is it? And then right down there off Long Wharf? That green bilge! Do you remember those summers and the water pooled in the rocks up in Maine? That was sweet and salty both. You thought I was mad when I tried drinking it. And then to throw the changing light of the sun on all that! Or the glow of moon. That's the very substance of life? But H2O? How boring."

He had no idea what I was trying to say. But that was my fault. I just had to find a better way to say it. Or so I believed.

And Aunt Jane was always there. Whatever else she had taken on whenever I was away, she had always made room in her life to spend time with me again when I returned. And with my parents gone most of each day, and off to one conference or another for a week at a time, or just on their own personal pursuits, it was Jane who raised me. "The son I never had," she said to me more than once.

After thinking over what I learned from my father for a day, I showed up at Aunt Jane's little house in Arlington during her morning writing hours so I was sure she would be there. I told her everything straight away.

Her first words were, "I told you that you were different."

"But a Neanderthal, for Christ sake?"

"Don't blaspheme. You are a child of God, like all the rest of us."

"I'm an experiment!"

"Not much of one, I'd say. Your father simply managed to do the hard way what everyone else does for the pleasure of it. But I told you when you were a little boy that you were different—more than just your size or the way you looked. And I was right."

This was no salve.

"What do I do now?"

"Do what you would have done anyway. What difference does it make?"

"He is going to publish his study of me one of these days."

"He would have done that anyway and you would have found out after the fact. Be glad your mother tipped his hand."

Jane is still a handsome woman. I am not sure if she was ever a beauty. Children don't think in such terms. Forgive me, but I've thought a few times over the years: I wish she was twenty years younger.

I said, "Where did you get your confidence? Ever since I was that little boy you told he was different, I have always been astounded by your confidence. Nothing like the arrogance of my parents. No assumptions. No presumptions. Just you on your way and the world folded around you."

"Thank you."

"For what?"

"For saying that. It's always been the way I have felt. At home in the world, so to speak."

"One day—One day I remember my mother telling you that they were letting you go again. I don't remember which time it was. But you didn't argue. You gave me a kiss on the cheek and a wink and slipped on your coat and walked out into the rain—it was raining terribly I remember—"

"I remember the day. Just a little rain."

"And it was as if the sun was shining. Your usual step. The wave. The smile. And you were gone. That's the way I always think of you."

"Good! Keep that. And when I'm really gone, I'll rest easy knowing that's the way I'm remembered."

"Not for your writing? Not for all your unpublished books?"

"Well, certainly, if they ever come to anything, that would be fine. I'm happy enough to have the time to write them, you see. But nobody cares about such things now. It's all slam, bam, thank you ma'am now. If they are ever read, that will be good too. But I will never know about that, will I? What I do know now is that the fellow I think most of in the world has got the right idea of me. For that I am happy enough . . . Here, have some tea and tell me what you think you'll do now."

I hadn't a clue.

"Do you have any beer?"

"It's too early for beer. Have some tea."

I would never tell Jane I thought my life was a joke. As much as she understands, she would not get the humor in that. Jane was, of course, my savior in all of this. She has the steady hand. I had some tea.

She said, "It's a good thing you're not easy to upset. If someone told me I was—well—not exactly what I thought I was, it would put me in a funk, I'll tell you."

The thought was unlikely. "I've never seen you in a funk."

"Well, that's because I go home and sulk. My mother, bless her soul, didn't believe in being depressed. She was a single mom from the time she was sixteen. We lived near an ancient hill fort called Cadbury Castle that some thought had been the seat of King Arthur. It was really no castle at all but just a pile of rocks, but when I was small she took it into her head to earn a little extra by taking tours up and down the hill, and me with her. At heart she was a romantic. She worked her job and took care of me, without a whimper, that I remember . . . Of course she was very religious. I think that helped. That, and the television. She was devoted to the shows. I would tell her, 'Mum, that fellow's a cad. He's going to take advantage of her. You can see that coming, can't you?' And she would say, 'Hush. You'll spoil it.' Funny thing now, when I consider that—maybe it was one reason for my starting to write. To fix those shows up so they made some sense . . . You've heard me go on about Ms Punaji. Our neighbor. That dear woman lived in a fantasy world six thousand miles away, but she believed in it so. Annapurna and Shiva. Ganesha. And the illusionist, Maya. It was only when I tried to write down all the things she said that I realized there was a story to it. It still amazes me."

"Unintended consequences."

"Yes. But you! You are not so easy. I've written about you, you know."

"I know."

"Yes. Well, that piece I showed you is just the tip of the iceberg, as they say. You fascinated me from the first . . . And one thing, especially."

"What was that?"

"You don't brood. There's no funk in you, I'd say. Maybe I learned my ways from taking care of you, after all. Even when you were a little boy and they taunted you for being so much bigger in the playground, it was like water off a duck's back. I remember some older boys came one day and before I knew it they had started a tussle. Of course, you had settled the matter yourself before I could help, but after, I said to you. 'Don't you mind what they say. You are not ugly. You are a handsome boy.' And you said, 'But they spoiled the game.' All that concerned you was that they had spoiled the game you were playing with the others."

I had been thinking a similar thought about Jane, and used the word handsome myself, to describe her, but I could not tell her that.

I told her, "I just don't take note of it anymore. I was in the dining room with Father and I caught a few of the stares. I

23

think he gets some sort kick out of it because they are looking his way too. He seems to like meeting me in public places."

She was caught on her idea then. "You never did brood. That's a fact. I don't remember you ever expressing hurt feelings to me. I wonder if that's just a part of your nature. Maybe that's one way that you are different."

That got me thinking.

When you read the old histories of Brits or Americans encountering new peoples—especially those they considered primitive, they most often note a certain passivity in the primitive when confronted with great distress. They usually ascribe this detachment to some sort of fatalism. But I think it is more likely a practical matter—facing constant hardship does not allow for the leniency of having 'hurt feelings.' If there is any dominant characteristic of Western culture, it is the raising of personal feeling above fact. 'How do you feel,' they say. When someone says 'How are you,' they are not asking about whether you are hot or cold or out of credits. They are asking how you 'feel,'

Now Jane was presenting a different angle.

I feel. I've always thought I had the feelings everyone else has. I just have them and then get on with things. What is the point of dwelling on a feeling any more than dwelling on the thought that you're cold. If you're cold, do something about it. If you're out of credit, earn some more.

But her thought had merit. It is something to consider. I am of a race that lived in extreme circumstances for hundreds of thousands of years. Perhaps there is some genetic difference. Any Neanderthal who spent time contemplating their navel would have quickly been lunch for another creature. Perhaps the unique quality of *Homo sapiens*—the difference that allowed them to succeed at last—was a greater capacity to dwell on their feelings. Maybe that weakness was, in the end, a strength. It is possible that my feelings are not the same as everyone else's. How would I know?

I left Aunt Jane's to go to work, already running late, and it had started to rain.

I avoid public transportation as a rule. The buses are always crowded and I get dirty looks as if I'm taking up too much space. But I was in a hurry.

I stood as far to the end as I could but with others near there was no getting by me in the aisle. The fellow next to me was reading a news report and looked up at me suddenly— stared me right in the eye.

He said, "Is this you?"

The lite-sheet in his hand had a headline 'Neanderthal Lives!'

Christ.

He was kind enough to let me read the first paragraph and then I got off into the rain even though it was not my stop.

'Harvard professor recreates ancient human ancestor in joint effort with MIT.'

Of course, the headline was wrong, but that did not matter now.

The thought on my mind was how I would deal with it. My guess was that Father had worried about my telling someone else before he could, and decided it was better to get ahead of the curve and release the information his own way. Being tried in a court of public opinion might be preferable to the judgment of an academic star chamber.

My immediate response was that I was angry.

I found a dry doorway and called my father. He answered immediately. As if he had just been waiting for me to respond.

I said, "Don't you think it would have been a simple courtesy to warn me."

"What difference does it make, Billy? Now we can let it play out. It will take weeks, maybe months or even years for the politicians to figure out what response will be most beneficial for them. In the meantime, we can make your case. 'Ancient race saved from extinction.' That kind of thing."

"Did you at least tell Mother?"

"No. I couldn't. I did call her. But it appears she's in a coma." There was not a hint of change in the tone of his voice.

"When did you find that out?"

"Last night. I called her to tell her what I had told the reporter. I got a nurse instead."

I didn't bother to say goodbye. I just pushed the button to dial my mother. A man answered.

I said, "Who are you?"

He answered back. "Who are you?"

I said, "I am Ms Rice's son, William."

He said, "Are you the Neanderthal?"

I said, "Who are you?"

He said, "I'm Greg, with the Bay State Mortuary service. We're just cleaning up here. What can I help you with?"

I called Jane.

She said, "Where are you?"

I told her. I told her about Mother.

She said, "Go home. Get dry. Get some sleep. We can talk in the morning."

Then I noticed the blinking light for messages. I usually don't get many messages. There were a hundred and seven.

I clicked the delete button until I saw a name I knew. That was from Joyce. Joyce was a girl I met at the club where I worked. We had dated for a while, before I found out her main interest was in a single part of my anatomy. I deleted that and the next twenty or so until the name of the club came up. I looked at the message they left. They were letting me go. They could not afford to have people hanging around the door just to see the Neanderthal bouncer.

And Jane had called before as well.

Her message was "It's just a little rain."

With no job now to get to, I went home.

My home is just one big room. The sink and half a refrigerator are in one corner by the biggest window, with the hot plate on top of the refrigerator. I think it was once the front parlor for the whole building back early in the last century when it was a single family home. The buildings there are all yellow-brick, three stories, flat roofed, connected, and face the Fens. There is nothing else of note along the way, so when I saw several television vans out in the street and a small cluster of raincoats at the entrance, I knew what was up. I went down the alley and in by the garbage cans. One enterprising fellow had staked that spot out and was just inside the shadow of the overhang at the door. He started to talk, but I didn't let him finish. I picked him up and set him down in the puddle behind me. He was cursing over ruined shoes when I closed the door.

As soon as I turned on the light, someone tapped on the window. I closed the shades. The tapping continued. I suppose the idea was that I'd give up and answer them.

My next problem was obvious. What should I do?

I flicked on the TV to obscure the muttering of voices outside. A reporter at the Bradbury Station on Mars was interviewing several new mothers. Making babies appeared to be the primary sport of that godforsaken place. I punched the button for something more diverting. The next picture I saw

27

was of me—an old one from when I had been arrested during an altercation with several BC students in Allston. It wasn't much of an event, but one of the other fellows was the son of a police chief and I suppose it had been covered for that reason. I had never seen it before. I flicked it off.

I needed to go somewhere.

Like a helpless little boy, I called Aunt Jane again. She said, come on.

It might have been difficult getting anywhere without being seen, but I knew from my job that the cabs get their gas at the station just around the corner. A bouncer has to be able to call a cab when he needs one for a difficult customer.

I packed my duffle with what seemed most important —mostly things like shoes that you can't get in the right size when you want them. I put the paper copy of the novel I was working on into a plastic bag along with my workboard. I slipped a couple bottles of beer in from the fridge, just in case Aunt Jane was out of stock, turned the TV back on, left the lights on as well, and then went out the back again.

The cabby wanted an exclusive on my life story. Given traffic in the rain, I had time to tell him the basic plot of a novel I wrote a couple of years ago. He seemed to buy it. I got out at the subway station in Harvard Square and went down and caught the T to Arlington.

To be sure, given the number of eyes watching me in the subway car, I got out one stop early. With the rain, and the duffle and the plastic bag, it made for a long trek.

Lots of time to think.

Starting with a fact. I was a freak. The life I had was pretty much over. What looked to be ahead was a freak show. Sure, the heat of the moment would pass, but whenever the newsies needed to fill some space, I would be their perfect update. You see it all the time. The latest chapter in the life of the first human being born on the moon. The girl with the neural implants who can do math faster than any computer. We know now that she likes barbeque sauce on her eggs. Did we have to know that?

Naturally that led to another thought.

I wanted to find out if there was indeed another of my kind walking the earth.

And the question that naturally follows—where should I look?

My mother had mentioned Zurich. Father had mentioned the Chengdu University. They had both mentioned the Dutch.

I slept on Aunt Jane's couch and hung my wet clothes from her curtain rods. She keeps a very neat home and this additional decor looked worse than it might have otherwise. She was immediately sympathetic to my new ideas. And she had a six-pack of good Menotomy Ale. We talked until she looked exhausted.

But she did make a lighter load of it: "How do you find a Neanderthal in a haystack? Look for a damned big haystack?" I smiled at that in spite of myself.

I started very generally scrolling through reference pages on my lite-sheet. That was boring. Especially at slow speed. Jane does not have a dedicated ether-connection. She does not even have a TV. She writes by hand in grammar school composition books, just the way she has since she was a little girl. I gave her a workboard about six years ago for Christmas, because she had mentioned the arthritis in her right hand, and it was still in her closet. Rather than her using the machine, she has even tried more than once to get me to write by hand. She says it would slow me down long enough to choose my words more carefully. I don't think it really matters. Neither of us has ever published a damned thing.

Even with the beer I couldn't sleep. I drank all of that and then spent most of the night sitting at her little kitchenette table drinking her coffee and referencing key words. 99% of the hits were from stories in the past day and they referenced me. That was boring too. I decided to get much more specific. If this other 'experiment' were born roughly the time I was, in 2020, there might be reports. I flipped through several years worth of *L'Hebdo* and *Beobachter* and *Topix*. There was nothing in there or in abstracts referencing Zurich. There was something in the *Handelsbad* for Amsterdam. My Dutch is really bad—just a queer sort of German to me. But anyway, the reference was cryptic at best. Neanderthal. Tissue. Experiments were done. Results achieved were inconclusive. No reference to an actual childbirth.

However, there was something odd in a *Dagblad* article concerning the efforts at the same lab at the University of Amsterdam. A study group from the University of Leeds, paid for by Bayerpharm, had been on site for over a month, participating in various trials concerning genetics.

I quickly found that Leeds had conducted some sort of study prior to 2017, funded by another pharmaceutical company entirely. Miles. Then, there it was. I looked back. *The Dagblad* referenced a visit from the same University of Leeds study group to Amsterdam in 2019.

I was raised in a household that kept secrets. And research being done was always a closely held secret until it was time to publish results. Failures were more easily obscured that way. Successes could be uniquely claimed. And getting to the patent attorney usually proceeded any publication. Some research was conducted out in full view, but usually that was of the publicly funded sort. Private research, where the cost could be recouped only through exclusive rights, would not be shared. Why would Amsterdam bring in Leeds on a private study?

Hadn't Mother mentioned Leeds?

I went back in my notes. And there it was. Leeds.

4.

I spent the next day at the Boston Public Library. I can walk about six inches shorter than I actually am if I have to, at least for short stretches, and I kept to the rush hour crowd. I was there at the library door when it opened. They have study booths and I would be away from people knocking at my door, but most importantly, the internet connection is faster.

Picking up on the lede to Leeds, so to speak, I started checking through news reports after 2020. That's a lot of material, even for a fast connection. But certainly easier in the period following the UN Free Press Directives. Many of the unsanctioned sources had disappeared by that date. "Bandit Journalism" had been outlawed. We had entered the 'New Golden Age of News,' as it was famously touted by the officially recognized press. There were less than a fifth the number of news sources for the scanner to check than had existed only five years before. But there still was nothing obvious to my eye.

Clearly, if the birth were handled surreptitiously, there should be nothing there. What I wanted was something else. Taggable anomalies. They could possibly have kept the child in a basement room, but that's unlikely. In the end, what does that prove? They would have wanted the subject to grow up as naturally as possible. They would have wanted to avoid the type of artificial influences that might skewer data.

That possibility opened up two other lines of inquiry in news reports. Academic results and athletic achievements. The easier of those—the one more likely reported by the news—was sports. I started with the academics. If the child was able to remember things as easily as I always have, then subjects like spelling or any sort of memory quiz would have been simple going.

The British love their quizzes. There were hundreds. Thousands, just in metropolitan Leeds over a three-year period from 2032 to 2038. I picked those years because the subject would have been between twelve and eighteen and that is when most such competitions for academic excellence are held locally and published for the eyes of proud parents in order to sell advertising space. No one stood out especially from the hundreds of winners. Many had won several competitions.

I had been regional wrestling champion in the intercollegiate games my freshman year. I dropped it after that. It was pointless to continue. But I got my name in the paper. I even had a fellow who said he was from the New England Patriots football team come by and invite me to tryouts. But that wasn't where I was going.

I did not understand just then that I was headed for being a bouncer at a nightclub.

In the morning edition of the *Leeds Mercury* for 2037 was a notice. The Bradford Bluedogs had defeated the Leeds United Women's Rugby Team for the first time in over forty years. The star, a uniquely athletic and notably large young woman, was one Elise Severn. She was a broad-faced and pretty girl in a green team jersey, with short blond hair held fast behind a red sweat-band, she was pictured being kissed by her mother and father on each cheek. The parents appeared to be at least half a foot shorter.

But protests had been lodged with the WRFL over her participation. In an interview several days later she had said that she was dropping out of play on the advice of her family.

The name was already familiar. Elise Severn had won three academic tournaments from 2033 to 2037.

There are many bright athletes. But I could not imagine another who looked like Elise Severn.

And she even had parents!

5.

The fellow at the Menino Building was immediately skeptical. He was not sure he should issue me a passport. He had no reason, particularly. He just had his reservations given the news reports.

He made me sit down again in those slippery little plastic chairs they have in the waiting rooms at every government office—the ones that makes your back hurt in about fifteen seconds. I suppose he was calling someone to check on me. I already knew I was the primary topic of conversation among the others scattered about that pale green space. This is not speculation. I could hear them. Some even knew my name. I was just thankful the office wasn't busy.

When you are doing something like this on the spur of the moment, it is easy to lose your confidence. I tried not to think about a number of things. They were, of course, the only things that came to mind.

The credit account Mother had put in my name was large, but not that large. It was clearly meant to make sure I could take care of myself when I started getting old. This was a matter she seemed to agree with Father about and would happen sooner than for the average *Homo sapiens*. I should certainly not dwell on that!

Father had not come to the cremation service the day before. It was far easier to damn him for the thousandth time.

In fact, there had only been about twenty people in attendance at the service. I'm not counting the reporters. They were made to wait outside. My mother's sister, Joan, was there. I've never called her Aunt Joan. She has never managed to spend more than five minutes in the same room with me before that singular occasion. I'd say she's afraid of me, but her behavior had started like that when I was still very little. I could not dismiss the possibility that perhaps she knew something.

The priest who said the prayer was the same one who came to visit Mother several times when she was sick. She told me afterward that she couldn't stand him. But then, Mother was not very religious and not forgiving of the tendencies of priests. The only one in the room who was crying was a rather tall woman who was Mother's last doctoral student. I could not shake the idea that the weeping was 'actually' over the fact that she would have to find a new thesis advisor and that would set her degree off another year.

Joan sat in a cold silence staring at the priest's feet, and that made me wonder about her again until I spoke to my mother's lawyer after the event.

'Mr. Grimm,' Mother called him that—his name was Grimolsky—came over to me after the service and handed me a small thin envelope with my name on it, written in my mother's hand.

No 'hello.' Simply, "I was instructed to give this to you," and the officious nod.

"What is it?"

"You'll see."

"You can't just tell me?"

Mr. Grimm looked both ways as if he was double-dealing in State Department secrets.

"Don't make a fuss. You don't want anyone in particular to put a court hold on this. She asked that I give it to you as soon as I could. And don't worry, your mother took care of all the taxes. It's a clear bequest. She even used the account you set up with her years ago when you were still a minor. It's basically what remains of her savings."

That was a complete surprise.

"What about Joan?"

"Joan will receive the proceeds from the sale of your mother's property—minus charitable donations and taxes."

Joan was by the door, talking to the priest, but she threw a look over at me and at Mr. Grimm and I knew then exactly what was making her so unhappy.

Mother's letter to me, in the envelope along with the pass card, was short and to the point, of course.

'You are likely to need this someday in the not too distant future. No need to be morbid about it. Just save it until then.'

No bid adieu. No affectionate good wishes.

It was well after dark when I got to Aunt Jane's and told her about this. She cried. At least.

After about forty-five minutes of waiting in the slippery plastic chair I went back to the fellow at the passport window. I told him there were going to be some unhappy people if he didn't give me the passport. I lied and said I'd been told to go to London and meet with some British authorities. I used the word 'told.' This implies higher authority. My authority was Jane, of course. She had decided to fly over and be my guide. She wanted to show me her homeland. (In fact, she had never been to Yorkshire in her life.)

This time I pushed some of the paperwork I'd photo-copied through the slot at the fellow. It all concerned Elise, though I knew he wouldn't read it. He simply looked at the headers. Much of it was from British Public Documents and was marked with the logo for the British Museum of all things. He looked at me again through the clear plastic grill like he was staring at a strange animal in the zoo, and then he issued the damned plastic card that would let me go.

That much was actually easy. But there were still a lot of gates to go through.

The unpleasant idea of getting on a plane had settled another problem in my mind. I've never liked small spaces. Not since that little room at MIT and the colorful buttons. I used to finish those sessions as quickly as I could, just to get out of there—hitting the right color almost as soon as the light came on. Aunt Jane could fly by plane, of course. Or airship. The Branson's were a little roomier than a plane, but the head height would mean I would be scraping the hair off my scalp every time I stood. And they took as much as three days, depending on the weather. Instead of flying, I would take a boat. I knew they were more expensive, but I was less likely to have a sudden attack of claustrophobia. I quickly discovered that this possibility was immediately closed to me, however. It was the wrong time of year. There were no passenger ships scheduled.

I looked again. There were, several cargo vessels scheduled to leave over the next ten days. I decided to take a tour of the docks. Only one of the ships looked busy. The fellow at the gate seemed oblivious to my presence. He was watching something that appeared to be naked, on a small screen. I walked on through to a flatbed truck in the midst of the hubbub. A fellow dressed in greys with the name of the ship on the pocket and a plastic identification tag clipped over that stared up at me like I was something they had to load and he didn't know if I'd fit.

I started right in. "Do you carry passengers?"

He said, "What? A little too hot for you around here?"

He clearly knew who I was.

"I don't like flying."

"Sure. I can imagine. But the answer is no. Not usually . . . But we've made exceptions before. You got a passport? How much are you willing to pay?"

I nodded and held the passport up to his eye level. "I can't afford much. How about the price of a plane ticket."

"Nah. Not worth the trouble. $20,000. $20,000 will get you to Blackpool."

I said, "Then I can't afford that. Thanks anyway," and started to turn.

He said, "15! That's only about twice the cost of an air ticket, but you get the rollercoaster ride and the bunk and your meals thrown in."

"Done."

I was seasick the entire ten days except for a stop in Halifax. Nothing I ate stayed down. The fellow in the greys, his name was Jose, had me drinking sparkling water and juice until I started peeing regularly. The bunk was so small I had to sit upright, but that was probably for the better. The room was higher than it was long. By that time we were in port, and I stepped off onto British soil for the first time in my life, it was Thanksgiving Day back in America. I was most thankful.

6.

I ate three helpings of fish and chips at a counter right on the street, within sight of the boat I came in on. An audience of sea gulls watched from the roof, and several children pushed into the spaces between the stools and stared up at me.

" 'er yuoo de cave man?"

I squinted at them as if sizing them up for my next mouthful. They moved off, at least out of arm's reach, but remained there until I left.

The counter man served me by pushing the paper plates across like I might grab his hand. After the third, he said, "D'you do those cave paint'ins I saw in France with the Missus on our honeymoon?"

I was at a loss. I said, "No. That was a cousin. I can't draw."

My next course was to get to Leeds. Jane would be ahead of me. There was a train through via Manchester and I bought a ticket. That trip took about six hours. Less than three hours of travel at reduced speeds against yellow caution lights and more than three hours of sitting on a siding while some problem with another train ahead was fixed.

And when I got off at the station in Leeds—right in front of me on the platform—there was a fellow flashing a press card and saying he was from the *Telegraph*. He wanted to know why I was there. I asked him how *he* knew I was there, and walked a bit faster. He ran beside me and said he had spoken to someone who told him. I said, if he wanted me to speak to him at all, he would have to actually tell me how he knew. He said another reporter mentioned it. I said that wasn't good enough. He then said a fellow name Jose from Bamburg Shipping Express had called him.

I asked the reporter, "Why do you think they use the name 'Express.'

He thought that was rather funny, and we got along fine from there. I lied to him about pretty much everything. I said I was there to see Jane, who needed some help getting around now. My only mistake was to add that she had been my nanny when I was a kid. This seemed to impress him. He liked the spirit of the thing.

"The old charge comes back to help the nanny."

He even said that aloud, as if testing the sound of the words.

I found Jane at the Hotel. She had been busy giving instruction to the staff, all of which they seemed to have promptly ignored as soon as I came into the lobby. They watched me come in like I was the King of England. Even the manager greeted me. I said hello and that I would be very happy if he could do everything Jane had asked.

She had managed to get an extension on the bed in my room and I had my first night's sleep in over two weeks laying flat.

The headline in the *Telegraph* the next morning, just below the latest death tolls from the para-flu in Jakarta, was 'The Neanderthal and the Nanny.'

At least it made me smile. Jane was not amused, but you have to have a sense of humor about some things.

7.

At the main building of the University of Leeds, an ugly construct of glass and metal and cement right out of the 20th century, I was met by a woman who appeared to be waiting for me. It was cool and she must have seen me from indoors because she came through the doors into the plaza to meet me.

Like Mother's lawyer, there was no, 'Hello, how are you, my name is—.' She was talking to me before I really understood it was me she was after. "I thought you'd come—I think we were hoping you would come. "

My first impression of her was that she must be in that vague territory between 50 and 60. A bit older than Jane. A little gray hair. Some wrinkles at the eyes. But still all the right shapes. It turned out she was seventy. I did not know the reason for her 'youthful' appearance until later. That doesn't really matter to this account, except, according to her name tag, she worked for Miles Pharmaceuticals and that evening I found out they were experimenting with aging and soon enough understood that Elise was somehow part of that.

Walking behind her, I managed to get her name as she escorted me up the hall, and an appreciation for the benefits of exercising the gluteus maximus after a certain age. Nothing more. She ushered me into a conference room and a table, held down by two fellows who looked like they needed a nap and I assumed were security by the fact that neither wore a jacket. Then she sat across from me and began to alternately explain what her own interest was as well as to ask questions about my life history. I tried my best to tell her everything that occurred to me about the main character from the very first novel I ever wrote. He was a big fellow too and at least that was somewhat autobiographical.

For every answer I gave I asked another question of her.

"I weighed one hundred and forty pounds when I was ten years old. Did you know I existed before this?"

"Of course not. We would have tried to contact you. Or Dr. McGuire. How much do you weigh now?"

"Two-fifty. About 114 kigs. Is Elise Severn here today?"

Most importantly, this Ms Evans assured me that I would be able to meet with Elise. Elise knew I was here.

"She is working in another part of the campus. She'll be coming as soon as she's free. Did you take the Park-Johnson intelligence evaluation?"

"Twice. They didn't believe the first set."

"Do you know your results?"

"No. It was never of interest to me."

Actually, my mother had administered the Park-Johnson every year from the time I was five. I knew my results very well. They were no one else's business.

The wait wasn't long. Elise came in with a frown already fixed on her brow and shut the door hard. The girl in the news photograph had grown a bit, but she still looked more like a girl to me than a woman. I stood and offered my hand. All I said was, "I am William McGuire."

That seemed to be enough to light the fuse. Her brow curled and darkened.

"I know who you are. I think half the world knows who you are, and your bloody Nanny Jane. What are ya doin'? They warned us you might show up. They even offered to give us a holiday so we could be somewhere else when ya did, but that would only prolong the embarrassment, wouldn't it. Let's get it over with now. "

I lowered my voice a notch. "I thought we should meet."

"Then ya should have sent us a letter. We're in the list. Instead ya've come in here like a parade, with the cameras and reporters under every bush and around every corner. Now everybody in Britain knows we're a freak." She seemed to catch herself, then. Her tone of voice changed. "I was just the great big ugly girl from Leeds. Now I'm really the bloody freak. What have you done?"

"You're not ugly."

She wasn't near finished.

"I know why I'm here! What did you think? I've known about my genes since I was eighteen. It wasn't that hard to figure out." Her tone shifted again as she spoke faster. "They were only too glad to tell us once they thought we could handle it. The question is, why are you here? Did you just want to bop someone your own size. Was that it? And once for the cameras, maybe?"

"What are you talking about?"

I had an inkling. A couple of the characters in my novels enjoyed active sex lives. The reporters might even have gotten into my databank. They could be reading my stories.

"We read about you in the news. Rather full of yourself, aren't you?"

"I don't know what you've read."

"What did you think you were going to do then? Whack us on the head with a club then and drag us off by the hair?"

"I was just going to tell you . . . to let you know . . . that you were not alone."

She suddenly quieted. She was obviously distressed. Upset. And I was a little worried. Lying to the press had taken a toll. There was a lot of false information floating around now and I was the source. Probably every bit of it recorded on phone so I couldn't deny what I had said.

Ms Evans was standing beside Elise and started to speak but I held my hand up in her face, like she was a schoolgirl crossing the street, to get her attention. As far as I was concerned, everything Ms Evans had said previously was as truthful as anything I had given out to the press.

"I've been trying to fend off reporters for the last couple of weeks. I've said a lot of things I probably shouldn't have. Giving them some tale crazier than what they were chasing seemed like the only way to break free of them. And it's true. I am a liar. I enjoy that. Lying seems to be the way I've always gotten along. I write stories. It keeps me sane—no—that's not fair. Sane is not exactly what it is. It keeps things 'balanced.' I don't feel like the world is falling apart when I can write a story and put it back together again. It's just what I do . . . I only found out about myself less than three weeks ago. I'd managed to pretend a lot of things before that, but I really wasn't ready for the truth. And then, almost immediately after, I found out there was someone else. I found out about you. And I just thought it was important to see you before everything else turned upside down on me. I think it was a good thing for me to learn that you were here. I felt—normal again."

She shook her head with a sudden jerk, "You're not. You're a freak!" She sat down. Ms Evans sat down. The three sleepy bodyguards sat up. Elise spoke then as if suddenly subdued by drugs. I knew the voice. I had used it a thousand times when I had found myself in a fix and wanted to keep things under control. She said, "Just like I am . . . We're both freaks. Genetic aberrations. Miscreations. Monstrosities. Grotesques. Accept it. Live with it."

Elise slumped in her chair. I think she felt a little defeated.

I sat down. "I for one, think I'm pretty normal. Maybe too damned normal given the kind of parents I had. But that was because of the infamous Aunt Jane you've heard so much about. She was in fact my Nanny. She raised me, not my parents. She taught me that the world is what it is and either I accepted it and lived with it, or I could try to change it, but I have no excuse to be unhappy so long as I had the choice. That I should not expect the world to change ,just for me . . . What about your parents. What were they like?"

This straightened her back a bit. I was looking directly into her eyes then—as blue as blue ought to be.

She said, "Simple folk. Normal people. They never really understood. They wanted a child and the paid-surrogate wasn't interested in the job, so I was this big baby nobody else wanted, and then I was just their daughter . . .Their big ugly daughter."

"Why do you say that again? Why do you use that word 'ugly.' Where does that come from? Did your parents ever tell you that you were ugly?"

She paused over that and Ms Evans took the chance to speak up. "It's just the way it is in school. Children say things."

I asked Elise, "But why would you believe it?"

Amazingly she said something outright which still surprises me to this moment.

She said, "Look at us."

I said, "I am."

"I'm— . . . WE are not normal!"

"I always thought I looked a bit Scandinavian."

She nodded at that once, like it was a smart-ass answer. "Alright! Very good! You are happy with the way you are. I'm not. That's just the way that is. And now you know that there is indeed another freak like you on this Earth. Now you can go home."

Ms Evans spoke again, but this time to Elise. "You don't want that. At least you should take some time and get to know one another."

Elise held her hand up this time. "Stop! I know what you want. You want to make another baby. That's ALL you want. Now is your chance to double your assets! That's all it is to you! The answer to that is NO! I'm not going to have any part of that. No sex. No babies. Mr. McGuire can go home and make himself as many half-breeds as he wants. I'm not a part of that bargain. And if you want us to keep working here, send him home, quick!"

Elise got up and left the room so suddenly one of the bodyguards fell backwards in his chair trying to keep his eye on her.

Her hair was not actually blonde. Sort of a dirty blonde, I think they call it. She did have the strong brow, but she also had the broad cheeks. Mine are rather soiled by a beard that grows almost fast enough to see, but hers were rosy. And her eyes were an unmistakable blue. The same blue I saw every morning of my life in the mirror and yet suddenly now, they were very appealing.

Jane was not at the hotel when I got back.

"Gone to see the Roman wall of Eboracum and the Shambles of York," said her note. My lite-sheet informed me that this Eboracum was an ancient name for York, and that it was only twenty-five miles away. She could be back in time for dinner.

When the front desk called later and said she'd be late, I went on to a recommended pub and filled up.

The only other interesting thing was that the fight I managed to get myself into in the pub was over those same two words. "Ugly freak."

I hadn't realized how much of what Elise said had affected me. The fellow who spat the words at me had repeated them when I didn't react the first time. He deserved to have his face cracked.

The police issued me a paper citation and told me to report to them the next day.

The headline for the *Guardian* on the lite-sheet, 'Cave man brawls,' seemed to me to be lacking in any wit.

8.

Aunt Jane returned very late. I was actually home from the police station by the time she arrived and I heard her in the next room, but I was in bed.

She called me at 7:00 the next morning and told me to meet her in the Breakfast Parlor downstairs. She was already at a table when I got down and immediately started in on blaming British public transportation for missing me the night before.

I asked her, "How did you like the Shambles?"

She answered, "Never saw it."

"The Roman wall of Eboracum?"

"Missed it . . . But I met this charming couple. The fellow is retired now but he used to work for the Postal Service. His wife is a dear. She makes jewelry from sea glass—Look!"

She pulled the strand at her neck out from within her blouse and displayed it in the gloom from the window.

"Very pretty."

"I had dinner with them at their home and we just talked ourselves to exhaustion."

"Where'd you meet them?"

"Bradford, I think they call it. The number 12-double-n bus to the number 2-e."

"That's east of here. That's not where York is."

"No. I didn't go to York. We can do that together today."

"I have to report to the police today."

"Why?"

"I smashed a fellow in the face."

"Why?"

"He needed it."

She shook her head with my hopelessness. "I have tried my best to teach you not to react to other people like that, even if they need it. "

"You've done your best."

"When are you supposed to report?"

"9 am."

"He's not dead, is he?"

"No. Just a bump. A couple of bumps."

"Well then, still lots of time to go to York."

"But I thought I'd go over and try to talk to Elise again."

"No, no. Let her be. Let her think it through. It'll be fine. She's at least as stubborn as you are. But she'll think it through and then she'll realize that at least you ought to be friends."

"It didn't sound like that yesterday."

"Well, what do you expect? Some women are fine and dandy with a headlong assault, I suppose. But I don't know of any. You have to take it easy."

"I'm glad for your confidence."

"It's just the way it is. Like you, she's good hearted. Remember, she's just been through a difficult time."

"How do you know she's good hearted? How do you know this whole thing isn't a terrible mistake on top of two very awful mistakes to begin with?"

"Because I met her Mum and Da."

"When?"

"Yesterday."

"Christ!"

I made the police office on time despite getting Aunt Jane to recount the gist of her near daylong conversation with Elise's parents. I was fined "200 quid." The clerk said that. The word 'quid' had a nice sound to it after reading it in novels all these years. They processed my card for 315 credits. The exchange rate, I suppose. All in all I thought it was a cheap price to pay for a great pleasure.

Aunt Jane and I were in York well before noon. It was not raining but it looked like it might. We were actually standing up high on the Roman wall, a place built two thousand years ago, probably by Pict slaves captured in battle, when Elise called me.

She was so furious her voice had dropped to that near baritone—difficult to hear in a steady wind off the Wolds.

"What is this then? Is it all just a big joke to you? Is that it? You care so little for yourself that you have made a joke out of your whole life? Did you actually come over here with a plan? How could you think so little of yourself? Now you're brawling in the pub we go to every day? Making a joke out'a both of us? And my parents! You sent your insidious Aunt Jane off to subvert my parents too! You are a monster!"

She did not let me speak. After she was off, I repeated most of what she had said aloud.

Aunt Jane apologized.

I had nothing relevant I could think of to say in return, so I said, "Let's go to London. Let's see some sights before we go home."

She objected. "London stinks like old rags. Let's go to Somerset. The heather smells good even in the winter. The air is fresh. And it's warmer. And I know a pub in Wincanton where they have manners."

She noticeably shivered to give that emphasis.

9.

The Leeds train took us to St. Pancras in London. There was no time to wander around that place in the dark of night, even if I had wanted to. I will have to go back some day.

A cab took us to Paddington. The Paddington train would take us Bristol. Even in the dark, the cab driver must have recognized me. His eyes were on his mirror more than the road.

"Yorkshire is cold this time of year. Better seen in July. Going to the west, are you? The late flowers are still in bloom at Falmouth, my sister says. I hope you have reservations. The hotels fill by Christmas." Jane grunted repeatedly in response without discouraging him.

When we were sitting in Paddington Station, waiting for the early train, a *Telegraph* reporter showed up with a digital rig and did his bit asking us questions, which we did not answer, but he kept shooting as if we just might if he stayed there near us long enough. I had a certain idea of what would happened with the footage. The big screen over our head showed a clip of the dead and the dying in the ongoing drought of northern Nigeria. A fire in Barnsbury. Then a picture of me, probably taken at the station in Leeds. I never noticed the camera at the time. I was talking in the picture and though I could not understand my own words in the echo of the waiting room, the reporter watched attentively and left me alone for a moment. Then, suddenly there was my father's face, outside his office at Harvard, explaining to someone else how his process was not cloning. It finished with the reporter asking Father if he had made any other clones besides myself, and my father's hand catching the light as it batted the camera away.

I stupidly turned to the *Telegraph* reporter when that was over, "There's para-flu in Jakarta, famine in Africa, and civil war in the Middle East, Tibetans are being slaughtered by the Chinese and Chinese are being slaughtered in Malay. Why do you want to waste your time on following me?"

The reporter said, "Because we got more eyes-on for the story we ran on you yesterday than we got for the rest of the sheet combined. Nobody wants to read about the starving children in Africa. They want to read about you!"

I fully expected the fellow to get on the train with us, but he was standing on the platform as it pulled away.

It may be a golden age for the press, with their stories filling every space that might be looked at by more than a few dozen eyes a day, but it makes for a sort of sur-reality where hundreds and thousands of moments in time, past and present, are competing for attention with the moment occupied by yourself. The odd fact has become king. What was once common—what we all had in common—was buried beneath. The story of a two-headed boy who could speak in two languages—but one of them only understood by his other withered head, did not appear to strike the audience as the obscene tragedy it was—a tragedy for the boy, and obscene for the news that carried the pictures and goaded the words for the audience. And this was especially cruel in that it ran just above an animated advertisement for baby food.

We had rented a van in Bristol. A van was the only rental that would allow me to sit upright. And I had paid for it in advance to save time. Another reporter met us as we stepped out of the train there and followed us from the terminal to the rental office. We tried our best to ignore her, but she stood then just outside the van and continued to speak to us as if we would suddenly find our tongues. She wore a light blue raincoat with an identification tag that dangled wildly through the windshield from her lapel, right in front of my eyes. The strategy seemed to be that her coat was unbuttoned just enough to offer a promise of pleasant things beneath. Aunt Jane rolled her eyes.

Not for the first time I wondered, what would make a perfectly healthy looking person do a job like that? Why was there so little pride? What exactly was the story behind that?

Aunt Jane does not drive. Never did. And with the distraction of gaping décolletage, it took me at least five minutes to get an idea where all the little buttons were. The steering wheel was on the wrong side, but the real problem was that all the buttons are reversed. If you are as left-handed as I am, you know the difficulty. During that five minutes the reporter asked every one of the same questions we had been asked before by every other reporter. Perhaps more urgently. I found that very boring.

And the pub in Wincanton was closed. Had been closed for over twenty years. It was now a shop selling cheddar cheeses and some of the local manufacture.

We bought several bottles of the local ale and some cheese and crackers and then parked in spaces designated by the National Parks service and walked up to the top of Cadbury Castle, 'which is no castle at all but just a pile of rocks.' With a view. Even in the rain.

Aunt Jane pointed out the familiar details from her childhood, with the clear voice of nostalgia. A black and white bull with a wet pink nose had once roamed over that fence on our right. Hawks nested every year in a particular oak above the pasture, but the branch was missing now, perhaps to wind or lightning. I easily imagine her walking there at her mother's side and a small party of visitors trailing.

Half way up there was a turnstile on a pasture fence to let people through but not the cows. I had never seen one before. Aunt Jane brushed her hand at it.

"Some damned tourist will steal the thing at least once a year as a quaint relic. The little barn down there by the lot has a dozen more. At least it did when last I knew."

The old woods surrounding the hill are deep and old and dense, trees gnarled in angry faces, and appeared filled with mysteries. This illusion she shattered too.

"There are fellows whose job it is to clear away what doesn't look just right. They trim the brush back and nurse the trees. They drive an artificial knot in the tree when its young to get those looks. It's all for the tourist, you understand. The weather has them off today, but if the sun were shining there would be dozens of them and that little lot would be filled and the traffic police would be issuing tickets to fellows dressed up in tin armour and ladies dressed in flowing gowns and they'd all be making their way up to the top and holding their dresses just so, "Aunt Jane demonstrated with fingers pinching a pleat in her skirt, "and the minister from the church in Castle Mead would marry them right there where they think King Arthur once married Guinevere."

"No." I protested. "That all happened up north by Carlisle!" She shrugged at me. "But I guess you can't tell people anything, unless it pleases them. Arthur was a Briton. His seat was Carlisle."

"I think she might have known, but Mother told them what they wanted to hear."

As we walked up the winding road to the ruin, she recited part of the spiel she had heard a thousand times herself. Her words echoed on the drift of the fog.

". . . And the fires could be seen all the way to the ships in the channel, and they would know what decisions had been made . . . "

The woods dripped great huge drops on our heads from the bare limbs in response.

At the top Aunt Jane propped our umbrellas up in the crooked arm of an oak tree that had squeezed itself out from a break in those big boulders and then laid a blanket down for us beneath that. We sat on either side of the drips from the middle and drank the ale first, and dangled our feet off over the lichen and the moss in the mist. The cheese and crackers were gone pretty quick, but we made the ale last.

I said, "You know, the story I told you about my mother and father sitting on the wall and her falling into the Charles."

"A good story."

"Do you think she loved him then?"

"Certainly. I do."

"How do you know? You were wrong about Elise."

This comparison of these two matters was not exact and got a queer look from Aunt Jane before she answered, "I'm not wrong yet. Not yet. But I got to know your mother pretty well over the years. She fired me six times you know. That includes the last. She was difficult, it's true. She had her own ideas, like we all do. But a woman doesn't just have a baby as an experiment. Not one as smart as your mother. She was under the spell of love. That happens."

I looked Aunt Jane in the eye.

"But never to you."

Her voice went suddenly sharp. "What do you know?"

"Not enough, I think."

"Not enough, indeed!"

"So, I take it you were once in love."

"Once. Once was enough."

"And what happened?"

"Well, I'm not going to say 'it's none of your business' after the mess I made with Mr. and Mrs. Severn, but I will say I don't want to talk about it."

"Was it in America?"

"No. It was here. Over in Taunton. I got a job there first thing, to get out of our little flat, and he was there at the store, and that is that and done so don't ask me any more."

"Do you know if he is still around these parts?"

"No. He's not. But no more. Please. You'll make me cry."

It explained something to me, though. I understood a little better why Aunt Jane wanted so much for me to find 'a girl.' Even such a big girl.

"Where did you live then?"

"Just below there, in Castle Mead."

She pointed out to the scattered roofs of orange and gray, darkened by rain.

"Was it what I hear called a 'council flat?'"

"No, it wasn't," she said that sharply. "My mother had grown up in a council flat and she wasn't going to have the same for me. We lived at the rectory of the church. It was a basement, but the back was open to roses on a stone wall and to the sun in the south and it never felt like a basement. Mum cleaned the church and the rectory and for that she got a place there that they kept for unwed mothers."

"You never told me this before."

"You never asked."

"I did. A hundred times I did. You just made something new up each time until I got tired of asking."

She shrugged that off. "I suppose I did."

"You know, I hold you responsible for teaching me to lie."

"I never taught you. It came natural."

"I suppose so."

She got up and straightened her skirt and pulled the umbrellas down from the tree. "So, now I'll show you Castle Mead. That should take but five or ten minutes. Then we'll go over to Wincanton. There is an old fellow there who'd better not be dead. I want you to meet him. I don't like my few relatives all that much so we can skip them. There will be obligations if we go to see just one. Maybe, if there's time, we'll check on a girl I knew in Yeovil. She was from South Cadbury and left home when I did and walked with me all the way to Taunton. We both worked at the Dell Brothers there. That place is closed now, but Kit married one of the Dell Brothers sons and I think it worked out for them. The last I knew they have a store of their own."

"What do they sell?"

"Same as the old place. Clothes."

"Do you think they'd have anything that might fit me?"

"No. Women's clothes."

"And then where to."

'We could just idle around."

I suggested, "We could go up to Cheddar Gorge as see about some more cheese."

"No, we shouldn't do. It's twice as dear there."

I said, "You look pleased to see all this. Would you like to spend a few days here without me?"

She did not hesitate to consider the idea.

"No. I left this place for a reason."

"I thought it was because your mother died. Or was that just another story?"

"A true one. But I left for another reason. And I have no story for that."

"The fellow that broke your heart?"

"I broke my own heart. It's what we all do a few times I suppose, trying to make something out of nothing. But after that, I never found all the pieces."

I had been watching two figures through the bare gray limbs of the woods, walking up the road from the parking spaces. One had a light blue raincoat and I was pretty sure who she was.

"They found us."

"Quick then. Down the back way."

I felt like a kid playing hide and seek, but the fun was in seeing Aunt Jane step lively on the boulders and then hop into the slick grass and find her footing like a goat. I didn't know that was in her.

She took me down a path that was invisible but for the near break in the trees and the narrow stones that came one after the other like steps.

Castle Mead is the smallest of villages, nestled at the foot of their once-upon-a-time fortress. The church is small as well, but it's the largest man-made object to be seen from there for miles. We came out from the path in the very middle of a narrow main street constricted by house walls and garden walls and walls that had no apparent reason other than to be walls, with a broad roll of green pasture beyond the houses themselves that made each one stand out starkly in the rain.

At the very first house Aunt Jane started talking as she walked.

"And here is where Mr. Wentsom lives. His daughter has cerebral palsy. He wheels her up and down the lane twice a day. She never speaks, but he talks to her all the time and hopes she hears . . . And this is where Mrs. Carl keeps her chickens— right there in that end of her house, like part of her family. I don't know how she can eat them, but she does. And that is—"

"Wait. Those are people in your notebooks. I've read about them before. Are they real?"

"No. And yes."

"I see."

"No. But I thought you'd like to see, because you always liked the stories."

She went on like that, house after house. The entire village populated by figments of her imagination. It took her more than twice as long as she had estimated, even without a halt in her pace.

"Show me the wall with the roses."

"Well, they are not there now. In season, those brown tendrils are blessed."

We stood by a four-foot high stone embankment that surrounded the church on all sides, ranging back and down to what must be a small run of water.

"Where did you live?"

"In the rectory. Behind us here." I turned around on the narrow road and looked at a rough stone house with its own high stone barricade. "The priests lived above . . . And I can even see the light on in the kitchen below. The unwed mother of the moment is making her supper."

A woman looked back out at us, eyes wide. I imagine what it must have looked like with me peering over the enclosure.

We walked on and around to the parking lot, and barely in the van before we saw the blue raincoat come down the road at a hurried pace, slipping repeatedly on the wet leaves.

"Now, enough," Aunt Jane said suddenly, "Let's go on back to Yorkshire where you want to be and get that much settled and then we can go home again. But first we'll go over and see Kerry, tomorrow after breakfast."

I had rented the only two rooms in a bed and breakfast cottage in North Cadbury. The bed was not as long as I had hoped. But they did have their own officially permitted internet access because the smiling lady who greeted us sold her homemade rosehip jelly all over Europe. Aunt Jane had a small package of that sent home. And I was happy then that the parking was at the rear and would not be readily seen by anyone searching for us. The smiley-lady promised to keep our being there a secret.

10.

In the morning, there was another van out front of the bed and breakfast when we were eating our eggs and Canadian bacon with tomato and toast. A paper copy of the *Weekly Times* lay open on the side table where we couldn't miss it. It featured a story on a British chemical manufacturer at the L-5 space colony going bankrupt and the Japanese company that had offered to take over management of the property. Just below that was an only slightly shorter feature on Aunt Jane and myself, which included a picture. The picture was of Jane when she was not yet twenty. Her local connections had been discovered.

At least the smiley-lady offered me seconds, which I accepted.

Thankfully, Aunt Jane knew another short cut.

The roads in South Somerset are narrow and walled by hedgerows or stone at both sides and though I supposed our van could be seen over the tops of the hedges, I drove a little too fast and was lucky enough to miss the brown goose at one turn. I have no idea if the TV crew hit the poor bird, but we lost them in the same area.

Kerry was a name I knew well enough. Through the years, whenever there was a question or problem that perplexed her, she would often say the words, 'I'd ask Kerry if he were here.'

I said, "Maybe I'll ask Kerry what I should do."

Aunt Jane said, "You won't have to ask twice."

The old man was ninety-two. Beardless. A wisp of white hair was left on a head that looked a lot like a spotted bird's egg. He popped up out of his thread worn chair when we came in, faster than I expected he could, after hearing the voice of his daughter saying who had come.

"Lord Bless us, it's Betty Jane."

Aunt Jane hugged him hard enough to hurt, I thought. He could not have been as fragile as he looked. His wool sweater had moth holes up the back. When Aunt Jane asked him later if he had a better sweater than that to show off to visitors, he said he didn't need it because his back was always to his stuffed chair.

"Is this the big fellow, as if I needed to ask?"

"It is. You've heard?"

"Lori tells me the news. I can't read anymore. But tell me now if you wrote your book! Lori will read that to me as well."

Aunt Jane shook her head in mock shame, "Not yet finished. A few more years are needed to get that done."

Lori, who stood by most of the time, quietly, nodding at answers, but rolling her eyes at her father's questions. The room was small and the furniture matched it well so I stood by Lori, and every once in a while I would catch her looking up at me sidewise.

Kerry had been born in this same room. Had spent the first year of his life close by the same hearth that was before us, darkened through all the years but for the red grin of several chunks of coal.

Their house was one in a row of the same gray stone, each built when Queen Victoria was on the throne. Kerry had been born in 1956. Another century—another millennium—

but as I watched, he might just as well be back there now. As if he had ever left.

When a word did not come quickly enough to mind, Lori spoke up to fill in the blank, and the old man scowled back.

"Let's see, we had the floods after you left, and then—"

Lori said, "It was ten year after."

"And then Mother died of pneumonia. And the boy went off to Australia. He's there now. Sells machinery of some kind. He sends me the brochures, but I can't tell what they do —"

"They process fiber."

"And Lori, she has stayed back, just to pester me, so I'll keep from passing alone. Now, you tell . . . Tell me about your big fella here." He turned back toward me for a quick glance.

Aunt Jane took up the topic without hesitation. "William came over here—dragging me along for protection you understand—to see if he could find a girl—of his own kind you might say—who lives in Leeds."

I started to say, "Not exactly—"

But the old man held his hand up at me. "We know all about that. The damned fool talked to the reporters. Why didn't you protect him from that? 'Adam finds Eve in the garden of Leeds.' It just isn't necessary!"

I defended myself, "That's a poor rewriting of a line from a book I wrote about an alien . . . I don't know how they got that. I didn't say anything—"

"Another writer! Is that it! You have raised the boy up with your own frustrations."

Aunt Jane objected, "That's not fair—"

I interrupted that, "If anything, she discouraged me. I probably did it more to trouble my parents."

Kerry said, "If she had stayed back in Castle Mead, she'd have written more, I think."

Aunt Jane defended herself, "I think not! I've written what I wanted. That's enough."

Kerry laughed, "Now, that's her voice! That's the voice I remember. Stubborn to the knees."

For thirty years, Kerry had built and rebuilt the stone wall that encircled the Church and rectory in Castle Mead. His never-ending job. And for some dear portion of that time a little girl would come out from the rectory and speak to him as he worked. He was in half a dozen of her stories.

The old man shook his head sorrowfully, "But you never married. One git and your appetite is spoiled for life. To think, some bloke is out there wandering the moors without hope."

"Bosh!"

He turned from Aunt Jane and looked up over his shoulder at me, all the lines of his face gathered in pity, I thought.

"So you've come to ask me what you should do, is it?. Well you should . . . Because I don't know a bloody thing about any of this, or less than that, because I've heard the 'news' and that has subtracted from my store of knowledge and sapped my energy just trying to comprehend such foolishness. And under these circumstances you have come here to have me offer a bit of wisdom over this matter that is so mysterious to me . . . Well, I can do that. I can, that! If you are here talking to me, then that means your brain is terribly addled—flummoxed. So let go of all that, and follow your heart and have done with it, whatever way it goes. That's what I can tell you. That, and stop talking to the damned reporters."

"Yes sir."

We arrived in Bristol after dark, but the woman in the blue raincoat was at the station when we got there. She seemed content to just watch until it was time to board. After we sat down and put our luggage away on the rack, she sweetly spoke to the gentleman in the seat ahead and asked him to move, and suddenly in one motion, flipped the back of the seat over and sat down so that she was facing us.

She said, "We should have time now to get to be friends."

Her raincoat was gone in a gesture, as well as the jacket she had worn beneath. Both were thrown atop a briefcase on the seat beside her. Her blouse was open again to the third button and her press card dangled from one side now to be certain it would stay agape.

Aunt Jane said, "You people have treated us very shabbily. I don't think 'friends' is in the cards."

The reporter said, "My name is Grace," she extended her hand. Aunt Jane looked away at the window. "And you are Aunt Jane. I am very happy to meet you. I've read so much about you."

"Little of it true."

"What did we get wrong?"

"Every word including 'and' and 'the'."

"Ah, that is from the American author, Mary McCarthy isn't it? How very sweet. However, it's not the press that has been telling fibs. Is it? We would have had the real story and been gone about other business except Mr. McGuire here has insisted on fabrication. His wild tales caught the public imagination. As someone who appreciates knights and King Arthur and all of that, I'm sure you will appreciate—now the gauntlet has been thrown, it's only fair we pick it up."

I said, "Actually, the gauntlet did not come into use until the eleventh century, I believe. Arthur lived in the fifth."

She took a short breath of dramatic surprise, "He speaks! And it's good to make your acquaintance as well, Mr. McGuire."

She actually batted her eyelashes at me. If She was going to be so arch, I had room to play.

"The pleasure is all your own, I am sure. As for blaming me for the fact that you are too lazy to do your own research, or know anything in fact about the subject you're writing about —which I understand is a tradition in your business—I reject the claim. I'm an author. Not a grotesque."

She raised a brow, "A bouncer, I understand. An author perhaps, but certainly an anomaly."

I tried to play with the words to keep my own temper. "In a world of anomalies, there is no reason to make a fuss over me, other than to fill some sad and boorish hole in the heart of mankind."

"Very prettily said. That's the author coming out, I'm sure."

I was riled. "The author in me is curious how anyone can be so lacking in principle and shame, much less human empathy, that she would keep at a job once she discovered it involved collecting the scum from the toilet bowls rather than simply flushing it, and then not wash her hands of it, or move on."

"How very descriptive—"

I had spoken with more pique than I wanted— especially given everything I had learned while lying awake in bed with cold feet. Propping my workboard against my knees is a habit when I cannot sleep.

I said, "No. Not good enough. Scatological comparison has a tendency to leave the stink behind. Allow me to withdraw the simile and try for something closer to the mark. Whores, famously, will do anything for the right price. But what is your excuse now? You earn something less that 2000 quid a week. As an old-time American journalist in the last century used to wonder, 'what's the rest of the story?' "

Aunt Jane's mouth was now agape as wide as the reporter's blouse. She had never heard me talk that way before. I winked at her. She shook her head at me in objection. I knew the look. I was being mean. Revenge was not a sufficient excuse in her view.

Grace had lost the sparkle in her eye.

"I see. You think you can put me off by attacking me personally—"

"No need for that. You've done that job yourself . . . I believe you grew up in a council flat in Manchester?"

The surprise was in the single flinch of her eyes. Otherwise she showed no reaction. She answered quickly.

"So did a million others. A less than boring topic. My job is to focus on things a little less common."

"No? Well, we have our public housing in America as well. Most people never escape the mentality of it. Or the diction. But very few go to the lengths you have. You changed your name . . . Twice, I believe."

"How would you—?"

"Research. You dangled your name tag in my face. I thought obliged to make use of the information. What I found was not what I expected. That name—your current name—suddenly appears for the first time nine years ago, when you started at the City College of London. Before that it was Shields, I believe. That was the name you used when you were turning tricks in Manhattan for 3000 dollars or more a night. That, I believe, is equal to about 2000 quid. In other words, you made as much as a hooker on one customer on one night as you now make in a week."

She kept her composure. I give her that.

"You are very good at your research. I thought that was well buried."

"So it was. Unless you look for the story in things. There is always more. Then you find the patterns. People change, but not wholly. Not completely. I was curious why you would quit one misbegotten job only to take another at lower pay? It's not that your looks deserted you. I really haven't a clue on that, and I can't seem to make one up. From Marta Poole to Greta Shields, to Grace Martin. Marta Poole must have been a very interesting young woman."

"She was poor. Not a crime, but a handicap."

"Well, Ms Martin. I was born with advantages you never enjoyed. I readily admit. And I was never made to sell my body or my soul, though I have been asked more than once. Researching you in the last day has made me appreciate the advantages I had more than ever before. Far more. And yet, for all of that, I'm still very curious. More than that. Mystified. Why did you spend everything you'd managed to save in New York on a Journalism school in London? Why not piano lessons. Or English literature?"

" I did that too. And the elocution. Don't forget that. I thought I would be a very good reporter. I had an idea I might be able to find the truth in things . . . And they all seemed like good ideas at the time. "

"And you did well, to a point. You remade a part of yourself, but not your soul."

"I don't believe in a soul."

She said this last thing having looked away from me for the first time. Her eyes were on her hands. The small recording device there was now turned off.

I said, "Then maybe you've answered my question, in your own way."

Grace Martin gathered her coat and satchel then as if she had reached her stop, but only went to the next car.

Aunt Jane shook her head at me, "At least now I know why you were looking at those disgusting pictures when I came to get you this morning."

"You didn't recognize her?"

"No."

"She was the woman with red stockings."

11.

The manager at the hotel in Leeds was happy to see us back again. It was off-season and I suppose he was renting extra rooms to the reporters from out of town. Two were doubled up in the room next to mine, and two more right on the other side from Aunt Jane.

After breakfast, I went directly up to the University. Elise Severn was not listed in the directory, but they have a telephone system with 'helps.' I tapped in the name 'Severn' and it dialed her directly.

I said, "Hello. It's William McGuire—"

She hung it up. I did it again, and she did that again a second time.

On the third try a computer voice offered to take a message.

I called Ms Evans instead.

I told her a lie. I said I just wanted a chance to sit down and talk to Elise for an hour. Maybe over dinner and a beer. I said that she had the wrong idea about me and I would be going home shortly, but I wanted to clear the air. Ms Evans was very happy to hear from me and said she would do what she could. But first, I must do her a favor in return. She wondered if she could interview me at one of the labs. It would only take a couple of hours.

The lab was a near duplicate of the buildings at MIT. Sterile Twentieth Century Academic with plates of colored plastic scattered here and there for visual amusement and enormously enlarged photographs of people and things that must mean something to someone but which offered no explanation other than the unstated possibility of simply hiding the sterile Twentieth Century Academic architecture beneath.

The first room was too small. I told her I would prefer something larger. Four or five times larger at least. She suggested an unoccupied classroom.

She was not alone. Three graduate students accompanied her. None of these people, two women and a man, seemed happy to have been pulled from their previously assigned chores. Only Ms Evans smiled.

The questions were as boring as the architecture.

"Do you feel lonely?"

"Do you feel anger over the way you have been treated?"

"Have you ever wished you were never born?"

Most of the questions I could easily turn back on the students for comparison.

This, they repeatedly told me, was not helpful.

When they got to the more speculative items like, "Have you wondered yet what your real mother looked like?" I had to answer a little more delicately. Her question suggested genetic memory to me and I was not ready to consider it.

I said, "I have thought she must look something like Elise."

This got an immediate facial tick from the male student.

Ms Evans asked, "Really? Have you ever dreamed about her?"

"I'm not sure I dreamed it. But I wrote it down that way in a story recently."

"And your father, what did he look like—not your adoptive father?"

"A darker version of myself."

"Very interesting."

"Why?"

By telling this little tale I might have caused another problem for myself. Of course I had always thought my mother looked like . . . Mother.

Ms Evans feigned reluctance. She clearly had a motive. "Well, if you must know, because Elise once told me what she dreamed her mother looked like. It was simply a bigger version of Mrs. Severn. And her father was a bigger and taller Mr. Severn. It seemed simple enough and I never made much note of it, but now I'm having a second thought. People so often see themselves as an extension of what they like. You did not like your parents, I take it?"

"No."

"Dr. McGuire was not a good father?"

"He was no father at all. More like a bad uncle."

"And your mother?"

"She did what she thought best considering the fact that she saw the whole thing as a great mistake on her part."

"I see.

The next group of questions I objected to.

"Do you date very often?"

"Not often."

"Have you ever had a longer term sexual relationship?"

"No."

"How many short term sexual relationships have you had?"

"I don't count. Anthropologically speaking, I suppose I'm not doing a good job of spreading my genetic material."

"Once a month?"

"I think you will have to settle for 'uncooperative.' "

"Mr. McGuire, you agreed to this. You must have known I would ask."

"No."

"Doesn't your father—or the team that works with your father—don't they ask these sorts of questions?"

"No."

"Are you serious?"

"I am. I refused. Once I saw the pattern to it I realized what they were pretending. It's not science. I found the report from one graduate student whom I'd mistakenly befriended when I was sixteen. He had made it part of his doctoral thesis. The presumptions were outrageous. It all made me an even greater admirer of Charles Darwin. At least Darwin tried hard to keep from such false narratives made whole out of insufficient data. Unfortunately then the public wanted something more vivid, like 'mankind descended from monkeys.' It made for a better graphic."

"But don't you see! Now we have two. Now we do have something more!"

"You have two. Importantly, you have a man and a woman. Any average social observer can tell you the differences between the two, male and female, are great enough for a hermaphrodite alien from Mars to presume they are from different species . . . But another thought just struck me. What is the difference between what you do and what the average reporter for the *Times* or the *Telegraph* does?"

The rest of the session was more combative and less relatable.

I think because she had her ulterior motives in place, Ms Evans followed through with her side of the commitment.

I met Elise at a faculty lounge. She was wearing a dress. I know this is not exceptional in America, but it is not the fashion in Europe. I was impressed. Very nice.

She had curled her hair. And that was quite cute. Better. Pretty. But she noticed me looking.

"I didn't do it just for you. My niece had a birthday party last night at my parent's house.

The place where we met was nearly empty, but all those who were there thought it best to sit close enough to hear a whisper. The fellow at the next table smiled when Elise mentioned the reason for curling her hair. I suggested we leave.

"Do you have car?"

"Yes. Though you're at least 10 centimeters taller than me. You'll have to bend your head a little."

"Four inches? Maybe. Any ideas?"

"I thought you would have something."

"I think you already noted that once—I don't have a plan."

We had made it to her car in the lot before she spoke.

"Everyplace we go somebody will be listening. I would even invite you to my apartment, but there was a strange little man outside in a car this morning. I can imagine the headline on that . . . We could go to my parents. They have some cake left. We could order take-out."

Her mother was not interested in having take-out brought to her house, though her father was not so disinclined. She made spaghetti.

Her father, a ruddy man, was fully a foot shorter than me. He squinted upward like he was looking into a bright sky.

"What do ya do?"

"I'm fine, how are you?"

"I didn't say 'how.' I said, 'What' "

The alternative statements in the press were simple to choose from.

"I was a 'bouncer' until recently"

"What's that?"

"I kept the wrong people from coming into a nightclub."

"Hah! I have a friend Eddy does that."

Mrs. Severn spoke up.

"Eddy did it until someone bounced his head on the road."

"Yes. He did. He works behind the bar now."

"What do you do, Mr. Severn?"

"Bob. That's us. I was a postman. That, until we was made to retire. Now I just pester my wife."

She rolled her yes. "I wish he pestered us more."

"Mum!" Elise was upset by something her mother had said which I did not grasp.

There was an 'electric fire' in the parlor and we all sat around there.

Clear ale bottles filled with multicolored fractions of sea-glass lined most empty surfaces. Each one had a date at the bottom written on a piece of tape.

"That one is what we collected in 2045. It was a very good year. There had been storms the season before and the beach at Weymouth that summer was filled with it like an open treasure box. I filled a dozen bottles in a week, but I gave them all away to friends. I can only make so much jewelry, you understand."

She lifted the strand at her neck up high enough to catch the light.

I said, "Very beautiful. A little summer in each piece."

Mrs. Severn smiled, "Every summer is right there in those bottles. Each and every one since Elise was a baby and she could scoot with the birds, and run just before the water on the pewter sand."

Mr. Severn had another thought, "Too crowded there. I think our girl was always happiest when we were up at the moors, the times we stayed at Ampleforth and she got to tramp through the heather from dawn till dusk, rain or shine. She has that wildness in her."

Mrs. Severn lamented, "She hasn't had that time for either since she went to work at the University."

Elise appeared unhappy at the choice, "I don't know which summer was the best."

I put in, "My favorites were the ones spent at the shore as well, at a little house my father rented in Maine. It only lasted for a few years, but it was nearly perfect. For a couple of weeks I lived at the edge of the ocean. No beach. Just seaweed and rocks, crabs and lobsters."

"Your parents are divorced?"

"Long since."

"That's too bad."

"Not for them. Not a good pairing." I looked at Mr. and Mrs. Severn to make the point without saying it. "Not so bad for me either, I suppose, because I got Aunt Jane to myself."

Mrs. Severn's voice rose. "Ah, Jane! She was a delight!"

Aunt Jane's visit was then recalled happily. I looked to Elise with the thought of her description of my 'insidious' Aunt Jane, and she appeared to know what I was thinking without a word. She bowed her head in apology.

When conversation slacked a moment, mostly from me trying to avoid the wrong questions, Mrs. Severn announced "Don't mind us. You kids just talk as long as you like."

Except that Mrs. Severn had to know the meaning of several words that were uncommon to her along the way and offered more tea as soon as the cups were down. And Mr. Severn corrected his daughter's recollections several times.

"You were the fastest. Not 'One of the fastest.' Until University. Body weight was the matter then. But before that, you couldn't be beat."

And again, "Not when I was around, you didn't." He turned to me. "She's not much of a whinge. Unless she took that all to her Mum."

Mrs. Severn joined, "No. Not an unhappy child. Not at all if you were at the beach, or up with us at Ampleforth and hiking on the moors. You know they had us up to the University a couple of times to ask us questions about such things. They didn't seem to like our answers. They thought we were hiding something from them."

"They did that to me today."

"You know then."

"A little. 'Bosh,' as Aunt Jane says. They are no closer to making a science out of psychology today than they were a hundred years ago."

Mrs. Severn wanted to know, "And what about Miss Jane? Is she a Mary Poppins? She didn't strike me that way?"

Seeing the confusion on my face, Elise explained, "Does she stick her nose into everything?"

I said, "I wouldn't say a Mary Poppins then. She worries about me. But she's . . . Aunt Jane. From what I can tell, she's what an aunt is supposed to be. I've only known the one."

Mrs. Severn immediately said, "Oh, thank God, not like my sister Matilda. Jesus, no. The life of the party, but she can't even remember when her own child's birthday is. She went off someplace—"

"Mum!"

"Not the first time."

"Da!"

After dinner Mrs. Severn said, "Would you like more tea with your cake."

Mr. Severn said, "Oh, Lord. Not more tea. Can I have my ale now?"

Mrs. Severn scolded, "You can't have ale with your cake."

"I'll skip the cake."

"But what about our guest?"

I took the chance.

"I think I'd like the ale better myself."

Elise smiled.

The cake, beneath a clear plastic bubble cover at the sideboard, was forgotten and we all drank ale.

Sometime close to midnight I suggested I should head home.

"So soon?"

"I have an early day tomorrow."

"Are you leaving, then?"

"I don't know. I'm not good with plans it seems."

In a high voice, Mrs. Severn said, "Let the wind take you where it must."

Mr. Severn objected at her. "You've never been on a boat in your life. You read that in a book!"

This comment was not well received.

"You ought to read more yourself!"

Elise was quiet once we were in the car and there were still a bucket-load of questions I had held back while with her parents. Now I didn't want to address any of them and spoil the moment. But one plagued me. Into the silence I asked, "What about the aging experiments? How long do they think we will live?"

It was rather inelegantly put.

She practically hit a parked car in passing.

"What? No! There's no idea! They threw that all out years ago. Didn't your people tell you? They can't find any genetic difference for that."

"But wasn't that part of the reason Bayerpharm supported the original project?"

She sighed, unhappy now to be talking shop. "I think, yes. But they couldn't find the markers with me. They must have been caused by some individual genetic stress in previous samples."

"What about Ms Evans?"

"What about her?"

"She looks like she might be dipping into the magic bottle."

That got a smile.

"She does it all. Whatever it is. Trouble with that, she can't tell what works and what doesn't. She worries over getting old and she not even living the life she has now."

I was happier at Elise's comment at that moment than at the new knowledge.

"Aren't you worried over the life you live now?"

She was unprepared for this. "Not worried, exactly. But not happy . . . I work with a lot with mice, you know, testing for harmful chemicals in new products and that. It's useful work, but some days I feel just like one of the mice. Because I know they're watching me all the time, looking for one thing or another. But I wasn't forced to take the job there. I worked for a time at Nat-Agro trying to increase the size of chicken eggs after I graduated." She caught the look on my face as she drove, "Really. I did! Until I was seeing eggs in my nightmares. But the university pays more. And I get a week more vacation every year."

"I couldn't do it. I wouldn't want anything to do with them."

"You think what they did is wrong?"

"Don't you?"

"I'm not sure. I'm here. I can live my life the way I want. They paid for my college education to keep me here. But I'm not in a cage. I'm free." She must have seen the change on my face. "What?"

"You are not free. But I suppose the delusion is not worse than it is for most people."

Her grimace at my answer was indignant.

"And you are not free to jump into the air and fly like a bird. None of us are really free."

I tried to back off.

"I do wish I could fly. I've always wanted to fly. I often find myself bounding into flight in my dreams. Floating above it all. But that wasn't the sort of freedom I meant."

"What did you mean?"

"We were getting along so well. The evening has been so good. Really good. I like your parents. I don't want to spoil it."

"What? It's just a simple question."

How was I going to avoid the collision?

"Have you ever smoked a cigarette? "

"A cigarette. Why would I smoke a cigarette? They're bad for you."

"Probably. But have you ever wanted to even try?"

"No!"

"Well, if you had, you'd discover you had to buy them from some odd character standing by an old car under a bridge somewhere. It's against the law. In America too."

"It's for your own good."

"You think that's okay, that someone else has decided what's good for you?"

She hesitated, already ahead of my line of inquiry. "I'm not sure."

"How do you learn to take care of yourself, then? Do the mice in your lab know where to go to get their kibble?"

"Yes."

"What would happen if the kibble wasn't there?"

"They would die! But it's a lab. Not the wild."

"I guess that's as much as I have to say on the matter."

She stiffened her back. "I'm sorry I asked."

She was quieter than before. In the dark, I couldn't tell if she was angry.

I tried again, "What would you do if you hadn't gotten a degree in biochemistry?"

"Why? Is this part of your lecture?"

"It wasn't a lecture. I was trying to answer your question. Now I've asked one."

"I don't know."

"Sure you do. You don't have to tell me, but you've thought about it a thousand times."

"How do you know?"

"I asked the question first."

"Really?" She paused and tipped her head from side to side. "If I had the choice, I would like to work on a farm. I'd like to be a farmer."

I gave that a full nod. "Truth is, I knew that. Your father mentioned it when you were off getting the ale."

"Then why did you ask?"

"Because I'm still giving you an answer to your other question. I wanted to ask why you decided not to be a farmer?"

"You can't just do that. There aren't a lot of jobs. You have to get permits and they're only so many issued. You can't just go out and start growing carrots whenever you want."

"No. I know that. Because you're not free to, even if you wanted. You can't fly and you can't smoke and you can't grow carrots."

"Are you any better? A bouncer?"

"I write stories."

"You and your Aunt Jane."

"At least we can do that."

The strange little fellow was asleep in his car outside of Elise's apartment. Her designated space was around the corner. After driving by once to check, we came around and parked with our lights off. The car was feeling too close, so I got out and said goodbye to her at the corner.

She said, "It's foolish not letting us drive you to the hotel."

"I need the walk."

"So you won't leave tomorrow?"

"Not yet. Not until you tell me to."

"Can we have lunch?"

"A quiet lunch with the faculty?"

"How about the bar where you 'smashed Ned Feathers in the face? The food is tasty."

"The owner won't want to see me again."

"He filled the place the next day. You made him a pot full."

Because I suddenly felt that time was running short, I kissed her then. More like a schoolboy taking his first peck, I'm afraid. But she kissed back.

And with that I said good night.

12.

The next day was the worst day of my life. Or nearly so.

"The lover's kiss" was the headline below the picture in the *Telegraph*. Very tasteful, actually. The little fellow in the car was not asleep.

But that was not the bad thing I learned first when I was awakened by my father's voice at 6:30 on the Hotel phone. Nor the realization that he was downstairs.

He was waiting for me at the elevator door. He turned me around on the spot and led me back in. We were in the closed elevator when he said it, holding the paper up to my face.

"You can't be kissing her like that. She's your sister!"

I don't know if he had spoken so loudly it was overheard, or if the information had simply traveled across the Atlantic by other means. It seemed to be known by everyone at the same instant. Later, it was on all the news reports, along with that picture of the kiss.

I managed to say, "You can't know that."

"Certainly I can. Who headed this project at Leeds? Moira Evans? The former Ms Moira Longoria. We used to call her 'Loingoria,' I should add. She was MY assistant the year before you were born. She knew how I did it! She was there for the first try—the one that failed. I had to let someone go after that, just to show good faith with the sponsors. Someone had to take the fall. And your mother was already suspicious." His face twisted with his anger. "I'm going to sue them for every penny they have in their coffers. That process was patented!"

"You patented a human life?"

"You know that! I told you that!"

"No, you didn't."

He shrugged that off. "Well, I meant to. It's a fact. In a manner of speaking, I own you. I just thought because of your temperament that maybe I shouldn't tell you at the wrong moment."

"Bosh." In fact I said 'Bosh.' I was suddenly very tired. I had not really slept all night. I was positive I was in love for the first time in my life, and now I had been told I was in love with my own sister.

The two reporters from the room next to mine were at the elevator door when we got to my floor. They were still tucking their shirts in, having realized I had left without them.

I took Father into my room, and sat down.

"How do you know for sure?"

"It takes years! She just didn't fly back here and duplicate all that in a few months! She'd worked with the Dutch after she worked with me. Probably slept with one of the heads of that program too. Right? How did she convince them to give up any of what they had? But they were . . . Well, Billy, you see, the Dutch team was working with the exact same material I was. Some kid that fell down a crevice in a glacier in the Caucasus about 40,000 years ago. They got to the Georgians first after the news reports hit. So I had to do some work behind the scenes, so to speak. I found a Russian geneticist who'd worked on the original excavation. He had put a little aside for himself, you understand. The body the Dutch got out just happened to be missing a few parts. So, whether Ms Evans stole it from me or got it from them, it's the same genetic stuff. The same DNA. You are twins, made from the same father."

"He was too young to be a father."

"Not a strong argument."

I sat in the chair at the desk and looked out through the drizzle in Leeds and felt pretty bad. I couldn't even get up when Aunt Jane knocked.

"What are you doing here?" were her first words to Father.

His kind reply, "Trying to save Billy from committing incest."

"Lord, Jesus!"

Aunt Jane had read enough to know about the process now. She did not ask for an explanation. She simply came over and put her hand on my head and pulled me to her breast.

Father had left for the University well before I could gather myself. There was lead in my legs and my butt. I don't know how long I sat in the chair.

I should have called Elise. I couldn't. I was totally without words. An unusual moment in my life.

The first I learned of the incident later that morning at the University was when I got into a cab in front of the hotel with Aunt Jane.

The driver turned to me. "Was that your father they took to the hospital?"

"I can only hope so. What are you talking about?"

"Professor McGuire, was his name. I know that. The big blonde—I 'm sorry, the young woman at the University that I read you went to see before—I think she assaulted him—I mean battered him. Or whatever the American word is. She bashed him up pretty badly."

There was a live television feed going on from the main gate of the campus when we got there so the helpful cab driver took us to a side entrance.

I found Elise in Ms Evans' office. Her voice was as low as I've ever heard on a woman.

"We are both monsters."

She stood back from me when I came in.

"It's not true."

"We are the artificial product of a test tube. Manufactured goods, as my Da says about cheap things."

Ms Evans actually looked remorseful. "I didn't know. How could I? I knew he'd bought his material from the Russians. That's all. I should have guessed. Knowing him, I should have guessed."

I tried to take Elise's hand. She pulled it away.

"But I don't feel like your brother," was all I could think to say

She spoke at the window. "How would you know? You never had a sister."

There was a silence. Maybe a second, Maybe a minute. I said, "What do we do now?"

Ms Evan started to offer an answer.

Elise said, "Shut up. You've caused enough." She turned to face me. "You should go home and live your life now, and I will stay here and live mine. It's what people always do when things don't work out the way they should . . . What they should do . . ."

I thought of English stiff upper lips for just a passing second before I saw Elise's lip begin to quiver.

While I could, I wanted to say one more thing to Elise. I wanted to say it out loud at least once in my life. I wished Mss Evans wasn't there. She'd probably just put it in her study report.

"I love you."

Elise began to cry. Weep, actually. I had not seen her cry, and I knew from Ms Evans response that it had seldom happened before.

Ms Evans actually said, "You're crying!"

Elise said, "Shut up," again. And then, to me, "Please go. This is not the time to sort things out. Go home. Please. And someday, if you can, write me the letter you should have written me before you ever came . . . Like these last few days never happened . . . I'd like to have that."

She left me standing there, feeling numb.

I did not visit my father in the hospital. But I was told he was not filing charges. The reason for this was obscure to me at first. Then I realized from a remark Ms Evans had made in trying to excuse herself of responsibility that they had spoken at length before Elise ever came on the scene. Elise pummeled Father for his bad behavior without a word. But something Ms Evans had told him must have been enough to hurt him or his career, or his reputation. Later, on the phone, Ms Evans would not say what that was. Why would she if it gave her such an advantage over him? He was not even going to file his lawsuit against Leeds.

And Elise had disappeared.

I imagined her roaming the heather alone and let that be.

13.

When I next saw the light blue raincoat, my first reaction was one of admiration for her persistence.

We were in South Hampton. Jane had booked passage on a Cunard cruise ship from there to Miami, Florida, and we had managed to get from Leeds to South Hampton without a hitch. Without being seen, or so I thought. I was getting good at it—that and funny walks. From Miami I would take the train north to Boston—or wherever. I had not yet decided. Aunt Jane had never been on a passenger ship before and was quite excited as she looked over the crowd for the sort of little details she loved.

Aunt Jane was the first to see the blue raincoat. "I don't believe this."

"It's great isn't it?"

"You don't see her yet. She's over there."

"Who? Where?"

"That woman, Grace. The reporter-prostitute."

"That's a tautology, or a redundancy, or some such. Where?"

"Coming right toward us at two o'clock."

There was a post blocking my line of sight that way and I suspect Grace had chosen her approach carefully, assuming I'd be the one to spot her first over all the heads.

I said, "Look away. Don't let her know you saw her."

"Why?"

I was shaking up a bottle of soda I had bagged for the trip.

Aunt Jane saw it and said, "Stop! Just because I'm here, you're starting to act like a school boy."

Reluctantly I did and we both stared at our pursuer as she made her way through the crowd, fully around the post and stopped directly in front of us.

"Hello. I see how happy you are to see me. But I tracked you down. Give me that."

"Very good."

"And I did it without a press badge. I am no longer a news reporter, as you can also see. Not for now." I will admit, from the way she looked, my first thought was that she might have returned to her previous profession. Then she answered that thought as if I'd said it. "And not that either . . . I'm going back to school. I thought I'd study a little history. There's a school in Michigan I've read about before. Maybe I can still be the reporter I wanted to be, someday. If they'll let me. But I thought I'd try some of your dream for now. I thought I would write a book. A few books maybe. I have several stories I'd like to tell. I have a unique perspective, don't you think?"

No argument with that. Just an observation.

"Yeah. You do. But perspective isn't everything. There is a lot of bad art out there that has all the windows the right size."

Grace nodded, "Right. You are right, just as you were before. It's really a matter of the story as much as the fact, isn't it."

"I think so . . . Did you track us down to tell me that?"

"No. I read the *Telegraph* piece that they ran instead of the one I never filed. It was bad. I admit it. Then I went back and read all the stories from the past two months. Then I read your father's curriculum vitae. And Moira Longoria's . . . I did my research." She nodded, as if affirming her words. She would deliver her lede now in her own sweet time. "You should always do your research, you know . . . And I discovered that Dr. McGuire was in Russia in 2018. For a conference, of course. That's how they get away with everything, all expenses paid. No taxes. I found out that he met there with Oscar Samuels, a Ukrainian geneticist. It was noted in the Russian press because Dr. Samuels was a relatively obscure man and your father was already one of the bright lights of the field. Samuels has died since. But Dr. Samuels was a man who often stooped to pick up a penny. He understood your father's ambition. And Samuels gave him what he wanted . . . But it was not from the Caucasian boy. All that remained of that find was in fact bought by the University of Amsterdam, a portion of which ended up in Leeds. What Samuels sold your father was from a previous Russian find at Belukha Mountain . . . You should read his paper on it. It was published in a memoriam volume and it's available on the Russian internet. I wonder if fifty people ever read it. But I had a bright fellow who knows his languages at the *Telegraph* scan it for anything I might want. And there is an interesting thing Dr. Samuels says." She unfolded a yellow scrap in her hand and took a breath. Suddenly, I could hear nothing of the hubbub that surrounded us. "It would appear these people did not simply have accidents, as we supposed. These places are far from the probable beaten paths. Desolate of anything but a clear passage to eternity. With this fellow's body there were flowers, still keeping their reds and yellows, which must have been carried to the site from far below. Just as there were with the boy in the Caucuses. It would appear that these Neanderthal, so primitive, knew these bodies would be preserved for the ages in the ice, and had wished that it would be so."

I was not breathing. Aunt Jane held fast to my arm for support.

Grace added, "It's amazing really. As if they were looking into the future and hoping that one day this loved one would live again. That's the rest of the story, isn't it?—As your old American journalist used to say. But Russia, Mongolia and China were nearly at war that year. He could not publish his findings then and he had no other use for the portion of this ancient man he had saved. It was just an expensive relic for an old professor from a small academic center. And then your father appeared. Your crazy father with American university money to burn and looking for a part of the Georgian find. Dr. Samuels had no private line on that. But he did know what was in his lab. So he told a small lie. And at least Professor Samuels did not die a poor Russian academic."

I thanked Grace—I actually kissed her and the picture of that was in the paper at Leeds the next day. I had a porter find my luggage. Aunt Jane wanted to continue with her own voyage. She saw no place for herself on the immediate road ahead for me.

I handed my ticket to Grace.

"Have you ever wanted to go someplace else in America? Miami is nice in the winter, they say. And you can even get to Michigan from there by train."

"Can you do that?"

"If you have your passport. Yes. I'm told a porter can fix anything. Let me ask—Here, . . . hold these snacks. But don't open that bottle of soda."

14.

Well, it's a bloody Cro-Magnon world out there. What's a good Neanderthal to do?

I found Elise at home with her parents. But I wrote her a letter first to say I was coming and had it hand-delivered by a newsboy I saw on the street who was making his rounds with paper copies of the afternoon edition of the *Leeds Mercury*. The one with the picture of me kissing Grace.

I won't tell you all that the note said. Most of it you can now guess.

But it began, 'I am William McGuire . . .'

**

That Little Old Lady and Me

She brought me down with a two-by-four across the back of the knees. My head hit the doorjamb as I fell. Hard headed or not, I think I was a little dazed.

I was lying then on a black and white tile floor in the half dark of that vestibule and looking up at the mouth of a model 17, 9mm Glock semi-automatic, when I first heard that voice.

"What'da'ya'want?"

This is a single word, in common use, but has problematic spelling. When I write stories now I often just resort to familiar forms, like 'What do you want?' Rather than be accused of stereotyping or pandering. I was actually thinking about this while I was lying there only half conscious. I had spent the morning at my one room apartment over in Cambridge, writing and dealing with the grammatics—that's my word for dramatic speech patterns—when Connie McGuire showed up and asked me to do him a favor. That meant he was going to screw with my regular schedule and put me on a job right away. He's been doing that less lately so I didn't complain. Just part of the job description. Besides, he's short on cash because of the economy and I'm on salary anyway, so it doesn't cost him extra to dump on me. I ran through a few more 'grammatics' in my head on the way over to the South End. I had to decide the way to go with the piece I was working on. It made a difference.

So there I was then, lying on my back with that little old lady staring down at me like a wrinkled kid in her pajamas. She was dressed in a loose grey sweatsuit and purple slippers. The half dark caught in the lines of her face and gave her eyes a fierce cast. My mind started to clear pretty fast.

"Your son sent me over. I'm from McGuire Security. He was supposed to call."

Mrs. Vento has a very steady hand. The mouth of that Glock, maybe three feet from my head, didn't waver a quarter inch the entire time I was studying the small black hole at the end.

Her eyes rolled. She has enormous eyes for such a small lady. She leaned the two by four against the wall by the door.

"Jesus. He would forget his head if he could. And just the kind of oaf Michael world hire. Big and stupid."

I said, "Thank you." Never argue with a gun, even if it's in the hand of a skinny little old lady who could not be more than five feet tall.

She says, "You look like a thug."

I say, "I've been told I look like a cop."

She shrugs, "Same difference." I was still lying on the floor at that point. I hadn't slept well the night before and I was about to get comfortable but she added, "You can get up now."

I say, "Thank you," again.

Standing up, the height difference was more considerable. I'm six feet four, but I think it's my over-all size that exaggerated the difference. I'm only hitting 230 these days. I've lost a little. Mrs. Vento could be a hundred pounds if she were wet. But still, she turned her head side to side to make a statement out of it.

"You can stand to lose a little weight, don't you think?"

I answer, "Probably."

She frowns, "How old are you?"

"53. How old are you?"

Mrs. Vento goes straight-face, like I had no class for asking. That was true, but I was feeling a little sore just then and didn't feel restrained enough not to ask. She said, "Old enough to be your mother and then some. You need to lose about twenty pounds. Do you exercise?"

I admit, "As little as I can."

She gives me a mother's sigh, "It shows. I was down in my gym in the basement when you rang the bell. Follow me."

The vestibule of the building had an ornate mahogany stairwell going up on the right, a small brass appointed elevator and a narrow hallway at the backside, and another unlit stairwell down on the left. I figure that was where she must have been when I used the keys Connie had given me and came in the door. She had not answered the bell and I had been warned she was elderly. I was looking up the stairs for an answer to my shout when she hit me. Now she disappeared into the dark on the left and I felt my way a bit more slowly behind her.

Her 'gym' was well appointed. Not counting the pipes and vents, the basement ceiling was over nine feet, and she'd installed a thick rubber mat, several benches, and an assortment of rigs on the wall. That kind of ceiling height in a basement is unusual for any building in that part of town and it gave me a clue as to the quality of the architecture and why she might be having problems, but I was going to let her explain all that. There was no sense in saying something just so she could correct me and tell me I was stupid again a second time.

She'd put her pistol away someplace I didn't see and pointed with an empty hand to a door in a back wall.

"There's a closet in there. You'll find some clean sweats. Michael comes over sometimes to keep me company. He's shorter than you are but he's wider. Get dressed. I want to see what you can lift. I don't want a bodyguard who's weaker than I am."

I said, "No thanks. You'll have to take my word for it. You weigh a hundred pounds? I can lift you and carry you a couple of miles if I have to. But I hope it's not necessary."

She dismissed this with a flick of the wrist and says, "Do you have a gun? I don't see a gun."

I told her, "I don't carry a gun. But I have one in the car. I can use it if I have to. But—"

She interrupted me, "You hope you don't have to. I got that. But you better carry a gun if you're going to be around me."

I was now aware of one of her primary characteristics. She is impatient. Her mind works faster than almost everyone else's and that has probably gotten worse through the years. Putting up with the human race when they're running at half-speed must be frustrating. Less than ten minutes after I'd met her I was hoping my brain would be as well greased as that when I was her age—so long as it did not require me to eat yogurt or bean sprouts and avoid caffeine, red meat, and ice cream. Or pasta.

Mrs. Vento says, "I should know your name, don't you think."

"John Finn."

She smiles for the first time, "I won't call you Huckleberry then."

I say "Good. I'll make the time pass a little faster if you don't."

She answers, "What? You in a hurry? What do you have to do? Is Oprah on? The Price is Right?"

I figured this was her trying to irritate me as some sort of test. I smiled back.

She shrugged and sat down on a bench and put one slippered foot into a stirrup and started to work her right knee.

I decided it was my turn to ask questions.

"Are you here alone?"

She didn't look up. "No."

"Who else is here?"

"You are, stupid."

I caught the look in her eye then. I was going to remember that. All those lines in that face made an easy map if I just kept track of the changes.

"No other tenants?"

"Not a one."

I asked why.

She raises both eyebrows so that the wrinkles all go up double rainbow fashion. "Somebody wants me to put my property on the market. They want to buy it. I don't want to sell."

Some of this I knew from Connie, who had gotten the call from her son. He was a teacher at the high school in Newton where Connie's kids used to go, but I wanted it from her.

I asked, "They're trying to force the issue?"

She rested back. "My husband, Frank, died three years ago. Charlie Norris was at my door the day after the funeral with an offer. If you know him you know he's a crass bastard. He offered me half what they were worth. I own the four

94

buildings on this side all the way to the corner. My husband bought them way back in the 1950's, for a song, during the Eisenhower recession. Norris offered me twelve million dollars. They're worth at least twenty. I don't know what he was thinking. I told him he was a dog and he should go sniff himself. Well," She shrugged as if it was just the way life tended to be, "since then he's chased out every one of my tenants with strange phone calls and flat tires and a few dead rats thrown up the stairwells. That kind of prank. And this last year he's had another piece of excrement from his real estate company come by every month or so with a lower offer. He thinks I'm going to panic. He's that stupid."

I knew Charlie Norris. Of him, in any case. I had only met one of his middlemen. All that was not the matter though. The matter was Charlie Norris could get most anything he wanted. It was curious why he'd let something like this drag on.

Norris' dad was an Irish punk who died in one of the Winter Hill gang wars back in the sixties. But his mother was Sicilian. I wondered if he had a soft spot for elderly Sicilian women.

Just for punctuation, I said, "Not a very nice fellow."

She looked up to check out my own reaction and then added, "Now I think it's him that's going to panic. The state wants to build a new off-ramp from route 90. I can sell the property to the state for twelve million and walk away. Norris just wanted the place so he could move his prostitution and gambling business from around the corner. Property over there by the theatres is getting pricier. He thought he could sell out there and buy over here and still have change in his pocket. Now he sees a new opportunity. He has connections at the State House. He could get them to pay twice as much to him. For three years I've been telling him to stick his nose up his ass and now I think he's the one about to panic. I've had Barton Security in here for most of that time, but now they've cancelled. The issue about the off ramp just hit committee up on Beacon Hill." She smiled. "Mr. Norris is going crazy, I think."

I say, "It won't be a long trip then."

She laughed out loud. All those wrinkles gathered at two neatly rounded and reddened cheeks and I could see right away she had all her own teeth. I was very impressed.

Then she says, "So you aren't stupid. I'll take that one back. But I'll bet you're an oaf. Can you dance?"

I wasn't going to let her off on this one.

"Dancing is for little people who don't have a lot of distance between themselves and the floor."

That got her to laugh again, and then she adds, "But you are an oaf."

All I knew in addition was that her only son was a math teacher in Newton who has a stomach, but not one for standing up to someone like Norris. She has one daughter. I knew nothing about the daughter.

She put her other foot in a stirrup and worked the left knee.

I ask, "So why don't you transfer the property to a holding company—some kind of a real estate trust. At least separate yourself from the whole issue. Probably save you on taxes when the time comes anyway."

"Does the financial advice cost extra?"

"Yes. You have to be more polite and stop hitting me."

No smile. Just a straight stare with those enormous eyes.

She asks, "How'd you get to be so smart?"

I answer, "I listened to my mother."

That broke the smile out again.

She tells me, "The trust part's done. We started that process a few years before Frank died. But the real matter is the sale. When that should be done. Who should we sell it to? The State could take years even if Norris' friends didn't hold the measure up. In the meantime I'm paying over ten thousand dollars a month in taxes, the building next door needs a new roof, and I've got no income."

Somehow, these were problems I would rather have than some others—Charlie Norris aside. When people already have money, their difficulties seem exaggerated, at least to themselves. Personally I was more used to pinching pennies to cover the monthly child support. And I had just discovered that I had a new landlord over at my place in Porter Square and they wanted to raise the rent. I was trying to write my great American novel every morning like I promised myself I would, instead of putting in extra hours with Connie to keep up with the bills, and it sort of skewered my take on anything else. If Charlie Norris got his way, Mrs. Vento would still have more money than I would ever see in a lifetime. But that's none of my business, is it?

Now my next thought was all very premature on my part. I had no business mixing things up. But the fact is, whatever would likely happen with this place, it was going to take a year or two. That's just the way things work in this city. An idea just hit me and I didn't see why not. At least, not just then. In any case, I was tired of Cambridge.

So I said, "I can't pay South End prices. I live over near Porter Square now. But if you give me a good rate, I'll move over here. And I'll bet I can find a couple others. It's a nice location if the rent isn't too high. But then at least you'd have some money coming back in. It'll be easier to rent if there are others already here. And the people I know are the kind who'll toss the rat back."

Mrs. Vento stopped working that knee and leaned on the backrest again.

She said, "You don't know me."

I said, "Yeah, I do."

How much better do you know anyone than the first time you meet them? That thought was rhetorical because I already knew my answer in this case.

She acted like she was thinking about all this, but I knew she was going to take me up on it from the first.

Then she said, "So, I'm supposed to give my boy Michael a gold star? We'll have to wait and see."

'Bay Village' is not really part of the South End anymore, since they cut it off with the trench they dug for the Turnpike back in the 1960's. In fact though, it is one of the oldest precincts, and the narrow streets date from the time when the 'Back Bay' was a swamp and Washington Street was the single high road out of town. Since the Turnpike was built, it has become a little too precious. This isolated nest of closely built brick townhouses and small apartment buildings is now a convenient neighborhood at the threshold of downtown Boston.

Mrs. Vento showed me around and I picked out a nice apartment at the back on the first floor, just behind the elevator of the same building she was living in. She was right above me on the second. With that done, I called up Connie and told him I needed a truck and then I called Burley.

Burley works out at a gym three times a week. He's fifteen years younger than I am, and he never smoked. I let him do the heavy lifting. He's been working for Connie in between acting gigs, which means mostly all the time, for months. He looks like a movie actor, but so far he's only gotten local theater parts. There are a lot fewer prime parts for black guys than you might think. Then again you might not. In any case, I can't keep up with him anymore. Besides that, his girlfriend has moved on again to New York with the production company she's with. This means he has a lot of nervous energy to work out. I asked him to do me a favor. I got him to help me move all my crap.

He was on duty with Connie that night, but he was free until then. So by dark I had most everything piled at the center of the floor of my new apartment. It wasn't much. Just one room again, but twice as big as my place in Cambridge, with an actual kitchenette. I could pull the curtain on my dirty dishes. Burley required pizza and beer and we were occupying my only two chairs when Mrs. Vento poked her head in. Burley got up. His gentlemanly instincts are better than mine. Given a slice and a bottle, my hands were full.

She sat down. Her wrinkles seemed less composed.

"My son Michael called when you were out. He was upset. His wife Marcia called him at the school, in hysterics. Someone keyed his car and slashed one of the tires. Right in his own driveway. In broad daylight. Marcia saw them. She was home. They smiled at her. Of course they were gone by the time the police came."

There were a number of thoughts that went through my head. But the first one was to keep a lid on all this for as long as possible. Panic would get nothing. Waiting was harder, but had the most potential.

After a moment, Burley said, "I'll move in tomorrow."

Mrs. Vento looked back at me. Like I might have a better answer.

I said, "Connie has some sweet equipment. Digital cameras. That kind of thing. He can put a few around. Here and at your son's house. We could use some pictures of Norris' guys. It could help, just so I know when one of them is coming up on me if nothing else. And the cops might be able to use them."

Her face did not change.

I said, "There's something else....What else?"

Mrs. Vento looked away as she spoke. "And my daughter called."

I'm pretty sure Mrs. Vento was trying not to cry. That was something I did not expect.

I said, "I thought you hadn't spoken to her since your husband died. But she called today? That couldn't be coincidental."

Mrs. Vento shook her head. "No....No. There are three names on the trust. Mine. My son's. And Carlotta's. Carlotta called Michael. He told her he'd spoken with Mr. McGuire about you coming in here to keep an eye on things. She told him he was stupid for siding with me and putting his family in danger." Mrs. Vento looked up at me with an expression that was at least sympathetic with that assessment. "If she gets Michael to give in, they'll be able to control the trust. And I think he's having second thoughts."

I asked, "Did your daughter call you?"

Mrs. Vento shook her head.

I was just getting mentally prepared to live in the South End for a while, close to everything worth being close to. I could eat dinner a couple times a week over at Jacob Wirth's. I like their beer. I could probably cover half the jobs Connie threw at me just by walking, or a quick trolley from Arlington Street station. Suddenly having all that taken away again made me just a little grumpy.

I asked Burley to finish the pizza for me and I drove out to Newton to speak with Michael Vento.

Newton is pretty much all residential. Nice houses. Nice shrubs. Big trees. There is no overnight parking on the streets in Newton. Not a lot of cars on the street. Lots in driveways. Michael did not want me to come over but I insisted.

When I arrived, there was a car parked on the opposite side from his house, just past the corner. Not just a car. Someone was sitting inside.

I rang the doorbell and got the wide-eyed face of a kid in the side window within seconds. A dog barked at me from behind the door.

Michael Vento did not look as soft as his mother had portrayed him. He had a good comfortable gut. He seemed like a regular guy right from the start. His twelve year old boy was right on everything. His wife Marcia and his younger boy were off to her mother's house for a convenient overnight visit.

The dog was a full sized black poodle. After we were introduced properly he turned out to be more of a pussy cat.

Pretty quick, Michael hit the only theme I was going to work on myself. Maybe he was not as quick as his mother, but I didn't notice the difference.

He said "I don't think I can be a hero on this. Whatever happens, the Commonwealth is going to take a big chunk of it anyway. I don't want to just give in. But if it keeps escalating, I might have to. I don't want Mom to get herself hurt. She has a temper, you know." I had nothing to say to that. Then his voice took an edge, "They woke my sister Carlotta up this morning. Called her. I don't even have her number, for Christ sake! I don't know how they got it. Whoever it was wouldn't say their name. They just said, 'there was a lot of misery in holding out.' She repeated that to me twice. She wanted to know what that meant. I couldn't imagine. Then, when she went outside to go to work, all four tires on her car were flat. And her windshield was cracked."

"Where does she live?"

"Up on the North Shore. In Ipswich...I didn't even know that until she called! She cut all the strings when dad died. It's a long story."

"What does she do? She married?"

"No. Divorced. That's part of all this. Mom hated her husband. He was a jerk. He likes to gamble. Now Carlotta's selling real estate for a living. In this market. I can imagine she's having lean times. And here comes an opportunity to get a real big fix if we sell that property."

His boy, Robert, sat through most of our conversation without a word. That, in itself, was extraordinary. But the whole time I could feel his eyes on me and it was like having his grandmother there in the room.

Robert suddenly spoke up after his father had finished describing the situation with his aunt Carlotta.

"She's not so bad. She's just alone."

This was a wise observation, under the circumstances. I thought there might be another angle on this. I asked the boy, "What do you think about your aunt? You like her?"

Robert shrugged. "Yeah. She just married the wrong guy, I guess. Her husband has problems."

Michael interrupted, "They're divorced now. That's all over. She just seems to have gotten way too focused on money since the divorce."

Follow the money. That was the rule. At least in most cases.

I told them both, "I don't think Norris is insane. More than just vandalism right now is pretty unlikely. He has to see if he can get his own way at the lowest possible cost first, before he gets really mean. And for the time being, I think we can keep an eye on things and let them know we're doing just that, so they get a little more careful about what they do." I looked at Robert. "You wouldn't go near someone in a car you didn't know, would you?"

The kid smiles at me. He says, "Not unless they had some candy."

I'm not good with sarcasm from twelve year olds. I've had my share of raising three girls and they all have wicked tongues for that kind of thing but I've never gotten used to it.

The dog had taken the spot on the couch next to me and had his muzzle in my lap.

I said, "Do you take the dog out for a walk at night?"

Michael nodded. "Usually."

I said, "Don't do that anymore. Not for now. At least not at night."

The main point of my going over there was to see if Michael Vento was badly shaken. The answer was no. He was angry. I liked that. His wife's worry was for the kids. That was fine too.

Before I left, I asked him about the car on the corner. He hadn't noticed it. But he suggested it might be the cops. They had shown up immediately after Norris's guys did their work and told him they would try to keep an eye on things themselves.

On the way out I stopped my car in the middle of the street to get a look at the fellow behind the wheel. I rolled down my window and said some gibberish to him. He rolled down his window and said, "What?"

It was not a cop. I took a picture of him with my cell phone. He let out a profanity that questioned my biological origins. Then I called the Newton Police and let them know about it and sent them a copy of the picture.

First thing in the morning I took a nice ride up to Ipswich. It was dark when I went out the door of my new apartment and I was a little tired. My mattress was still on the floor, but it was comfortable. I just wasn't used to the night noises yet, and that would only come with time. I'm a light sleeper.

Not wanting to have my tires flattened, I had taken the precaution of parking my car in a garage over near the *Boston Herald* building and was still exhaling the fumes of urine from the bums who use the place as a toilet as I went over the Charlestown Bridge. I had not eaten and my stomach roiled. It was not a good start to the day. Traffic on Route One at that time of the morning is not a pleasure either. I got to Ipswich in a foul mood before eight and stopped in a café there. And suddenly everything changed.

Mist was rising up off the estuary. A pearl pink sky was opening up to a French blue. The smell of salt water is a fine clean thing in late spring. The cafe there had eggs and ham and homemade bread for toast. Life was good again.

Sometimes you cannot imagine the way people are going to look before you meet them. All the evidence is insufficient. When I went in the door to Argilla Real Estate I knew I was looking at Mrs. Vento's daughter even though they had only one thing in common. The woman had short black hair tailored to the shape of her head like a cap. Very stylish. She was wearing a skirt that hugged actual curves. She was at least five and a half feet tall if I discounted the high heels—about as tall as her brother—but she had boobs, and she was very pretty. And it was all in the eyes.

She looked at me like I was going to attack her. The eyes widened. She took a firm grasp on a three-hole paper-punch at the edge of her desk.

I introduced myself and got a sneer in return.

"What a waste of money. If we sold out, we could all walk away with enough to live well for the rest of our lives. Who cares if Charlie Norris makes a killing? It's his business. Not ours. What is she trying to prove?"

I was in a great mood now and not likely to be disturbed by someone who wanted to sell their soul to the devil for a buck. It was their soul, after all.

I said, "You know your mother far better than I ever will, Carlotta. It's really her property. The Trust was just something to keep the State from taking it all in inheritances taxes. Without it you'd have gotten a lot less in any case. Whatever her reasons, why don't you just let her do things her way?"

She sneered again. There was no color in her eyes but black. "You can call me Miss Vento. I go by my maiden name again, thank you. And all of that is none of your business."

I kept a bit of my smile on. For some reason I was not ready to give up on this lady. I think I wanted to believe that Mrs. Vento had not totally failed to raise a daughter worthy of her.

"Miss Vento. I'm not interested in your business. But your mother has hired me to protect hers. That's all I'm doing. Nothing more. And whatever your differences, I don't think you want to see her suddenly dead. Which is exactly what she will be if all this plays out badly."

Carlotta Vento straightened her backbone enough to project everything else forward.

"All she has to do is agree to sell the property. Then it's done. Over. We can all go our own ways."

I shrugged. "She won't do that. She doesn't want to be told what to do. I think you understand that much. But there's more, isn't there? Is there something about your father in all this?"

She gave me a flat-faced cold stare for stepping into territory that was not a public space.

"Go away."

I said, "I can't. I'm just trying to do my job. You may not want my help, but you're in some danger now as well. Or haven't you noticed."

She clinched a jaw. The jaw was something she had probably gotten from her father.

"Like I told Michael. It would all be over if she would just agree."

"If it were just a matter of money, I am pretty sure your mother would give you enough to get by until this thing is resolved."

"Please go."

I turned to leave.

A thought occurred to me. There was nothing to lose on the speculating. It just made sense.

I turned back. "It's your husband, isn't it? Your ex. He's in debt to Norris, isn't he?"

There was a time stop. One of those moments. Then she sat down. Her eyes were turned away.

I said, "You still love the guy, right? And he's in over his head. Gambling? Right. That's all this is. This is all about Norris taking advantage of your husband's gambling habit. Right. And Norris probably let him run up a big tab for exactly this reason." I gave that a second thought. She was just sitting now, looking out the window toward a field of new green salt hay. I raised the speculation. "You only divorced him because you wanted to separate him from the estate. That's what this is all about. And your mother never liked him anyway. She wasn't going to pay off his debts."

I turned to go again, and then turned back a second time.

"You know, your husband is a bigger fool than just being sick with the gambling disease. He's given you up in the bargain. How stupid can a guy be?"

I left on that note. I figured it would give her something to think about.

That afternoon I helped Burley move into the building next door. He was happy to be out of his parents' house again. We brainstormed in the cab of the truck as we weeded through the traffic from Dorchester. We needed two more fools to take a spot in the other buildings. One I had in mind already, but I couldn't tell Connie his number was up until the right moment. The fourth was still a mystery.

Connie has been living in the family beach house in Hull since the separation. He hates the commute. The house isn't properly insulated for winter use and he's forced to turn off the water whenever a deep freeze is coming. The stove sometimes backs up on him if a stiff sea breeze hits the flu and he'll come into the office stinking of the wood pellets he uses to heat the place. Besides, he could rent the whole thing out in the summer months and make his money back and then some.

That afternoon Connie had Jim Lunz and one of his other technicians in, putting up camera's and setting up equipment, so I figured it was the right time to go wandering. Mostly I just wanted to do some more brainstorming and that always seems to come easier when I'm moving around. I rounded up Burley and we walked over to Stuart Street and then around to Tremont through the theatre district. On the way we looked over Mr. Norris's real estate holdings.

I asked Burley, "What happens when one of these theatre companies come into town with a show. Where do the actors stay?"

He was ahead of me before I finished the sentence, but he played with it. "Wherever they can. Anything that's cheap. They room with friends. They do Craigslist. But it's always a problem. Mostly a problem because they can never be sure of the length of the stay. Will the show be held over? Will it close early? It's a pain in the ass. So you've got an idea, I take it."

We talked about ways to get the word out. He suggested he could call his girl in New York. While we walked I called Mrs. Vento and talked it over with her. Theatre people were not her first choice for tenants—too transient—and she wanted to be charging a lot more in rent than I suggested. But then she was down to second choices. A more modest income was very much better than no income at all. The location was right. And actors are used to rats.

Our stroll was interrupted by a phone call from Becky. I had forgotten to tell her I had moved.

She says, "I was going to surprise you. You tell me I'm not spontaneous enough, and here I am standing at your door and your apartment is empty. I don't think I've had such a sinking feeling in years. Where are you?"

I had about three hours before Burley needed to be at the job he was doing that night as a bodyguard for some Rocker at a club up by Fenway Park. It wasn't really enough time, but it would have to do. I asked Burley to hang in with Mrs. Vento and I went on to Cambridge to mend fences.

Rebecca is very sensitive about time. She will murder one of her archeology students who doesn't show up when they're supposed to. If it's three months in upstate New York excavating some colonial fort on the Mohawk River, that's fine. It's her job. If I go away for two days without telling her where I am, she's upset. That's the way it is. But it's nice to be needed.

Besides, I hadn't seen her in a week. I went almost directly to her apartment, but called in an order and picked up some Chinese food on the way to kill two birds, so to speak.

By the time I got back, Burley was at the front door of the building. I thought he was upset because I was a little late. That wasn't the matter.

He gets very cool and casual when he wants. He said, "You missed the cops."

"Why were they here?"

"Because of the break-in."

"What break-in?"

"They came in through the back of the basement of the building on the corner. I think they were after some of Connie's equipment. They get a piece of that and they can figure how to go around it. I bet they didn't think it'd be working yet. Or if it was, that I'd be right here...Connie tried to call you first. Is your phone still turned off?"

It was. I hate to be disturbed at the wrong moment.

I switched it on and it rang in my hand. It was Mrs. Vento inviting me up for dinner. I could still taste the Chinese I had with Rebecca, but I figured it would be a good time to talk. Besides. I like Sicilian food better that Italian food and I love Italian food.

I washed my hands and went up.

Right off she says, "You missed the fun. I thought you were here to protect me."

"I had other obligations. And Burley was here."

"Your girlfriend?"

"Yeah. How long did it take you to get that out of Burley?"

"Under a minute."

"I bet."

Her apartment is four rooms, one at the back, one at the front, and two at the side. I came into the living room at the front and she had a table set for two over by the kitchen. Down low I could hear some old Rock and Roll, mostly Buddy Holly and Roy Orbison.

She says, "Did you eat?"

I say, "Yes."

"Good...Still hungry?"

"Sure."

"Good. That's what a little exercise will do for you."

I did not want to discuss my recent exercise, and I was pretty sure she was working the double entendre anyway, so I just moved on.

I sat down on the side away from the kitchen. Never get in the way of food service if you can help it. I said, "This is going to get expensive if you intend to feed me as well."

She said, "It already is. I'm the one paying for that equipment they tried to steal."

I weighed that before saying anything more. She took some bread out of the oven. It smelled homemade.

I asked, "Are you still sure you want to hold out?"

There was no hesitation. "Positive. And don't worry yourself about me. I just felt like cooking. It takes your mind off things. I'll be letting your girl friend take care of your needs, food and otherwise."

No smile. She just opened a decorative ceramic dish at the center of the table and through the steam I could see veal and some sort of green I didn't recognize. The day had been a veritable feast from start to finish.

My cell phone rang in the dark. Because my mattress was still on the floor, I didn't have far to reach. It was Peggy from McGuire Security. There was another break-in alarm signal. They had called the cops already.

"Where?"

"Where you are. Building three. On the roof."

I use the same .38 that Connie gave me the day I agreed to go to work for him. It's a nice little gun. Good enough for me. Since Mrs. Vento had told me to carry it with me I had taken the advice, but I usually remembered to pull it from the car when I locked up, anyway.

I got my pants on and went up the stairs barefoot.

Mrs. Vento's door was locked. I went up to the third floor in the dark and paused to let my eyes adjust to the vague illumination from the skylight above. There was no sound at first, and then some stirring from below. I had managed to somehow awaken Mrs. Vento, even though I was trying to be quiet about it. Both doors on the apartments on the third floor were locked. I went up to the fourth. The doors there were locked as well. There is a red emergency sign on each floor that was blinding in the dark so I took it slowly as I went up the steps to the roof. That door was bolted.

At that point I looked down the stairwell and saw Mrs. Vento staring back. She was aiming her Glock right at my eye.

The cops finally came about fifteen minutes later. I had my shoes and shirt on by then. We went out the roof door together.

At one edge, there was a cement block with a rope attached. The rope was dangling toward the street below, but it was clear what had been done. It was simple harassment. The building across the alley was six floors high. Someone had gone to the roof there and swung the block over simply to see what effect it would have.

Mrs. Vento was standing by her door as we came down. She had a look in her eye that worried me. My dad used to get a stare like that on occasion. That was the time to stay out of his way. He would disappear into his workshop in the garage and not come out until it was over. Mom was always worried he might kill someone, but he never did—not that I know of.

Bright and early the next morning I call Connie. I woke him up actually. He was covering the job last night with Burley, which he shouldn't be doing, of course, but he's a cheap son of a gun and money has been that short. Besides, it's an excuse not to sit in the office out on Morrissey Boulevard.

He's not happy about being awakened. He says, "Don't tell me the client is dead. Not before I've had my coffee."

That's as close to humor as Connie gets.

I say, "Not yet. I've got an idea."

"Another idea, you mean."

"Exactly. Have you made any new friends in the real estate business?"

"You mean since we blew off all that regular weekly income for keeping an eye on the marble in lobbies just so we could protect forty year old rock stars while we watch them score on chicks that should be doing their home work or washing the dinner dishes and watching American Idol on television at home."

"Yeah. Since then."

"No. I didn't have friends like that even when we were still keeping an eye on slabs of marble for a living. What's your idea?"

I told him. Basically I said, "We need a bigger fish."

He comes right back at me, "You mean a 'boat.' When you are dealing with a shark, you need a bigger boat."

I say "No. Wrong metaphor. I mean we need someone bigger than Norris to keep Norris in line. We can't handle this."

I had to bear in mind that Connie hadn't had his coffee yet. There was about a minute of silence where I figure the main thing on his brain is wishing he had a cigarette. Then he says, "We want Cooper, Dodge. Private banking. The old guy there's what's left of 'The Vault.' All a bunch of Yankee stiffs. They own half the financial district."

I asked, "Can you get me an appointment? This morning?"

Connie says, "I don't know who their real estate man is. I'll have to check."

I say, "No. I can't negotiate anything. I need a quick yes. See if you can get me in to see the old guy."

Next I wake up Burley and tell him I'm going to need him to cover for me here with Mrs. Vento.

Then I showered, shaved and ate. I was on my second cup of coffee when Connie called back with some good news. Hale Cooper could see me between 9:45 and 10:00.

I was there a 9:40 and sat in a small waiting room that wasn't any better than the one at my dentist's office but without the magazines. The secretary who sat across a low partition was suspicious of me for no reason I could fathom. I took the book out of my pocket and started reading. I'm reading Washington Irving for the first time. I avoided him all the way through school and never thought of him again until I read George Borrow's *The Bible in Spain* a few months ago—that for some background research on something I was writing—and the introduction mentioned Irving's *Alahambra*. Suddenly I had a whole new author to read and I was right at the start of it. I settled in.

At 10:00 a tall, thin, fellow in a rumpled tweed jacket and corduroy pants that had probably never seen a crease but looked very comfortable was standing directly in front of me.

He says, "What are you reading?"

I say, "*The Alahambra.*"

He says, "Good. I believe a great uncle of mine published that in the first edition. I've always intended to read it myself. Never enough time. What can I do for you?"

I stood and shook his hand and introduced myself, but we were still standing there in the waiting room and there were two or three other people there as well. He caught my discomfort, and guided me down a short hall. His office had one small window that faced an alley. On a single desk there was a 9 x 12 professional photograph of a beautiful woman in a spring dress somewhere that was probably not on this continent. The desk was cluttered. An old rotary phone sat to the side. Several shelves of law books were held in place by odd objects—a jar of pennies, a white rock, a rather large snow globe—behind him. The fluorescent light recessed in the low ceiling above our heads bleached the color from everything. I sat across the desk in a wooden chair without cushions.

He says, "What is it you need?"

It was only later that I discovered that this particular office was actually where Cooper, Dodge conducted a charitable trust and most visitors were there looking for a handout. I suppose I looked shabby enough myself to be in some need.

I told him about Mrs. Vento, the property, and the problem with Charlie Norris. He actually seemed very interested and peppered me with short questions along the way. At the end of it he shook his head.

"Fascinating. But what can we do?"

I went with the idea, plain and simple. "Take an 'option to buy' on the property. You don't have to exercise it. Unless you want to. A best offer type of thing. Put it writing. That would lock Norris out. He would have no option in the matter. He would leave her alone. She's seventy-five. She'll sell it all eventually."

Mr. Cooper sat back. Behind me was a map of downtown Boston. His eyes scanned the area of Mrs. Vento's buildings.

"That's rather funny, you know. My father owned property along there in the 1950's. He sold it for some reason."

I kept my trap shut and waited.

After a minute or so he said, "I turned seventy-six last year. Odd thing. Feels about the same as sixty-six."

When I got back to the building with my news, Mrs. Vento was gone.

I called Burley. He didn't answer either.

I knocked on her door. I knocked on his door. Nothing seemed amiss. But of course, it was. Burley should have called me if anything was going on. I called the McGuire office to check. There had been no alarm.

Maybe she went shopping and Burley went with her.

Maybe not. Their cell phones would not be off.

I think sitting in my room and waiting for an answer is not a good option, so I take a walk.

Charlie Norris' office is on Harrison Avenue and I moved a little faster than usual. The sky had gone stone gray and the day grew colder, and I figured it was about time for it to rain on the whole deal. I had no idea what I was going to do.

A block away and I can already see Burley hanging in a doorway a couple of buildings over from Norris' address. He doesn't see me. I use my thumb to text him for fun. I can see him look at his phone. I can read his lips as he talks out loud at the air. He looks up, as I cross the street.

"Damn. I was hoping this would all be resolved before you got back. I don't know where the hell she went."

"How long ago?"

"Half an hour. A little less."

I said, "We might as well go visiting."

This was a funny moment. It reminded me of when Connie and I were kids in Hingham. We used to play ice hockey on an old millpond that had a deep end. We played there a hundred times. No problem. But there was always one stupid kid that had to try the ice out there beyond where we had our markers. A puck would go awry. Tommy Steele would be the first to say, 'I'll get it.' Like he had a button in his brain. We'd all yell, 'Forgetaboutit.' But Tommy couldn't resist. We had to pull him out of the water at least four or five times. I have no idea if he's alive today. But the thing was, you had a feeling right away when you were out on the ice. The hair on your neck would come alive. You knew where not to go.

The hair on my neck was yelling at me.

Norris' building isn't big. It's a brick built for some well to do family in the 1890's. It had probably been through a dozen different uses since. Where a wide oak front door should have been, there was now a cheap glass affair with an aluminum crossbar.

The entry hall has been turned into a narrow lobby, lined with paneling and with a single chair for somebody to sit and keep an eye on things. Right off I notice it's a little dark before I see the glass from a light bulb and part of a cheap chandelier scattered on the floor in front of the elevator. The plaster rosette where the remains of the chandelier still dangled was chipped through the layers of paint to a white gash surrounding a small black hole. The fact that there is no guard there makes me look on the floor for something worse, but there is nothing else on the tile but the glass, and a puddle of what I thought was water.

I texted Connie and told him where we were. There is a directory on the wall that has Norris' name on the third floor. The second floor is an import export company. The first floor is mostly occupied by an escort service which appears to be closed. It's not quite noon, so I guess lunchtime isn't big for the escort business.

Burley and I took the stairs two at a time and as quietly as we could. We didn't get beyond the second floor. We could hear her voice on the other side of the stair door marked with the name of the export company.

Now, it's important to note here that I did not have my gun. Burley doesn't carry one at all. We made a few judgments with this in mind.

I could hear her words. "Give me a reason I shouldn't shoot your balls off?"

I opened the door right up, already talking while I did. "It isn't necessary. Everything is taken care of."

My big worry at first was that she might shoot me. By accident. Thankfully, she was not as out of control as I worried she was.

She let out a sigh.

It was the sigh of a mother who just found out her child had come home after being out all night. I've heard that one before.

She had the big gun held out there with both hands and Charlie Norris, in a blue suit and silver tie, was sitting at a desk with his hands on his head like a kid in kindergarten playing one of those games. Behind him, standing backed-up against a wall was the guard from the lobby with a dark pee stain on his pants leg. It was a picture.

Norris looked at me with the surprise on his face of finding something under a rock he didn't expect. I thought he recognized me, and this one fact was a bother to me. You don't want to be a known character in the universe of the likes of Charles Norris. Burley went around to the back of the desk by Norris and pulled a gun from the drawer. He emptied the shells on the floor.

There was another gun on the floor at Mrs. Vento's feet. I said, "Sorry about the inconvenience," to Norris and picked the other gun up and emptied it as well. Mrs. Vento just stood there, all five feet of her in a yellow rain coat and a red felt hat, as if everything were just as planned.

I check Norris a little more carefully. My first real chance. He is not a big fellow. He looked worried. Tired. He had caused a lot of people I knew a lot of worry over the years. In another world there was a better justice than this. But for now, this would do. I said, "You might as well give me your cell phones too. I'll drop them all in the mail box on the corner."

You never know who's going to show up in a place like that, so the best thing for us to do then was to move along.

The walk back was time enough to tell Mrs. Vento about my meeting with Hale Cooper. The idea that he wanted an option to buy back for twelve million what his daddy had sold to her husband fifty years ago for less that fifty thousand seemed to entertain her enough to put a smile on her face. Good enough. I was just a little bit worried about Norris trying to get some retribution, but that's another story. The only thing that happened right away was more grief for Norris. The United States Post Office may be on hard times, but they still get upset when their mail boxes are broken into, and one of Norris' guys was arrested later that night trying to do just that. We got to read about it in the newspapers.

***

Seely's Surfside

The hanging road sign for Denton Real Estate offered a constant chirping against an intermittent wind. It was a small and familiar voice to Burk as he approached Seely's Surfside Diner. The murmur of tires on passing cars was dampened by the new snow. With the hood of his parka pulled tight against the cold, most other sounds were obliterated by the rub of fabric against his ears and he had to keep an eye out for the car lights through breath-fogged glasses as he made his way from his apartment.

The blaze of neon from Seely's was not comforting against the black and white of snow and night ahead. It never was. Even on a hot evening in the summer it was joyless. Tonight, it cut through the falling snow more pink than red. Burk had thought before that it was an odd thing, how the color in the sign seemed to change depending on the weather. He had mentioned it once to Pat, but the observation was shrugged at. Ignored

Burk stopped in the glass box of the vestibule to the diner, stomped the snow from his boots, and unzipped his parka. Then, as he did almost every night when the weather was cold, he wiped his glasses with a tissue from his pocket. With the glasses clear, he briefly tested them by scanning the community notices taped to the glass around him. He cleared his throat. He used the tissue a second time to blow his nose and then slipped it back in his pocket. Then he pulled the quarters from his pocket and slipped them into the slot in the newspaper box and grabbed a paper. Finally he ran his fingers back through his hair and opened the inner door to the moist warmth and thick smells within.

Pat smiled at him from behind the counter. The exact same smile she offered to every other person entering the diner. The same smile she had offered him for over two years. Burk nodded and went to the stool at the end furthest from the bathrooms.

Burk knew she was not beautiful. Neither was he for that matter. She was a near blond except for the darker dye still visible at the ends of her hair bundled by a rubber band at her neck. But she was smart. She did her own plumbing. She could fix a toaster. She had some personality. And somehow, over the last couple of years he had grown attached to her . . . Maybe not. Maybe it was simple lust. She had a great body.

"What'll it be?"

He heard the words before they were spoken. The exact same words every night. He answered with a small variation on his common request.

"Bowl of chowder. Extra crackers. Coffee. Apple pie."

He did not look up to deliver his order. He knew she was not looking in his direction in any case.

In the summer, when the tourists were thicker than the flies, he liked to watch her as she moved back and forth over the black rubber mats in a near continuous waltz. She often stopped to flirt with the male customers then. They didn't realize just how much body language she put into the effort because she wore a full apron. But from the end of the counter he could see her backside, her bare legs, and her butt in the tight shorts. She wiggled that butt mercilessly as she spoke to the young guys. The top of her apron buckled with the sway of her breasts beneath the fabric. They saw that, of course. But they didn't see her butt.

He looked up now as she pushed his bowl of chowder onto the counter in front of him.

He said, "Thanks."

She didn't answer. She seldom did. Her lips turned inward briefly, as if to withhold the courtesy.

He would have assumed long ago that she disliked him personally if he had not seen the same service given to nearly all the regulars. She was never rude. Never gave cause to think she was being rude. It was the service of someone too busy to offer more than was necessary. Or someone who hated their job, not necessarily the people they served.

He unfolded the paper and began to read the news with no more expectation of something extraordinary than what played out in front of him day to day.

"Burk!"

He lowered the top of the newspaper. Beyond the six or seven heads in the booths between, George Parker, a mechanic at the Sunoco station, stared back at him from the far end.

"Sir?"

"You hear anything about Dick Johnson?"

"No sir."

Del Parker, his wife, turned around in her booth-seat across from George to look back at Burk. "You heard he took a head-on collision down Route 6 yesterday, didn't you? The

Medevac took him out in a helicopter all the way to Boston. No one has heard if he's dead or alive."

Dick Johnson sold wine at the Eastham Market. A good fellow for a story and a laugh.

Burk asked, "What happened to the person he hit?"

George answered with a shake of his head, "Nobody knows. Car was empty when the police got there. Odd thing. I thought it might be in your paper there."

Theresa, the red head from the barbershop who often filled in at the diner when business was better, had followed the conversation back and forth from the booth closest to the door.

"It had just started to snow, you know. They sent out a search party. But they couldn't find a thing. Nobody. They think whoever it was might have had some sort of concussion and be in a daze. You know. But they never found them."

Burk answered back, "Nobody came in the shop today. Exactly nobody. So I never heard. Everyone's hunkered down with the weather I guess. I cataloged every piece of copper pipe in the place. Pete's going to hate me."

Several people laughed. It was a small joke. Pete never used copper anymore. Burke snuck a look at Pat. She was busy scraping her griddle.

In the beginning, when he had first arrived, after completing his six year hitch in the Army, she had flirted with him as well. He had learned a bit about her then—what she was willing to tell.

She once said, "It's a small place here. A narrow place. You can find out too much about people, way too quickly. Good and bad."

He could not remember his answer to that. But he remembered the look on her face. Her eyes were gray and conveyed her sadness as easily as a smile.

Another time, soon after seeing her cleaning the griddle late one night as he passed, he had asked her if she ever went out with friends.

She had said, "Most people around here are just visiting. You don't want to find out more about them than you need to. The rest are retired."

That wasn't completely true of course. She knew that. She was simply putting him off.

He had persisted. He told her something about himself. She seemed interested in his writing at first. Not to read it, he thought, but in the fact that he did it even though there was no realistic chance he would ever be paid for it. She had never gone to college herself. She did not read novels.

"What's the point. It's all made up. It's not the truth about anything. It's just the way someone wants it to be or the way they're afraid it really is."

She never told him what she did when she wasn't working. He had discovered that by accident.

Her small interest in Burk had lasted a month or two at most. Then, as the summer wore on, her conversations had shortened. By the autumn of that first year he had already fallen into the pattern that continued to the present. He had changed jobs that September so that he could stay on the Cape, leaving the kitchen at Arnold's to work the counter at Pete's Plumbing. But he had not done it for her. No. He had done it just because he needed the job. Mostly. His father had been a plumber, and Burk knew enough to get along there on his own.

Besides, his boss was a decent sort. Most days Peter was gone, off repairing pipes in the cottages that were not properly shut off for the winter, or drains clogged with sand. Burk had the store to himself. Between customers he could read his books. He lived in the front apartment above, facing the traffic of Route 6, with a small slice of Town Cove visible from the bathroom window if he raised himself up on tip-toes. The back apartment was the seasonal rental. In the winter that was empty. Life was quiet.

In all other matters, his life was pretty good. He was saving his money. The Army had paid off his college loan. He had plenty of time to write, which had been his objective in staying on the Cape from the beginning. In better weather he ran five miles on the beach three times a week, plus the three miles from here to there. In bad weather he walked the distance. His health was good. He had recovered as completely from the accident as he could hope. The pain at the center of his leg would be with him to the end now the doctor said. Pinched nerve. That was that.

'That was that'. Who said that so often? It was Pat, of course. He could even remember that first time he had heard her say it. Or a version of it.

He had asked her once why the place was called 'Seely's Surfside', given that the surf was at least three miles away.

She had leveled her standard stare at him and answered with a question. That was another of her habits. "What side of the road is this?"

He had said "Ah."

She had said, "So that's that."

Such responses were the reason he seldom attempted small talk with her. He had never been glib. The right words did not often come to mind until well after the need.

The morning at the beach when he discovered her secret, he had not spoken to her. He had known it was Pat from a quarter mile away, just by the way she stood. Because she was concentrating, she saw him only as he came close. She was facing the inner bay over the marshes, where the water was silvered beneath a steel sky. She was wearing a broad hat, tied beneath her chin. The plain cloth coat she wore was scared by smears of old paint. Stunned and wordless he had approached further to see the small canvass but she shook her head at him and said, "No. Please. Go away."

He remembered that face too well. He had disturbed her in some way far beyond mere interruption.

And he had never mentioned it to her again.

Burk looked up from his newspaper at the thought. Pat was at the register, oddly dancing from foot to foot as she punched at buttons and a customer waited. Even with long pants on, her butt was worth a peek.

The register suddenly tilted forward at her as if alive. The open drawer sloshed loose change at her apron as Pat fell backward to the floor. Stiff-armed, the man across the counter held out a small black pistol.

The gun cracked. Contained in the narrow room of the diner, the sound was not much different than a larger firecracker. The glass front to the pie display shattered and collapsed around Pat's head. The man in front of the counter pulled the cash register back to him with his free hand before it also fell. The cash drawer gaped.

"What the fuck? I told you to keep quiet and keep still. Now, get me the money!"

Someone said, "What's happening?"

The gunman spun around now, looking at the half dozen faces that stared back at him. "Y'all stay in your seats! I got no business with you." Then he turned back to Pat. "Stand up bitch. Get the money!"

Pat shook the shards of glass away and stood uncertainly, while using one hand to reach into the open drawer. Burk could see only half her face, but he knew the whole. He had seen her kick rowdies out the door during the summer. She could look fierce enough. She held her other arm at her side, as if it were hurt.

The man with the gun was at least six feet tall. Overweight. Or something was stuffed beneath his parka. He had a thick black mustache and black hair that had the look of tar protruding from beneath a baseball cap. The parka was dark green with the hood down and Burk could see that the inside of the parka was maroon. The man's skin was oddly yellowed as if he had used the liquid tanning lotion tourists sometimes tried in the early weeks of the summer. All of these details Burk cataloged one by one as if calculating a sales slip at Pete's plumbing.

Pat set the loose bills from the drawer down on the counter and the man swept them up in one grab and stuffed them in his jacket.

"Where's the rest?"

Pat said, "What rest?"

With that the man pushed the register forward again and it nearly struck Pat's feet as she danced away.

The man's voiced raised to the level a scream. "The bank, BITCH. What you keep aside. I want all of it!"

Pat turned to the collection of packaged teas in various boxes that filled the high shelves beside the ruined pie display. At that moment, George Parker came out from the bathrooms. He was headed toward the corner booth, asking his wife why she had the funny look on her face. He never saw the shot that killed him. The wallop of sound gone in an instant. Del Parker screamed and collapsed to the floor beside her fallen husband.

The man with the gun took careful aim and shot again directly at her head. Burk did not understand the action until it was too late. The sound of the second shot made more stunning for being watched.

The gunman said, "SHUT UP. All of you!" and turned back to Pat. "Give me the money!"

Pat's face had gone slack and expressionless. She handed him a box of green tea. The gunman slammed it to the counter, breaking it apart and grabbed the bundled bills with his free hand, and stuffed them into his pocket with the others.

Headlights scanned the ceiling of the diner as a car turned in from the road.

The gunman looked back at Pat. "Do you want to die?"

He said it with his jaw thrusting forward. Pat shook her head. Her hair had broken loose from its clasp and hid her face from Burk. He imagined how she might look. She would not be scared. She would be angry. But she would hide that now.

The car had pulled up. Even through the glare and blush of moisture on the glass, Burk could see that it was an Orleans police cruiser. The headlights went off. The two officers got out causally and stepped toward the door. They could not know what was going on behind the fogged glass.

Burk realized that the situation was about to get worse. Behind him he knew there were wooden highchairs stacked to be moved to the booths for children as necessary. He had never really looked at them closely but he imagined they were heavy enough. He would have to lift a chair with one motion or else the moment would be lost. He was going to get shot. He would have to survive that the best he could.

The chairs were stacked too tightly. The top chair did not come away easily from the rest. It was three chairs he flung at the window and it took all of his strength to elevate them above the near booth. He felt the bullet before he heard the crack of the gun. The glass shattered outward as he lost the strength to keep his balance and he folded to the floor. His head hit the black and white tiles first.

Burk awoke to a room hazy and half dark. His glasses had fallen loose somewhere. The sounds he heard were not what he was used to. Only the small fluorescent at the top of the pie display still shone over the room inside.

With his cheek hard against the tile, he could turn an eye to see one corner of the broken window above. Cold air flowed down at him in a steady stream along with flakes of snow. Outside it appeared to be daylight . . . No. Those were bright lights directed at the diner. Beyond a dark pool of liquid that trailed forward from his own body, Burk followed the lines of the tile along the floor until they blurred to gray. He could make out the shadow of a leg protruding from the opening at the center of the counter. It moved. Someone was sitting there, with their back against the griddle. No one else was visible. No one else but the darkened bodies of George and Del Parker where they lay at the far end.

The blue strobe of another police cruiser grew brighter and halted somewhere close.

Burk's right hand was caught beneath his body in a cold pool of blood. He knew that much. His left hand felt numb, but it moved. Thinking through all of this hurt. He had a headache.

There was a whimper.

The leg on the floor at the center moved slightly with the shout. "Shut up!"

Burk reconsidered the situation.

Given his position, Burk was not visible to the man who was sitting there on the floor. In the time Burk had been unconscious, the other people in the diner, those still alive, must have been corralled behind the counter, probably so they could be watched by the man with the gun.

The sound of expanding metal popped. An odd sound. The sound of a radiator perhaps. No. It was the stove. The griddle was on full blast. The gunman was keeping warm.

Burk tried to move a leg. He was unsure if there had been a reaction. He wiggled a toe. He felt nothing.

As it was, he would probably be dead fairly soon. Just from loss of blood alone. His options were limited.

A voice came from outside, magnified electronically by a loudspeaker.

"You in there. Why don't you come out? You are not going to be able to leave on your own. You know that. Just throw your gun out and we'll take you into custody with no more harm done."

The gunman pulled his legs beneath him and crouched forward. Burk could see his face now. The mustache was gone, along with the baseball cap and wig.

He yelled, "I tell you what. If you put any of that fuckin' tear gas in here I'm going to shoot these people dead, one by one, before you can get through the door. Do you hear me?"

There was silence.

The gunman leaned even further with the scream in his next words. "Do you hear me?"

The answer came, "Roger that. We hear you."

Burk closed his eyes. He was sure he felt the man's eyes on him. He heard the thump of the man's knees on the tile as he moved in Burk's direction. When he parted his eyelids again, he was looking up at the back of the man rising on his haunches to peek from the broken window.

Burk checked off the possibilities again. What would be his best move? If his legs did not operate, moving at all would be folly. But then, he would just die a bit faster. Whatever he did, it ought to be effective. He shouldn't waste the chance.

Before he completed the thought, the gunman shifted away. He cackled. Burk could not remember ever hearing a man cackle before who was not on television.

Still on his knees the gunman lunged back inside the counter. Then his hand rose above and pulled a tin pie plate, covered with the gleam of plastic, out from the shattered display. It was a lemon meringue pie and it shimmered in the light of the display as he brought in down. A whimper followed. Burk thought it was from Therese. He had heard no sound from Pat.

Burk pushed through the pain in his mind. Where was it coming from—exactly. He concentrated on shifting each part of his body. He began to faint. Fought that. Concentrated on controlling his breathing first. Clearly his key problem, other than loss of blood, was his right lung. Every breath was excruciating. That must be where the bullet had entered. Close to his sternum. He had faced the gunman in that instant after he released the chairs at the window. The continued turning of his body had saved him for that moment. The gunman was an excellent shot. He had fired at Burk's heart and missed because of the turning of his body by a couple of inches.

The pain of Burk's effort to move took his senses away for an instant.

Then he heard her voice.

"It's cold over here. Everyone is cold."

Then the gunman, "Shut up."

During those first summer months Burk had actually learned a great deal about her. He had always liked to watch

131

people and he had gotten to know most of Pat's ready expressions and a few of those faces she reserved for unexpected moments. He got to know what it meant when she stood a certain way. He learned the tones of her voice. All of it unbidden. She had never really teased him with possibilities beyond the counter at the diner. Her flirting was always just that.

He remembered one big fellow now, a lifeguard from Marconi Beach. She had chatted with him several times before. Then one evening he came in from his jeep without his tee-shirt on. The sign on the door could not be missed. She told him to leave. He thought she was kidding. A major mistake. The police station was only a quarter-mile away.

Burk tried once more to move his left leg. After a delay that seemed surreal, it shifted forward. He moved it back in place and then tried his right leg again. It buckled at the knee. He twisted his ankle. It moved side to side.

Once, when she was still making the effort to chat with him—that was the first August wasn't it—he had foolishly asked about her father. The picture on the wall by the entry was of her mother, father, and herself as a girl of eight or nine. It was taken the day the diner opened. Her mother worked the morning shift from 5 am to 1 pm. Pat came in at noon and worked till 9 each night. Fred and Albert, two short order cooks came in five days a week when they were sober. That was the entire staff. He had seen Pat through the windows mopping floors after hours. Her mother was in every morning by four working up the dough that had been set aside so the yeast could do its work during the night.

Stupidly, that day in August, Burk had said, "What happened to your dad?" Just that much. He had gotten a cold stone stare. No answer. That might have been the start of when things changed between them. Certainly, when the flirting had stopped.

A broadcast voice broke the silence.

"Tell us what you want? What is it you want? Talk to us. We'll see what we can do."

The gunman came forward from his place behind the counter. Back and forth he looked for odd shadows against the glass of the windows. Burk closed his eyelids just enough to see the figure of the man as he moved.

The diner was raised about three feet off the ground. That made the windowsills at least seven feet high. But this spot was well chosen at a turn in the road and slightly higher than anything close-by. Across the street the land fell away to trees in a lot that was nearly a swamp. The tree limbs were bare and neatly outlined by a topping of white, offering little concealment. The only taller building nearby was Denton Real Estate. From where he lay on the floor, Burk could just make out the roofline of Denton's faux Cape through the glass. He knew there was no second floor there. Just the gray blur of an air vent.

The gunman moved in Burk's direction, waddling back and forth, this time in a crouch. When he reached the booth below the opening of jagged glass, he rose a bit to see what was there before he spoke.

"I want a truck. Get me a pick-up. Four-wheel drive. Gas tank full. I want some pizza. Put a hot pizza in there. Leave it in one of those delivery packs. I want it hot! And a bottle of Coke. A big one. And money. What you can get . . . No. I want ten thousand dollars. You can get that. I know it. And I want it all in half an hour."

The loudspeaker voice began to answer quickly
"I'm not sure we can—"

133

The gunman screamed, "Shut up! Shut up! Listen to me! I'm gonna shoot the waitress if you're a minute late. Two minutes, I'm going to shoot the one who whimpers. I'll shoot'em all and then you can come and get me. I know my chances here. No games!"

The gunman made his way back to his space behind the counter before Burk had steadied his breathing enough to try to move. The trick was to keep the breaths shallow to avoid significant pain as well as to avoid being noticed.

Burk shifted his left leg again. It responded quickly this time. That was his good leg now.

Funny thing. He had left the Army after jumping out of moving trucks and helicopters, and rappelling down fifty-foot cliffs over and over again until he could do it in the dark by feel alone, and after nine months in Afghanistan where no two feet of ground were the same height, and two years at Fort Benning Georgia where he used to do the obstacle course just to keep himself in shape, he had come home and jumped a rain puddle in Allston one night after drinking a few too many when the Patriots won the Superbowl and ruined his right knee. That was the way life was. He had gone to his local diner for some chowder and gotten himself killed. What a pain.

Burk shifted his right leg. That leg seemed to be good enough, but it was that knee he had damaged and it had never really been a sure thing since.

He moved his left arm. It was the most visible part of his body so he had to be careful that it was not seen. He brought his hand up to his face where he could see the skin clearly. It looked pale, even in the small and distant light of the florescent from the pie display.

About a foot in front of him on the tile beneath the table of the near booth was an angled piece of what appeared to of his eyes as ice. That could not be. It was an angle of window glass. But if he reached for it, his hand might be seen. If he dropped it, it might be heard. He waited.

After a moment the gunman stretched up toward the pie shelves again. What he grabbed this time was Burk's piece of apple pie. It was the last one in the case, and Burk had taken note of it as he came in. It seemed life was going to make this experience as painful as possible. His killer was going to eat Burk's piece of apple pie. Burk took the chance then and grabbed at the shard of glass. He grasped hard enough to feel the sharp edges of it bite his fingers to be sure he didn't drop it. Then he pulled it back and manipulated the largest end into his palm.

Something odd had changed in the moments since he had last looked across to the end of the room toward the window that faced Denton Real Estate. A small dark triangle had opened at the peak of the roof. Blurred as it was, Burk was sure it had not been visible before. The air vent had been opened.

He felt woozy. He had to keep his head. Burk had no idea of how much time had passed before the loudspeaker squawked again and the voice became intelligible.

"Trucks here. Tank is full. Pizza is in the cab. Ten thousand is in a paper sack on top of the pizza. Ready to go. Twenty-five minutes."

The gunman yelped as if outraged as he shifted across the floor toward Burk.

"The Coke. You forgot the Coke!"

"No, No, the Coke is there too."

"Better be."

"What now?"

"Now? Now I'm coming out for my pizza. I'm going to have the one that whimpers at my back. I'm going to have the waitress in front of me. You want them alive, you keep me alive."

On the gunman's last words, the glass high on the window at the far end of the diner changed to a gauze of fine gray cracks. The gunman grunted with the impact of the first bullet. The glass shattered as a second bullet came through.

The gunman screamed. In one furious movement he leapt back toward the counter screaming, "They're dead! They're all dead!"

Burk rose up directly behind him. Without the use of his right arm he used the weight of his body to bring the gunman down, just as a large iron chowder pot swung out from the opening against the man's head. The gunman's hand flexed against the trigger as Burk rammed the shard of glass into the gunman's neck. The shot, muffled beneath the man's body but so close from the awkwardly bent arm, was deafening. Through the haze and the intense ringing of Burk's ears that followed, he saw Pat's face. She was standing close above him. But he had never seen exactly that face before.

****

She Knows Her Onions

You want me to tell you about Zim? I don't know you. And I never forget a pretty face. . . . Sure, I worked over at the *Mirror* years ago. Probably before you were born. There wasn't a single dame in the entire room back then. I guess times have changed. For the better, heh? But if Barry George sent you over, then you must be all right. . . . Cass, is it? Just call me Jim. Is that shorthand you're doing? Geez! Chicken scratch. Nobody's gonna be reading over your shoulder. But let me tell you about the old days. I had a stubby pencil and a little note book and the best I could do was to spell the names correctly. . . . Yeah. I got canned. That was because of Mayor John F. Hylan. Sonofa—I'd tell you what the 'F' stood for but — . . . But that's why I gave it up.

Right. So this is what I know. At least what I've heard. The part that I think is true.

No. Cream. I can get you some milk out of the icebox if you want it?

So. Despite what you read in your own paper, it wasn't Joan who caused any of it. She might not be innocent, but she was a bystander right up to the end, almost. . . . Joan? I did my time waiting in that office? Smart cookie. But I never got to first base.

It was Florrie that was the first guy to get a hook on Zim. This was something of a surprise to me, you see, because Florrie was the last guy you'da thought needed the help.

You know Florenz Patterson. Sure you do. But you probably know him better by the name of Gunther Grab or Forrest Fern. You've might'a read some of his '*Ready Evans*' stories in *Black Mask*. He wrote under a lot of names. There were issues of *Wild West* that he wrote almost single-handedly using five different monikers. Not many of the New York guys have ever been on a horse or much else west of the Poconos. Hell, Clarence Mulford even writes his '*Hopalong Cassidy*' stories from up in Fryeburg, Maine, for Christ sake! But they are all good at making the best use of what little experience they know.

Florrie once woke up from a dead drunk down at the police stables, nestled in a pile of manure for the warmth. It was winter at the time. He never remembered how he got there, but that resulted in the '*Fast Burk*' series. You've read those maybe. The jockey detective? No? In any event, Florrie was a generous guy for a tight-wad sonofabitch penny-a-word man. For a while there he was churning out stories so fast that the pennies were adding up to dollars. He bought a Packard. Got drunk. Wrapped it around a tree up on Pelham Parkway. Went right out and bought a Cadillac. But before that, he was the one who first discovered George Zim.

Have another cup a' joe? Yeah. This might take a while. The answers to some questions aren't so simple.

No. I can say this for sure, though, not as simple as a cheap headline. When that hack Vince Fosdick walked into Bill Grogan's office at Power Publications last week and shot poor

Bill in the eye, it was just damn lucky he didn't get Bill's good eye or you guys would have never had all that ready-made material. Vince always used a typewriter and not a pen to churn out his line of dreck anyway, but still, you all got it wrong. That was not Bill's sword. Bill was in the Philippines, and in Mexico, and in France, but he never carried a sword. That was his granddaddy's sword from the Civil War. Bill just kept it up on the shelf there behind him for sentimental reasons. And there was no fight. No tussle. Bill stuck that sonavabitch Fosdick up against the wall like a butterfly with one thrust. Bill wasn't one to waste any energy. Especially when he was about to take his last breath. You guys just couldn't resist the easy one-liner about the 'sword is mightier than the pen' after all. Three cartoons in three papers the same day all working the same angle. You all should be embarrassed.

Yeah. I was talking about when Florrie met Zim. But it's related. Right? Or why would you be in here asking about all that old news now?

So, it all started one evening when Florrie was down to the Chelsea Diner on Ninth Avenue. It's where a lot of the guys went when the pay-day came because Sally took their checks and they all ran tabs. Besides, she's a heavy reader. And it's where Florrie was that summer night, right in the middle of a feast. He'd just gotten Kennicott over at the *Blue Book* to pay up on a couple of stories from the year before. This would be in early '35. Florrie was ready to celebrate. By himself, naturally. No one in the per-word trade would think of breaking bread with old Florrie otherwise. No one liked him.

Just then, this guy comes in and sits down at the next stool and orders soup. This fella is wearing a good Burberry coat that's a little frayed at the cuffs, over the remains of what must at one time have been a three-piece suit. But the guy just orders soup. Sally starts to go get it and then stops and says "Don't I know you?" The guy looks innocent like 'Who, me?' Sally says, "I know you! You shaved off your beard, but I know you. You couldn't pay for your dinner last time. Right? You stiffed us for a Salisbury steak. Right? Right? I remember you. You're the phony writer!"

The guy looked pained to hear that. But Sally reaches below the counter and pulls out some coffee stained pages. She says, "You gave me this! What am I gonna do with this? Heh? It's not even finished. Bad enough you talked me into taking your goddamn story for the price of a meal—-I get to the end and it isn't even finished. What kind of trick is that. What kind of deal is that for a Salisbury steak?"

Now, this fits with Sally—her heart's made of butter. She'd given me more than one cup of coffee through the years when I was working the penny-a-word trade and didn't have the nickel. Now the guy is looking pretty sheepish. He finally just says, "I couldn't—" chokes on his words and starts to leave.

But remember, Florrie is flush. He's got most of fifty bucks in his pocket. *Blue Book* used to pay more then. Up to a three cents a word—when they paid. And Florrie's been watching this little drama for full entertainment value. But when the guy gets up to go, it pulls a string on Florrie's heart. Right. Hard to believe he has one. Not like with Sally. Florrie used to be a newspaper reporter, you see. Yeah. Just like you or me. But he walked out on a wife and kids down in Philadelphia when the *Enquirer* found out he was making stuff up. Now, Florrie's thick skinned. He just turned around and started writing fiction full time. And we all took him for what he was. But something about the other fellow that night just got through to whatever was still beating in Florrie's chest and it makes him speak up.

He says, "I'll pay for it. I'll buy his dinner, Sally. And if you give me those pages, I'll pay for the Salisbury steak too."

The deal was done.

Then Florrie proceeds to chat the guy up for a couple of hours or so while they eat. And it turns out he's an interesting guy. Says his name is George Zim. Florrie vaguely remembers the name from years before. He was with the *Minneapolis Star* just after the War, but made a name for himself working for *Asia Magazine* in the late 20's. Made his way all over China and India. Florrie knows a little bit about airplanes from time he spent pushing broom at an aerodrome over in England during the war so he uses his two cents to loosen Zim up a bit.

Now I found out about a good deal of this well after the fact because I got to know Sally a little bit better later on, as you know, but this was before we started trading recipes. So, don't quote me.

As I understand it, George Zim was born in 1900. Turns out, when school got boring in St. Paul, the kid ran away from home and joined the circus just like '*Wash Tubbs*' in the Sunday funnies. That lasted a season I guess, but Zim got tired of washing down the elephants and juggling apples and oranges at the ticket counter, and shoveling out the horse stalls. When the circus closed down that winter Zim found himself in Winnipeg, Canada during one very cold Christmas. I can't imagine that. We're the same age and about that same time I was still hugging on to my teddy bear.

There was no work to be had up on the farms in winter, naturally, and there was a war on, so Zim turned a six into an eight on his papers and signed up with the Canadian Expeditionary force right out of Winnipeg. By July 1916, on his birthday, he was in Paris, France, and later got to see action at Morval during the battle of the Somme. He was injured there.

141

A concussion, I think. Well, it was about then the Canadians were losing pilots so fast that they were asking for volunteers in the field and Zim up and joined the Royal Air Force. And that's where he stayed until 1918.

Zim ran away from St. Paul for the second time when his job at the *Star* got to including too many farm reports. He went to Chicago. He was the one who covered Jack Knight's transcontinental airmail flights for the *Times*. He interviewed Major Macready before he did the first non-stop coast to coast. He could fly a plane pretty well himself so Macready took him right up there with him during test flights. And it was from Chicago that he later went on to China.

But for some reason no one knew that night at the Chelsea Diner, the guy had fallen on hard times. So, the two of them talk right through a full roast beef dinner, four or five cups of coffee and a pack of cigarettes.

And that night Florrie takes the story home that Sally gave him and reads it. And damn! It's the goods. Florrie is gobsmacked. This guy Zim can really write. Only it isn't finished. Just like Sally said. The story isn't complete. So, Florrie finished it that night. He knows right off how it should end. He retypes the whole damn thing before dawn and hands it in over at Daring Publications the next morning. But now, it's got his own name on it.

Get this, Florrie goes down to the Daring Offices on Madison and 23rd and sits right down on the desk of Herbert Glick—Glick was editing *Daring Detective* at the time—and refuses to leave unless Glick reads the first page. If I pulled that stunt with Glick he would start laughing and wouldn't stop until he'd managed to throw me out onto Madison Avenue. But Glick reads the first page, and then the second. And the third.

He reads the whole damn thing right there on the spot. Bingo! Sale!

And *Daring Detective* pays up front. Florrie is riding high now. He buys a bottle of good rye, finds a lonely gal on the closest corner and takes her home to his hotel room. . . . Sorry. You're a reporter. You've seen worst. So, Florrie was living down at the Champlain on 22nd Street at that time. Nice place. No roaches. No bed bugs. Twenty bucks a week. I stayed there myself once.

Now, to be fair, the pulp trade is a hard grind for most guys. They have to be able to produce two or three stories a week to pay the bills. If they don't have families to support, they have other habits. You'll see a lot of guys out there on the street these days who were once in the trade but couldn't keep up with it. As fast as the magazines eat the stuff up, there is always some punk with a fresh face and a new bag of tricks.

My figure is that Florrie must have been getting tired. The easy mark was the one to hit.

Well, then, the next week Florrie can't get anything to crank. No ideas at all. *Daring Detective* even calls him for something else to put in their next issue and Florrie tries to steal something from the daily rags. . . . Yeah. Sorry about that. Everybody does that. You guys never tell the whole story anyway. Just pick a good headline, change the names and add the ending. Easy as pie! But this time nothing works. The next week, the same thing. And then another week. After a month Florrie's closing in on broke again. He's going to have to move out of the Champlain.

And then, right there, shoved into the shelf next to him, he spots that original story from the guy at the Chelsea diner. He pulls it out and sees there's an address on the top.

That's when he first got the bright idea to go down to Avenue A and look up Zim. But Zimm's not home.

Now Florrie is still Florenz Patterson of the Philadelphia Pattersons. That is to say, he's a schmuck. He has no intention of telling Zim that he's stolen the guy's story and published it under his own name. He just goes down there and sits on the stoop until Zim gets back. And the whole while he's waiting he's staring at a pile of trash on the curb and watching the bums come by and pick it over and then wander away.

Finally, the guy arrives. But Zim stops at the curb before he even sees Florrie. He looks stunned. Then suddenly he throws himself on that pile of trash and starts to sob as he roots through the mess. Florrie gets up and moves closer, but there is not much he can do, until Zim finally rises up with a small black book in one hand, and a smile on his face through the tears. With that in his hand, he just sits down again, on the remains of a chair.

This is a thin guy, maybe 5' 6" tall, in a brown Burberry that would have fit somebody thirty pounds heavier, and a battered black fedora—looks like that new guy at the movies, Humphrey Bogart, but on a bad day—and he's sitting in a pile of trash hugging a little black book like it has all the answers to life itself.

No. It's not a Bible. It's just a little note-book.

Florrie realizes that the pile of trash is really just the contents of the room Zim was living in. After a minute, when he thinks Zim has calmed down, Florrie reintroduces himself. Reminds Zim of their conversation at the diner and of the meal Florrie bought him. He asked Zim what's going on.

It turns out, Zim's rent was only eight dollars a month with occasional heat, but the guy was three months behind. Florrie's mind is working fast now. He tells Zim why he came by. He needs some inspiration. He's run dry. And from their previous conversation, Florrie got the idea that Zim might have a story or two to share. Florrie says he'd be willing to pay for it. Zim says no problem. He's got more ideas for stories than he knows what to do with. Right there, on the curb, Zim holds this little black note-book, up close in front of his face and pages through it.

Florrie realizes that Zim is running around without glasses. The guy is nearly blind now on top of everything else.

Well, Florrie can't wait. He rings the bell for the building super and chats him up. They make a deal. Florrie pays that month's rent for Zim in advance and the last month's rent and promises to catch up on the rest at a later time if Zim can stay. Deal!

Then, with Zim still in the chair on the curb looking at his little book, Florrie and the super move the rest of the pile of trash back into Zim's room.

Finally, Zim closes up his little black book again and after a minute he says. "There is a fellow, a scientist at Columbia, who is fading out. Just disappearing. He wakes up one morning and looks in the mirror to shave and sees the shadow of something right behind him. And it's not an optical illusion. Everyday it's getting worse. He goes to the doctor. The doctor tells him it's true. He's never seen anything like it. He's becoming transparent . . ."

Right there on the sidewalk at Avenue A, Zim tells Florrie this great tale. Well. you know the story, X rays and all. '*Shadow Man.*' It was the top title in *Daring Adventures* for 1935. They strung it out for three issues. Somebody else even re-stole it and gave it the Hollywood haircut for a film with George Brent. Big hit. But what you don't know is that only the end of that yarn was all Florenz Patterson. Zim had given him everything except the end for it. No finish. And if there was one thing Florrie knew how to do, it was finish.

The next week, Florrie is back again. This time, seeing how the guy is looking a little pale, he offers to take Zim out to dinner. For the price of a liverwurst sandwich and two beers at McSorley's, Zim opens his little black book again and sticks his nose down in the pages.

And that story? That story was even better than the first. That was *China Dawn*. Yes! That made it all the way to the *Saturday Evening Post*. Florrie knew a good tale when he had it. He didn't waste it on the pulps. And he used his own name on that one too. That one made it all the way to Hollywood right after *Shadow Man*. Yeah. Gary Cooper. Madeleine Carroll. You saw that, right? Foreign correspondent in Shanghai trying to get the missionary's daughter out before the Japs take the city. Lord! Madeleine Carroll! What a woman. And for that one, Florrie got full credit on the film too. He was rolling in dough then. That was when he bought the car. You know all about that, right?

But it was before that when everything really started to fall apart. The *Post* didn't run *China Dawn* until later in '36. Meanwhile Florrie had his rent to pay at the Champlain. And now he had Zim's rent to cover down on Avenue A, as well.

About once a week, Florrie starts showing up at Zim's door and takes him out to dinner. Zim was very grateful. That was probably the only substantial food he was getting at the time. But a man cannot live on liverwurst alone. Even with the two beers. And even Florrie could see that. So, each visit he would stuff a couple of extra bucks in Zim's pocket when they parted. Very generous.

What? You're wondering what Zim is doing with himself the whole time. Right? We don't really know, but it seems he used to go to the museums or the library a whole lot. Some place to stay warm, I guess.

And in the mean-time Florrie is moving up the food chain himself. One week he has something in *Argosy*. The next month he's in *Blue Book* again. A *Black Mask* here. A *Dime Detective* there. Even the *Post* took another one. Florrie is eating well and the girls on the corner are seeing him every week. But Florrie's real problem was the bottle. When he was short on cash, a quart of rye might last a good two weeks. With his pockets full, he was knocking down a couple or three quarts a week, not counting his visits to McSorley's with Zim.

And when Florrie was drunk, he talked. I know this first-hand.

When Christmas came that year, Daring Publications had their annual soiree. They rent the Hibernian Hall on Fourth Avenue and invite all the other magazines to join in. A good affair. Lots of schmoozing. All the editors and writers show up for the free booze. But more important, all those secretaries show. And that's where the real trouble is. And I was there. I saw it all unfold.

Pete Barron from *Thrilling* never liked Florrie and that situation was only magnified by the fact that Florrie never sent any of his work there. Now, with Florrie hot in the market, Pete's boss, Leo Margulies, wants to know why, and this has rubbed things a little raw. Everybody wants a piece of the hot pie before it cools off. You know.

Florrie had said things here and there over the previous months that had people wondering. Just a bit here, and a bit there. Now, all together in the same room, the word was going around. Florrie was getting his stuff from somebody else! And Pete Barron puts two and two together. He knows the trade. He knows all the authors worth knowing. Hell, he'd started with *All-Story* back in the first days of *Tarzan of the Apes*. And more than once, back in the 20's, he'd encountered pieces by George Zim.

What is it about some material? You can tell who wrote it without the name. Even with Florrie's re-write, Zim's mark was on the stuff. Running food relief by aeroplane into Sikiang during the siege. Flying into a forest fire in Montana to save a bunch of railroad workers. Fighting a dope ring on the docks in San Francisco. Chasing off bandits along with a dinosaur hunter in Mongolia. This wasn't the world of Florenz Patterson of the Philadelphia Pattersons. Even the fantastic stuff was outside of the usual fare. Who in 1935 was envisioning another planet in a balanced orbit around the sun exactly opposite to the earth? Hell, who understood enough about nuclear physics to imagine a bomb the size of a Studebaker could wipe out New York City?

It was Zim.

Zim had gone to Germany in 1924 for the *Chicago Times* to hitch a ride on Hugo Eckener's first Zeppelin flight to Lakehurst N.J. But the flight was delayed, so he stayed a while in Berlin with an aunt who was a secretary to some Hungarian physics professor there. He and the professor got to be beer buddies. And let me tell you, that one had cost *Astounding Science* a small wad when the government made them pull the whole print run. But Florrie still got paid. Twice, as a matter of fact. The Federales paid him afterwards not to write about such things again.

Well, it was Pete Barron who guessed what was up. Right there, on the floor of the Hibernian Hall, with all the secretaries kicking it up to the sound of some orchestra, Pete Barron said as much. Pete's problem was that he lacked about thirty pounds weight and six inches in height. Florrie took him out with one punch.

But too late. Now the news was out. And nobody can be more resourceful than a pack of pulp writers who smell a wad of dough. And now each of them was in it for themselves.

The next up in line was Phil Parks. Phil had been a hot shot on Wall Street before the crash. He never used his own name because there were too many investors still looking for him. You might know him as Donald Crimmins from *Daring Adventures* or *Daring Detective* or one of the Thrilling books. But his big hit finally came with the '*Fanny Pierce*' series—You know, the minister's daughter trying to make her way in the world as a nurse, smart as a whip, chaste as new fallen snow—she just can't stay put when there's good to be done. The set-up seemed old fashioned. Sure. But the fact is, it was real. That character was based on Sarah Fearing—really, just the same character everybody fell in love with in *China Dawn*. It was Reverend Thomas Fearing's daughter that George Zim had fallen in love with during his China days.

And for reasons we will never know, she had rejected him. And then it was too late. You might have missed the short bit in *Time Magazine* about her going missing back in '32. She was up in Manchuria by then. I think it was politics that kept it quiet.

Rice pudding's a dime. Yeah. We put a little extra egg in it.

Well, the '*Fanny Pierce*' series would have run forever if Phil Parks hadn't gotten himself killed. After he'd extracted that scenario out of Zim, he could have run with it all by himself if he'd been smart.

And then there was Charles Jones. He started going to the bank every week with the '*Chris Tell*' stories. Better than selling encyclopedias which is what he did door to door until '31 when a lot of people stopped buying such things. Charles fancied himself an 'intellectual' because he'd spent so much time reading his sample copies. Funny thing was he didn't know much of anything beyond the letter 'g.' But lumberjacks who investigate murders? Not a common area of endeavor. You gotta remember, George Zim had worked up in Idaho and Montana for three years after he came back from China the last time. George wasn't big enough for the saws but he could handle a truck and understood the chains. I think George tried to lose himself up there. But I guess when the long nights came, he couldn't forget Sarah, the missionarie's daughter. And you know that *'Chris Tell'* character had the matter of fact quality people like in a hero. Not a lot of nuance. Straightforward. Honest. A little naive. I think even the girls were reading those issues of *Argosy*.

Geez, even you? See? Refill?

I think it was Finley Barnes might have been the first one to figure out where George Zim was living after the word got around at the Daring Publications Christmas party. He has the nose of a bloodhound. He used to sell insurance and he could always smell a prospect. And when people started cutting back on insurance, it was that ugly nose of his that made him successful over at *Black Mask* and *Thrilling Detective* and the like. But his stuff was getting stale by 1935. Hammett had covered the 'Pinkerton' type story in Spades, so to speak. Yeah. Sorry. But then Finley suddenly came up with the *'Chicago Sam'* stories.

I know. Reports hate those. It doesn't matter that a crime reporter can't really spend the time Chicago Sam does on getting the facts. It's the detail that makes those yarns work like little Swiss watches. And the description—like when the jewels were hidden high in the alabaster bowl suspended beneath the ceiling light at the Chicago Public library. The grain of the stone hides everything but the glow of the ruby. "Like a drop of blood, suspended in the milk of the light." I love that line. You know right then he has his man—or, in that case, woman. Finley Barnes went to town with what Zim gave him. At least a story a week. Even Hollywood was sniffing around again.

And all three of these guys knew how to finish a story, you understand. Never kill the kid or the dog—well, the dog can die but only if he's lost while saving the kid. The hero always gets the girl. The girl always keeps her knees together, if you'll excuse the expression. The bad guy always gets what he deserves. Right there you have the whole problem with Zim. That's not the way it had worked out for him. He could make up a thousand stories, but it was never going to work out the right way for him.

But I think the problems really began when Phil and Finley and Charles started bumping into each other. Remember, these are writers, not fighters. A couple of writers in the middle of a fight is a comical sight. I've seen a few. So, after one or two altercations, they just made a deal. They had it all figured out that Florrie never showed up at Zim's except on Wednesdays. The reason for that was not obscure. It had to do with his ex-wife. She'd got tired of waiting for the check in the mail and used to come up from Philadelphia on Wednesday morning to collect the alimony in cash. So, on Wednesday afternoons, Florrie was broke. That, plus he had just about recovered from his weekend bust with the bottle.

Still, Florrie discovers right away that his situation has been made. He no longer has a private line on Zim. And he has two alternatives. Maybe three. He can make a deal with his competitors. He can kill them. Or, I suppose, he can quit.

You wouldn't know this, but Florrie could take pain. He just couldn't take much. In 1918 he shot off his small toe so the Army wouldn't send him to Europe. They sent him anyway. He was assigned to KP for six months and then cleaned engine parts and cement floors at an aerodrome outside London. So, in this situation, he decides to keep the rest of his toes. He makes the deal. The four of them divide the days of the week up. They figure Zim might get a little chubby if they try to see him on weekends—given his sedentary habits during the day. And they leave one day free for emergencies—that is when one or the other can't show up on his assigned day for some other reason.

Geez, I would have loved to have been a fly on the wall during those negotiations.

And what was Zim thinking the whole time? . . . He must have guessed. He might have known. But what was in his mind. Here he is playing Scheherazade to a bunch of thieves. I can't even begin to speculate. The life he once had was gone. Life wasn't worth living any more, I suppose. One too many crashes. One too many concussions. His eyes were shot, so he could never fly again. Not to mention, he'd lost the love of his life. And he was a German Catholic, so he wasn't going to take the easy way out and commit suicide. Suffering was part of the deal for him, I think.

Every day he went out to the Library, or to the Museum of Natural History. I bumped into him myself up at the Metropolitan once. But I didn't know it was him until I figured it later because Finley Parker was following him around like a puppy dog taking notes.

No. Actually, it was Sally who figured that all out. Plus, she listens. Amazing what a guy will tell a pretty girl across a counter.

When I finally saw Zim that first time at the library, he didn't look so bad. He was eating better by then, see. Four meals a week. He had the same coat, but someone had bought him a new pair of glasses. He must have been very grateful for those. He was a little pale. He looked more like the kind of guy he must have been once, but just a bit threadbare.

I can imagine those guys coming to Zim for material four days a week. Begging him. And him opening his little black book and reeling off yet another yarn. Day after day. By the summer of thirty-six, Zim must have been responsible for a lot of what we were all reading every week. I can only guess at that from the frequency of certain noms de plume—Is that how you make a plural out of that one? Pen names. You know— Well, there must have been some of Zim's stuff in every story magazine that Union News carried. Westerns. Mysteries. Ranch Romances. And then, of course, the flying stories. Barnes had the lead serial about that time in *Zeppelin Adventures* under the name Holly Andrews.

Did you know that George Zim had been up in the *USS Shenandoah* earlier on, and had filed one of the first reports from Ohio when it went down because he'd flown out to the scene himself? That was when he was still working at the *Times* in 1925. And then he went to China the next year.

And Zim keep poring over his little black book and pouring out the plots. My guess is that those creeps were making upwards of five hundred dollars a month while it lasted. Probably more. Besides Patterson and Barnes and Jones and Parks, there might actually have been others. But we can be sure of those four because of what happened at the end.

And my guess is that Zim knew nothing about it. He didn't read the pulps. He didn't even read the *Saturday Evening Post*. All Zim wanted to do now was write novels. That and spend his days down at the Museum of Natural History, or at the Library doing research. Otherwise he stayed away from the human race. And every night he sat in his little room on Avenue A and tried to finish something.

Yeah. Novels. He had an old Royal Number 10 and typed out fifty or a hundred pages at a whack. Only he never finished a story. Not one that we know of, anyway.

Well, the problems really escalated when Florrie got so drunk one night he was still drunk the next day when he showed up down at the Daring Publications office on Madison and 23rd.

Nice building. I worked there myself for a couple of years back in the twenties. Copy-editing, mostly.

So, Florrie shows up, like God's gift, and wants to talk to Doug Kirk. Doug is managing editor and chief bottle washer over there. He's always too busy to sit down. That, and if he did sit down he'd need a high chair. When he stands at his desk he looks like a fire hydrant waiting for the dog. . . Yeah. Don't you think? It's the bowler hat that does it. He won't take it off because he's balding. But he keeps a rope on the budget. That's why Daring made it through the financial crunch in '32 and '33. Not a nice guy, exactly, but okay. Fair.

And he doesn't like drunks.

And Florrie comes in and accuses him of stealing one of his stories.

Well, that was bound to happen, I guess. Zim had related one tale or another more than once. Florrie had submitted a story to Daring and it was rejected because Florrie wanted too much per word. He was on his high horse by then. And then Herbert Glick later ran a story by Charles Jones with the same plot and characters in an April issue of *Daring Detective*. Florrie was outraged. Doug is not interested in outrage from a penny a word man on a winning streak. So Doug throws Florrie out on his ear. Bingo. Florrie wants the fight. Doug tells him to get lost. Florrie starts to brag. He says he has more stories like the ones Doug had bought before and Daring Periodicals will never see a word of them.

Now, this is a mistake. Why? Because Doug Kirk has a secretary. And this is where Joan comes in. Nice girl. Corn fed. Out of the Indianapolis School for Women. The blond isn't real but the curves are. And she had made the mistake of going out with Florrie a few times. That was before he was flush and he was on his best behavior because he wanted to get his stuff in with Kirk. He was just using her, of course.

Well, Florrie had disappeared for a while when he first discovered Zim and got the piece in at Daring. Then he got a couple more with Street and Smith and a few at Popular Publications. And by then, he had already hit the big time with *China Dawn* at the *Post*. It was after he got the check from the *Post* that he shows up one day and takes Joan out to dinner at the Stork Club. No telling what lines he used, but he gets her to drink too much. Then he takes advantage of her. . . Well, we don't actually know that, but we can guess. She suddenly hates his guts.

So, now we're back to the day he comes into the office at Daring again. And he's bragging. Everybody knows now he's sold the movie rights to *China Dawn*. He's in the big time. And he comes in not just to brag, but to accuse Doug of theft! Got that. Doug Kirk was the thief! And like I said, Doug throws him out. Never pick a fight with a midget!

And that was when Joan puts two and two together from the Christmas party and all. And Joan, being the kind of resourceful secretary Doug Kirk would hire—she's from Indiana, you see, and her Daddy is a Methodist preacher as well as a cabbage farmer, so she knows her onions. She gets on the phone and puts that farm girl's arm on someone she knows who knows just what's going on. And finally, it's her that goes down to Avenue A to tell Zim what the real deal is.

The person Joan had called was Kelly O'Toole. Kelly is the secretary for Herbert Glick at Daring Detective. Kelly is not the smartest gal on the beach, but she has the reddest hair. For Kelly, gossip is a team sport. Kelly was at the Daring Christmas party along with the other girls. And Kelly knows more about this than anyone because she's been seeing the encyclopedia salesman, Charles Jones, ever since he started turning up with the 'Chris Tell' stories and getting a regular check. She knows all about George Zim. Mr. Jones confessed it all to her the first night Kelly was willing to let him master the mechanical geometry of her bra clasp. . . . Sorry.

Well, you can guess that Joan has never been down to Avenue A. It's a tough neighborhood. She gets off the IRT at 14th Street. George Zim lives off the corner of Third Street. She's got a long walk and she's wearing high heels. In the meantime, Kelly has confessed to Charles what all she's told Joan and that Joan is going down to see George. Charles is not a brave fella. He sees he is about to lose something he can't replace—i.e., a meal ticket. He likes all the comforts that more than a hundred bucks a week can buy. Besides. He'd probably lose access to both Kelly and her bra if he doesn't have his story fix every Tuesday. Tuesdays are his days to visit George Zim. But now it's Thursday.

Thursdays are reserved for the insurance salesman, Finley Barnes, to buy George's dinner. Charles calls Finley and gives him the scoop. They decide to head down together. And, of course, if they are going, Phil Parks ought to have a piece of the trouble. And between the three of them, they haven't got a clue what they are going to do once they get there. They can't make it up. All they know for sure is, they better go. And one other thing. They aren't going to tell Florrie.

The three of them take the BRT express right down to Houston Street and walk over from there.

What they don't know is that Florrie has already decided to get revenge on the whole lot of them. He figures Zim is his goose and from now on he's not going to let anyone else have the golden eggs. Florrie, you see, has not just spent his money on cars and hookers and Canadian Rye. He has bought himself a cabin in the Catskills close enough to Grossinger's to smell the pastrami. And he is going to take George Zim away on a 'vacation.' In that he had just gotten this brilliant idea, he has no idea what he's going to do after that.

Now, have I forgotten anything?

I've got Florrie heading down to Avenue A in his blue Cadillac.

Yeah it was dark blue. I know that.

I've got Charlie and Phil and Finley all headed down together to Houston on the Broadway line.

And I've got Joan going down on the IRT. . . Right! Oh, yes. I forgot one important detail.

Joan didn't wander into her secretarial job working for Doug Kirk at Daring Publications in Manhattan fresh out of the Indianapolis School for Women just by accident. She took the bus. And she knew exactly where she was going. Joan wanted to write romances. *Ranch Romances* and *Daring Romance* were her favorite publications. Doug Kirk hired her before she could sit down. She's been the artist's model for every cover of *Daring Romance* since 1934. And get this: she has no idea. She doesn't think any of the girls on those covers look like her. Doug buys one of her stories every few months just to keep her happy and gets the price back by under-paying her for her secretarial skills. Now, that's about the whole picture, I think. That, and the fact that she came up out of the IRT at 14th Street and asked the first cop she saw where she could find number forty-one, Avenue A. And the cop told her.

Now, that was October 16, 1936. One year ago tomorrow. Which is why you're here. Right? Sally makes a good cup a joe, but you're doing the anniversary piece on the unsolved murders. And no, I didn't see what actually happened any more than anyone else, but I won't forget it. The week before that, on October 9th, I proposed to Sally. Sally quit her job down at the Chelsea Diner. I quit writing for the pulps. And six months later we opened this place. Best thing I ever did.

No. That has nothing to do with the story. It's just a time frame. You see? The way you can remember things. That's all.

No. I don't know what happened after that. I've got no more finish on what happened than George Zim did on his stories. But I can do better than the police report I read in your paper. "Pen Pals Massacre." What kind of crap headline was that?

Look, I see it this way.

She's just come from the office. She's in high heels. The cop she'd asked directions from reported she was wearing high heels. I believe him. Even an ink stained wretch like you would notice something like that. She can't walk far. So she hails a Checker cab and right off she probably tells the driver if he can step on it she'll double his fare with the tip.

Yeah, I'm talking about Joan. Who else? You got that down?

But when our three guys show up at Zim's apartment, he's not there. Right. It's six o'clock, and that's when Finley

Barnes was supposed to meet George for dinner. Right? All Zim's trash is laid out around the room like it usually was. The Royal Number 10 typewriter is there, with a sheet of blank paper turned in and ready. Yeah. The police report says the paper was blank, except for a spot of blood. You read that, right? Hell, The *Daily News* put the whole thing on page three. . . And his bed is unmade. The towels are on the rack by the sink. His toothbrush is there. But he's gone. So what do our three guys do? They start to tear the place apart looking for the little black book, naturally. Right? They don't even need George Zim, do they? All they really need is the little black note-book. And he usually doesn't carry it with him. So it might be there. Someplace. In all that mess. Dirty laundry. Unfinished manuscript pages. Stacks of old books.

And that's when Florrie shows up. He sees what they are up to and he goes into a rage. He goes nuts. They start to argue.

At least one knife was already there. The police said there was an apple peel in the sink, so it must have belonged to Zim.

I figure, someone lost their temper first. Then the next. They would have started to fight. The room was small. There wasn't much space to take a big swing. I figure they wrestled. That's what must have turned all that sad furniture upside down. We know that Florrie had a knife wound too, but it probably didn't kill him. What killed him was the back corner on that Royal Number 10 that someone slammed down on his head. So I figure that at least two of the three held him down. Then, they turned on each other.

Ya see? Now there was a murder done. The one who could get out alive could go his own way, and it might look like the others did themselves in. That's the way a pulp writer might figure it. That's the way they think.

Well, it's an explanation, is all.

Four bodies? How else? They ended up killing each other and none of them got out alive.

What about the little black book? Now that's the mystery! There it was in Phil's hand. The blood on it was his. There was blood on the pages and in the wire wastebasket too. Right? So I see it this way. Phil is already on the floor there, bleeding to death. Maybe he's the last of the four alive. And he can see the wastebasket in front of his face. And there, in the basket, is the little black book. He musters the last of his strength to reach in and pull it out. He opens it up . . . And it's blank! Blank! Page after blank page, like the police report in the *Mirror* said, he was 'clutching a blank notebook.' You see, all those ideas for stories were just in Zim's head. Those blank pages were just the catalyst. . . You know, 'catalyst.' It's a chemical you put in that makes the other chemicals work. Like sulfur in gunpowder. Yeah. Like that.

What George Zim had was writer's block. When he looked at a blank page it started him thinking. His problem was he couldn't finish, for whatever reason. Get me Sigmund Freud, will ya? What do I know about that?

So, my figure is this: maybe Joan did get there in time to tell him some part of what was going on. Maybe he threw that little black book in the trash can himself because it was the catalyst to his problems. I don't know.

What I don't buy is the idea that Zim killed those guys himself. I believe that Joan must have got there ahead of them all. She told Zim what the deal was. Or she didn't right away. Maybe she just told him to come with her. You know most guys

160

would follow a girl like Joan into a dark alley if she asked them to go.

We know the cab picked up two people, a man and a woman, at 5:58, right at the stand on the corner of Avenue A and Houston. The cabbie says he didn't see any blood. They looked fairly calm. He was wearing a Burberry. She was doing all the talking, but the fellow didn't seem to be paying attention anyway. Like he was in a daze. And maybe the talk was something about writing. That's what the cabbie said. But it was her that paid the fare when they got out at Grand Central. That's important. What gal pays the cab fare? It had to be them.

Where?

I have no idea. I can guess as good as the next guy. I just don't believe that George Zim killed those hacks and then committed suicide by jumping in the East River. And besides, where is she? Where is Joan? Did he kill her too? She hasn't been heard from since, has she?

If you ask me, I think they're together. I think George Zim finally found his preacher's daughter. And this one knows her onions. It's no mystery. It's just another *Daring Romance* for Christ sake.

You ask me, that's my answer. And, you can quote me on that.

If blood were orange

a pastorale interrupted

1.

She was wearing a loose, green flannel shirt—dark green and very loose. And jeans. The jeans were loose too. There was not much to see there but that she was tall. After a moment I took note of the L. L Bean hunting boots and the heavy belt that brought the bulk of her shirt to an abrupt termination at her waist. I could see right there that she was not fat. Nor thin. But all that was secondary.

What I saw first, from a hundred yards away, was her hair. It is the first thing anyone would notice. Everyone does.

That day she had her hair gathered to her back and tied loosely by a single thick strand of unbleached gray-brown wool cut from the skein she'd been working with during the early morning. As you know, the hair is orange. If blood were orange it would be this color, not more yellow. The burnt orange of a French liqueur, but marbled here and there with an errant strand of bright metal gray that makes it certain to the eye that the orange is real.

She waited by an open gate where she had crossed the empty fields from her house on the hill above and, with her eyes on me, I was immediately self-conscious about the way I walked and how I might appear to her, and that brought enough natural rebellion against the predetermination of things that I started immediately to look for other matters of interest. Unsuccessfully.

Her dog was with her, a dark coated German Shepherd who stayed down on his haunches and studied me in return with his mouth closed. He was clearly ready for business but had received his instruction and would not have disobeyed. His name was Fred.

Margaret's eyes are more green than blue though it is the blue you see until you are close, which is a trick of their color in the setting of her hair and the ruddy pink of skin so heavily freckled.

You must remember that at this moment I did not know whom she was other than that she owned the property I wanted to rent for a year. The name she'd taken on at the time was her mother's. Abernathy. And she was only famous for being Maggie Flynn.

Did I recognize her at all? Yes and no. I certainly understood that I'd seen her before but must have instantly doubted that recognition as impossible because I had Margaret Abernathy on the piece of paper the realtor had given me and nothing more was said about it and this was 1996. The Maggie Flynn I knew of was a younger woman by twenty years, which was when I'd last seen her in a movie. And I had never seen the woman in person before.

There was a tick to the small finger where her right hand braced at her hip and thrust her elbow out in a neat triangle. I was certain this was impatience. It was, of course.

But my response, just as much of an involuntary twitch as her own, was opposite. As I have said, I've a tendency to rebel against predeterminations. I slowed to look at the open fields around us as I approached her at the crest of road. The last strides were felt in slow motion.

I said, "A gorgeous fabulous wondrous spring day."

She said, " 'Beautiful' would have been sufficient."

She said it like a teacher would in class. Her voice has settled. Deepened. Nearly husky now after thousands of cigarettes, though she no longer smoked. I did not recognize any familiar tone to the sound of it.

Contrarily, I said, "Beauty is never sufficient."

She tilted her head at that. A pose, I thought. As if telling me she was reconsidering her decision to rent the house. Still, I did not see the actress.

She asked, "Have you ever lived in New Hampshire before?"

She had not yet introduced herself. We'd spoken briefly on the phone that morning and she had spoken to the realtor the day before, so there was no mystery to that. Just the formality.

I answered and put a hand out. "Hi. I'm Jim McNeill."

She took it reluctantly, I think. It was a womanly hand, and not weak but I instantly thought that the intimacy of a handshake was more than she wanted. I answered, "And yes, many times. I went to camp here as a boy. And I've rented houses up this way before. I gave a couple of references to Ellen at the Realty."

Ignoring this, she asked, "Why did you walk?"

"To get the feel of the place. And I like to walk. My truck is down on the main road." Wanting some humor, I added. "Nothing to do with the fact that it's a bit battered and I didn't want to give the wrong impression."

The tilt of her head straightened just a little to let me know she approved of that.

Fred watched all this intently, as if he were reading lips. I bent down to him and showed him a hand. His nose was as cold as the day. I gave him a scratch on the neck.

She said, "He bites."

I stood and gave back a smile. "I hope he's not hungry."

She had not yet smiled at me. She was not wearing makeup that I could see but the wrinkles that touched the curve of her cheeks and flayed at the outer edge of her eyes and neatly furrowed her brow against a bright sun did not appear to be the product of frequent frowning.

She turned away from my scrutiny and pointed further along the road as it dipped down again to the filigree of leafless maple and oak in the next intervale.

"The house is there."

With the bright white of the clapboards laced in the foreground by the gray of fat and budding limbs, this was the one-and-a-half story Cape that was advertised. Or not advertised, as the case was. Ellen Macomber, the realtor in Madison, had the information set aside, along with a single photograph attached, on a sheet that she took from a drawer after giving me the third degree. I thought she had done so reluctantly.

Ellen is that busty sort who wears too much jewelry, an unmistakable perfume, is brusque, and yet has an immediate intimacy to her manner. I'd rejected the half-dozen other rentals she had available. Most of them recent second homes built with the good taste of building contractors in a hurry and on a limited budget. I wanted something old. She repeated that it was the wrong time of year unless I just wanted a place just for the summer.

She handed me the sheet and said the owner of this one, Miss Abernathy, would show it if it seemed to be the right sort of place for me. "But Maggie is as particular as you are." And I was warned then that it might be a problem in winter. It was an old building and the insulation did not seem to keep the drafts out. "And there is no heat to speak of."

That sounded even better for my purposes. I smiled, and Ellen Macomber frowned with doubt.

Now, under the owner's scrutiny, I studied the perfect simplicity of the house from the distance and knew it was far better for me than something grand. "Looks beautiful."

Miss Abernathy caught the intent of that comment as we began to walk.

"Pretty, perhaps. But that's the best I can say about it. Ellen said you were looking to stay through winter. That might not work. There's no real furnace. Just wood heat, except for an old hot water heater in the basement that has it's own thermostat. The thermostat has been known to freeze."

"I don't mind the cold. But what if I bought enough insulation to seal up the center room at least?"

"You haven't seen it yet. You ought to look it over first."

"I will. But I've lived in drafty places before. If you can get one room right, it's a good refuge on the worst days."

"Yes. . . . That's true." The agreement was spoken as if to counter-weight her previous disagreement, the word, 'true,' tossed out to lose itself in the air ahead.

Though nothing was said to Fred, he had followed just behind and I was already feeling a touch of admiration for her command. I had a dog for nearly twenty years. He was a mutt but mostly Border Collie. He was a friend and companion but never gave much of a damn about anything I had to say. But then, most of my friends are like that.

I asked, "Where do you live?"

"Back there," She swept her hand up and around toward the crest again. "Behind those trees at the top of the field. I have the view. But my house is new. Nearly new. This little place here is where Isaac Abernathy lived for ninety-three years. And his father before him. He was born in the keeping room beside the chimney. He never seemed to mind the drafts."

I immediately thought of how I might make use of a keeping room. "I'm sure I'm not the man he was. I sit a lot, and sneeze. But I could use a cozy place to work."

"You're a writer?"

I nodded.

She said, "I think you'll find it's a good house for that. Cozy may depend on how much wood you burn. But then, what do I know."

I did not expect such phrasing. I was already certain that she knew a great deal. Ellen Macomber would have told her I was single. My age was on the sheet as well.

"I'm hoping you know enough to keep me out of trouble up here. I just want the peace and quiet."

"You're out of luck, then. Between the birds and the chipmunks and all the rest you're going to have to get used to a lot of noise. Except in the dead of winter. And then it's the wind."

"I'll settle for the peace."

"Maybe you will get that. We'll see."

Large flat fieldstones set in rough uncut grass made a walkway from the road through the collapse of a stone wall tied by dried vines and withered weed. Several gnarly and naked sugar maples followed the road to the West with the largest of these close enough to the walk to make good shade when summer came. Closer, the house seemed smaller, and the entry low and narrow, though I was only expecting four rooms, including the kitchen.

The door opened silently on fat iron hinges. Not brass, and not decorative. The interior was colder than outside. Not unexpected, but a surprise nonetheless. In the front hall and directly ahead, a shallow stair wended upward from the entry along a hip of rough chimney stone. I figured this must lead to the "unfinished space I could use if I wanted," mentioned by Ellen the day before. Miss Abernathy had stepped into a room on the left but I went directly at the stairs. The treads protested each step with a squawk. A small door opened at the top to a tent-like attic of rough hewn beams which had evidently been covered over in some distant past but the space was now long empty and smelling of the plaster which had broken loose from the lathing and dropped in clumps to the damp-stained floorboards. A single window at either end threw in light as if it were an afterthought. The upper chimney there appeared to squat at the center of the floor before tapering quickly for its exit up through the center of the roof. I could see slivers of daylight at the edges of the stone.

She said, "My aunt told me the kids were all relegated to that space as soon as they were weaned. She hated it up there. And they all left home early."

A cold thought.

"What if I stuck a little something into those cracks too? Just to keep the weather out?"

She was just below me at the bottom of the stairs and I looked down into a concerned face.

"So long as it is not 'construction.' I'm trying to leave the house as much like it was as I can. There aren't many of the older homes left that haven't been made convenient, if you know what I mean."

A lungful of chalky air fortified me against her caution, but I was immediately aware that I was on tender ground.

"I understand. But you could lose the whole house if the weather keeps coming in like that."

Her expression hardened. "I can't pay for it. I have no budget for that."

"I can handle that much I think. A little flashing, shingles and tar along with some fiber glass shouldn't be that expensive."

She nodded without answering. I imagined she was wondering if she let me do that much, would I want more.

Downstairs and to the left of the entry on the East was what would have been a narrow dining room. At least this was bright. An unused door there on the opposite wall led to a small porch I hadn't noticed on the outside. I discovered later that the shed roof there had rotted and been pulled away and the remaining floorboards were unsafe.

Another and wider door to the back of the dining room led to a large kitchen.

"I keep that door shut tight so that the heat that rises from the water heater will keep the pipes from freezing. The water is turned off now, but you'd have to do that as well."

The kitchen was at the North side, darker in spite of having four windows, and smelled of stale odors that I could not identify. Even in shadow, the pattern of the linoleum on the kitchen floor was clearly worn away in the most frequently used paths. Nearer the back door, there was no pattern remaining at all.

The refrigerator suddenly came on with a rattle and I opened it reflexively. The little light showed it to be empty and well cleaned. An electric stove nearby appeared to be even older than the refrigerator. A small clock glowed yellow on a rear panel of the stove, with the wrong time by an hour.

"The stove is still good. But the last person I tried renting too turned the oven on and left the door open to get the heat, rather than cut wood. I asked him to leave."

I ignored the edge on this statement.

At the center corner of the kitchen, the original dark maw of a massive cooking hearth was agape, as wide as it was tall, and looking ominously dark within. The space in front of this was blocked by a broad-topped black iron cooking stove with bright nickel trim that could have been in service shortly after the Civil War. I ran a hand over it with some obvious awe, while opening the firebox and looking into the lightless interior, not knowing what I expected to see.

"My Grandmother didn't like to cook. I've heard that she could make bread and would keep a pot filled on the stove top with what was handy."

"Why do you think Isaac married her?" I meant the question as a joke and smiled with the asking but she did not rise to the bait. The green eyes turned away.

"Probably because he was getting lonely after fifty years, and she was handy."

There appeared to be a hint of humor in that remark so I persisted in my own weak attempt. "A handy woman is a good thing to have." I smiled again to make sure she understood, and then had second thoughts about possible implications.

Miss Abernathy seemed unperturbed. "Well, she was that. She could milk a cow, plant a field, and cut hay as well as a man, or so I've heard. She was also good with horses."

I gave my own effort up.

A door beside the hearth that opened beneath the rising stairs from the front hall revealed the cellar and another stale odor when I opened it. A light came on automatically and I looked quickly but the space was low and I decided not to stoop and snoop just to see the water heater and the ancient unused cistern she said was there.

The back door by the sink opened on a small decaying porch, patched for use over the years, but in obvious need of repair.

A bathroom had been installed immediately beside the kitchen at the back, filling most of the space where the ancient 'keeping' room had been. This was sensible, of course, making it accessible through from the other side by the bedroom as well. There were few toilets in houses when this one was built, or when Isaac had been born, and his bride had not been sentimental about a better use of the space.

Leaning in at the bathroom to show due diligence, I saw a claw foot tub below the window. This sported a shower attachment on a rubber hose. As I looked at the odd configuration, I must have said, "Too bad," aloud, because it was my thought at that instant, not about the shower, but the loss of the original room and my prematurely conjured idea of writing there.

Still keeping her distance behind, Maggie Abernathy spoke to me from the kitchen. "The new cistern and well are just up the hill on the other side of the road. That was my grandmother's doing too. She was frugal and didn't want to spend a lot on copper pipes, so she put the bathroom in there. I don't think she ever intended to have any children herself. No need for a nursery. She was over forty when she married and she was never particularly fond of children. But even though old Isaac married late, he managed to get three kids out of her in twice as many years. One good litter he liked to called it."

She might have smiled then but she was out of sight.

The remaining portion of the space was divided into a narrow closet space set against the chimney stone. Beyond was the bedroom, empty except for a lone wire hanger on the naked cedarwood floor. This room was narrow, like the dining room, but darker for being on the northeast corner. It was big enough, though not a space I planned to use more than was necessary.

I said, "The beds were smaller in those days. I guess the making of children was inevitable."

This could be taken as something of personal remark, or as simply another bit of my weak humor. But I thought Miss Abernathy had already opened the door on that.

She didn't answer.

Other than the kitchen, the largest of the rooms was the 'parlor,' around to the front again. There, another large fireplace faced out from the center corner; this one a lower affair with a polished red granite mantel, but this hearth was also blocked, here by a smaller wood stove. This room was bright with the slant of afternoon sun. The wide yellow pine of the floors was honeyed by the light and I could easily imagine spending time there in a clear morning light.

In the yard, after the inspection, she stood on the flat stone of the walk and waited again. I took my time. I had made up my mind, but I liked that moment and wanted it to last for as long as I could stretch it. The first moment. Maybe the beginning of something. As always, my imagination was getting ahead of me.

The front door, a sturdy plank-and-batten of oak heavier than most anything you could buy today, opened between a battered sill and jambs and lintel that were themselves as thick as the posts that supported the beams of the house. The space between was narrow and low and I stood cramped in the frame of it for a moment, enjoyed the sense of filling it with my body, and studied her there, standing on the walk. That little finger on her hand began to tick.

"Well?"

"This is what I want."

She had yet to really smile. She squinted at me instead.

"Don't complain to me when the winter comes."

"I won't. I'll celebrate! I'll shoot off fireworks on New Years Eve! Do you think the neighbors will mind?"

Almost a smile then. "Alright with me, though Fred might worry. He was trained by the State Police and he's heard guns before, I know—but he was a reject." She knelt, rubbing his neck with her fingers, "Weren't you. A cull!" speaking the word 'cull' like a compliment, or at least in recognition of her own good fortune. "He didn't pass some test or another and I bought him from an ad in the paper." She stood then and pointed off through the trees behind the property. "And Harold Jenks, over that way, is deaf. His cows aren't, but they hardly move when it thunders. Bob and Marie Ferrell down the road there go to Florida right after Thanksgiving. Terry Bills and Georgina Greider live in the house you passed as you came up. They have a daughter in California and after the holidays we don't see them back until April. But I'll tell you, it's February that's the longest month for most people."

"And you stay?"

"That's the best time of all! On a clear night when the moon is down you can see all the way to the ends of the universe."

She looked up toward the crest of the hill again with her words, as if to say she had often done just that.

And I added the thought, "To the end of time." Which was the way such star gazing often felt to me.

She frowned at some new concern then as she looked back at me. "Yes."

2.

I bought two thousand, four hundred dollars worth of shingles, tar paper, tar, aluminum flashing (because I couldn't afford the copper), fiberglass insulation, as well as a couple of basic tools, and loaded them in the bed of my pickup and it didn't seem like a whole lot beneath the tarp next day, standing in the rain and reconsidering what was needed. I had already decided to limit my roofing to the north side where the moss was thickest at every seam.

The distinctive feature of the house was the chimney with its two great hearths. This massive fieldstone monument was nearly twelve feet wide at the base where it disappeared into the litter of gravel in the cellar space beneath the house. It was certainly the reason the home had endured. I was in love with the place immediately and the chimney became the centerpiece of that affection. Even without a fire in the hearth I found my eyes on it at all hours, like another living presence. Perhaps a shade of old Isaac Abernathy himself. I imagine he had spent many hours there warming himself as he considered the burn of time.

Surprisingly there was very little rot, possibly because the air so freely circulated, but I did not express this opinion to Margaret. She might have stopped me from my project.

I write in the morning, often starting as soon as the coffee is made. It was my habit to eat breakfast during my first break sometime after eight. By noon or one o'clock I'm pretty much empty of ideas and my hands start to hurt from too many years pounding the keys. I usually took a walk then before setting up to work on the roof by about three o'clock and pushed that through to the last twilight, as the spring days grew longer. Margaret might have the morning views to the east above, but I had the sunsets from my roof.

And I had other thoughts about the place. The foundation for the original barn was quite clearly visible from the roof, a shallow but level depression in the earth just away on the downward slope to the West and I started thinking about a little garden for myself there. I could shovel any debris from the interior and dump some more soil in. And closer in, there was a small shed that had fallen down and I picked out the pieces of wood that weren't punky and set those up in the attic to dry for some future use. I only learned the purpose of that little structure when I found the quarter-moon carved in a buried door plank.

The brown stems of roses bristled out of the collapsed rock along the road where a low wall had once been. Close within the yard two gnarled apple trees bowed their limbs to the ground and were already covered with the starting buds of their white blossoms. Judging by the remnant stumps scattered about, those two were the remains of an orchard that must have stretched all the way down the slope to the west toward the rim of oaks and maple and beech that now trimmed the farthest reaches of field.

Someone had obviously brought a bush cutter into the field at least once a year to keep it from being overwhelmed by scrub and second growth. I assumed that was to allow for a seasonal pasture but there was no fence, only a string of metal posts and I finally figured that part out when I found the ceramic knob for an electric wire in a kitchen drawer.

Each day in April Margret came over to watch me on the roof, we chatted then a bit. Not much. She would disappear after a short while.

Early on I asked, "Who uses the pasture?"

"That would be Harold. He still has at least a dozen milk cows. It's against the law for him to do it now I guess, but he makes cheese and gives that and the milk that's left over to his grand kids when they visit, or just gives it away. It's very good. Some days you can smell him cooking the milk in his pots. The cows are getting old and he won't ship them off. He sold most of his own pasture so he could afford the taxes."

"I'm glad you can afford it here then. I like cows."

"I can't afford it. Not anymore. That's why you're here."

And then she disappeared.

Fred followed her up the road when she came, zigzagging from side to side as he checked out one thing or another. When she got to the yard, his special interest was the wall where I had begun to pull up the loose stones and set them back in place, one by one. This was where the chipmunks lived and he had a cause to mind. Margaret did not seem to take note of my own effort there but I was sure she had. I figured that particular project would take me through to the fall if I did a little each day.

Another time, later in May, she walked around to one of the apple trees, blossoming wildly then and putting honey in the air.

"What did you do?"

"I trimmed it just a little."

"You should have asked."

"I'm sorry. I meant to. I only did what the book explained. You should know that I sprayed too."

After a short examination of the branches she said,

"Good." And then she left.

The roof took me a month of afternoons. I'm wary of heights and though the house is not tall nor the roof so steep, I was constantly feeling like I might misstep from the supports I'd set, and this slowed me considerably. The 864 square feet of it—that is about half of the roof—took me over a hundred hours. If I had to earn a living doing this, I would be even poorer than I am.

But on my daily walk at noon I made it my focus to find out a little more about the woman that was occupying a great deal of my thoughts.

I started with Bob and Marie Ferrell on my very first Sunday. Marie was in their yard raking up fallen branches from the wintertime and freeing the early flowers from the wind drift of debris. She seemed friendly enough but despite her direct questioning of me I got the sense that she was being very purposely circumspect about Margaret.

"Where you from?"

"New York."

"What do you do?"

"I write. What about you folks?"

"My husband used to manage the Aubuchon Hardware before the Walmart came in. Now he leases tractors. I do a little of this and a little of that. I sell some real estate for Ellen Macomber when I can."

"Have you known Margaret Abernathy long?"

"Since she came."

"When was that?"

"A few years ago."

"She didn't grow up here?"

"No."

I decided to slow down my inquiry and asked about the black Labrador retriever that danced around us both, looking for attention.

I said, "I'd like to have a dog again."

She seemed more enthusiastic about that. "You gotta have a dog up here. Life's too short without 'em. What kind did you have?"

"Border Collie."

"Now that's a writer's dog for you. Smarter than most people. I once knew a fellow who wrote. He used to go to the writer's colony down near Jaffrey. He had a Border Collie and we took care of her when he was down there. Stubborn little thing. Never minded."

"Well, this is my attempt to achieve a writer's colony of my very own. A colony of one. By the way, where is that fellow now? Maybe his dog had pups."

"Oh, he's dead. Twenty years ago. But I know that dog had lots of pups. She got around on her own. Maybe you'll come across one of her great grandchildren."

I figured I might have already had one.

The following Sunday I got down the road in the other direction and found Terry Bills and Georgina Greider both outside at once, putting together boxes of assorted junk left over from a yard sale they'd conducted on the main road with several other families the previous day. Most of it appeared to be children's toys so I used that to start the conversation. Their kids were all grown. Terry sold insurance and had a local franchise on a steam cleaning business. Georgina knitted authentic Irish wool sweaters which she sold through a craft store in North Conway. I saw the same natural gray-brown wool that I'd noticed more than once in Margaret's hair, on a skein with a dozen others.

"Does Margaret knit too?"

"Oh, I taught her. She's good. But she doesn't work at it like I do. She has her flowers and chickens and things. You have to put in the hours, or you won't get enough done to pay for the time. I've told her she has to get herself a dish antenna. If she had one of those, she'd get all the television shows and she can have them on while she knits. It's the only way. But she won't have a television in her house."

This was the singular piece of information I acquired from my attempts to pick up more information on Margaret. Little else. Her neighbors were unlike any I'd ever met before. They did not gossip. I was impressed.

I would make the parlor my writing space and set up most my shelves and desk there when I got them out of storage. In the mean time I pitched my tent right in the middle of the open floor for safety against the rampant mosquitoes and any possible rain leaks on the first nights. The dining room I now considered my sitting room because it was there that I would read and listen to music, at least in warmer months. I could put my reading chair up close by the window, on the south side facing the road, where the light was best and the largest and oldest of the maples would throw shade midday in summer and I could open the window for the breeze. For the time being I propped my typewriter up on the plank with the half-moon inscribed in it, feeling rather good about any symbolism to that. I would eat my meals in the kitchen which was more than big enough for the pressed-metal topped table I bought the very next Saturday at the Spring Auction in town for five dollars. I bought two mismatched chairs to go with it for an additional ten.

The 'Hotpoint' refrigerator that was already in place (a contradiction in naming that befuddled me) was thirty or forty years old and chugged a little when it switched on and off but kept everything plenty cold. I quickly decided, based upon evidence, that I'd better invest in a dozen plastic containers at Walmart, immediately, to keep the mice out of the rest of my food—whenever I finally got a chance to really go shopping. For the first weeks I got by using the Quick-Mart at the gas station.

At the same auction where I'd bought my kitchen table, I purchased a Browning 12 gauge over/under manufactured in 1938, as well as a more recent Browning .22 long rifle. The .22 was for target practice. The shotgun was to get the feel of the thing, having never fired one before. It was about time. I had gone to the auction for the guns. The table was a bonus. Still, I was $1260 out of pocket. The cost surprised me.

Years ago, I'd bought two hand guns, one a .32 Colt Police Special and the other a .9mm Smith & Wesson, at less than half that price. These had been necessary for the mystery series I was writing about a private detective, loosely based on an uncle. Both of these were in a safe deposit box now, along with a few odds and ends that passed for the McNeill family jewels, along with some legal paperwork. I hadn't touched a gun in at least a dozen years. As I thought about it, I realized this was probably about the same time I'd taught my son how to shoot. He had been fourteen then. Now he was twenty-six and a first lieutenant in the military and handling weapons I could only read about.

But my purpose for being in New Hampshire for the year was to write a story about my grandfather, Daniel 'Buck' McNeill, and he had owned a shotgun and used it to great purpose on several occasions. He swore by Brownings and I had to take his word for that.

Something more about the economics. I don't really have any money. A little in random royalties. An article now and then. But most of my usual income is from whatever book I write each year. One every year. I'm that methodical, give or take. And my agent had yet to find a home for the last one, so I was feeling the pinch.

"You are a romantic in an age of nihilism," she told me once. "You have to let go of the old conventions. 'Boy meets girl' is now 'boy hooks up with girl'. Love is now simple lust. Even better if it's the girl who's doing the lusting. Danger is not enough. You need a body count. And in the end, boy always loses girl. The bloodier the better."

I've never had a real bestseller, despite what the cover blurbs say. The Cold War thrillers I wrote in the 1970s did well. The mysteries I wrote in the 1980s did well enough. My two travel books did better than the mysteries. The horror novels I tried writing in the early 1990s had been a waste of time. Now the bank account was running fairly near empty. So, I want to admit right here that I took on that little house, and the expense I knew was there, because of Margaret. That's just how smitten I was. And I didn't like that one bit.

3.

More about Margaret.

Harold Jenks may be deaf but he never stops talking. The cows seem to enjoy that. When I went looking, I found him fixing the hinge on a barn door and I stood back, intended to wait for him to turn around. He has a little dog that is of no particular breed but reminds me of the sort of small hounds you see down South. The dog barked like crazy as I came down the unpaved road between Margaret's land and the property owned by Bob and Marie Ferrell. Harold didn't seem to notice as he turned a shiny new bolt into a rusted hinge plate and fastened the nut at the other side with his free hand without looking, but he started talking just as I got close enough to hear.

"Charlie doesn't bite. I wish he would, but you can't train a dog to bite. They do or they don't. Now, I had a dog once that would bite me as soon as he would a stranger. I kept him around because he liked mice and rats and was the only dog I ever had that was smarter than your average rodent. But Charlie dances. I can see him dancing out of the corner of my eye and I can tell by just what sort of dance it is who might be comin.' Like for a waltz, when he goes side to side, one foot to the other, I know it's Marie. He loves Marie. But if it's Margaret, he just goes quiet and disappears because she is never alone and he has no affection for Fred. And if it's the postman, he turns flips. Every damned time. But not for you. He hasn't figured you out yet so he doesn't yet know what your dance will be. You had him practically going in circles."

Harold had tightened the nut with a wrench until it got a grunt out of him and then he turned around to me.

He is as wiry as the scrub trees that line the gravel road. He has a baseball cap and a white fuzz of beard grown thick from lean cheeks after the last week's shave. His coveralls looked like they were just out of the wash and bright at the knees from wear. I stuck my hand out and said my name and he pulled his glove off and took it.

"Say again?"

"Jim. James McNeill."

"Your family from over by Manchester?"

"No, sir. New York."

"New York?"

"Long Island, actually. But my grandfather came from down around Exeter."

"Hemph. . . You staying in Isaac's house?"

"Yes, sir."

"Cold in there come winter."

I nodded, "I've heard."

He asked me what I did and I told him as best I could. He told me about a writer he met once that used to live over in Fryeburg, Maine, who wrote westerns. I told him I grew up watching those Hopalong Cassidy westerns on television, but he didn't quite understand me and I couldn't see an antenna on the small house there that catty-cornered to the barn so I gave up on that.

Then he said, "What do you think of Margaret?"

I was unready for this and fumbled over any sort of brief answer that would be easy to lipread. He laughed at me.

"She does that to fellas. I'm just sore that I'm too old to make my game. I would if I could. But you watch out. She'll take your head off."

I tried a direct approach

"Where is she from, do you think?"

"Hollywood."

"Where's that?"

Of course, I was thinking this had to be some other place in New Hampshire that I wasn't familiar with.

Harold laughed hard enough for me to be sure he had a well-used set of dentures.

"You know where that is! And I'll bet you know her!"

So, I drove down to the library that afternoon.

In fact, though I'd seen her in half a dozen films, I knew very little about her—but that was intentional on my part. I had long ago dismissed her from the world I wanted anything to do with. And that prejudice is easily explained.

The 'Joe Parker' series, my first success as a writer, had been optioned by Universal Pictures in 1975. And the essential plot of that storyline had been hatched out of my three year incarceration with Army Intelligence. My job there was as an analyst. I sat at a desk, in uniform, and read translated copies of Soviet, Bulgarian, Rumanian, Hungarian, Polish and East German documents (the Chinese were sent to another section). These had been translated by some poor schmuck more unfortunate than myself who'd also been drafted as I was and also probably majored in some aspect of the liberal arts but had mistakenly opted to minor in a foreign language (clearly and not necessarily the one they were made now to translate).

Thankfully, I had majored in English literature and minored in writing. To the Army's way of thinking I was made for the job they gave me. I was stationed at Ft. Belvoir, in Fairfax, Virginia. I left to work every morning at seven. I got home at six. I lived in a small two-bedroom house in Arlington that I shared with another officer. I was, indeed, an officer. A second and then a first lieutenant. I never made it beyond that. And I was bored stiff. So, in the best Walter Mitty tradition I dreamed up an alter ego. That was Lt. Joe Parker. He also worked in Army Intelligence. But unlike the department of the Army he and I both worked for, I invested Joe with actual intelligence. He was naturally curious. And he was continually seeing connections between odd scraps of information which his superiors thought worthless—like the number of potato chips eaten at a particular East German army depot. By a process of elimination, Joe Parker figured out that this depot was actually a secret missile site that housed twice the number of known personnel. Stuff like that.

Most importantly, the object of Joe's great affection was Molly Lynch. Joe had met her during training, and fallen in love. Molly was in fact an actual agent for Army Intelligence, and one who was assigned to dangerous duty. And those assignments kept her in Europe, while Joe was chairbound in Fairfax. So Joe took it upon himself to keep an eye on her, even to the point of re-enlisting and eventually rising in rank to Captain. He was her guardian angel. Against rules and regulations, he followed her progress on paper from place to place and spent his own free time analyzing information that concerned the area of her postings. He would inevitably pick up on some incipient mortal danger and warn her surreptitiously (she did not know where her tips were coming from) or give her something of real interest, like the potato chip problem. Unlike James Bond, Molly had little luck seducing the subjects of her inquiries, not because she wasn't a beauty, but because Joe kept putting obstacles down to foil any possible romance when need be. The comic element of this reverse on the usual 'lover and spy' was what made it work for me. I thought it was a good and humorous take on the entire Cold War situation of the time. The fun for me was working out the segments of cloak and dagger interwoven with the daily humdrum.

But my real problem was keeping my own identity secret. The Army frowns on soldiers writing novels that poke fun at their activities. And the first in the series got an advance from Simon and Schuster before I was officially out of the Service in late 1973. That caused a little dustup in the papers, and got some needed publicity for me that the Army could have done without in those dark days.

It was that publisher's option on the Joe Parker series that fueled several bad decisions on my part, including getting married and buying a house in Seacrest, New Jersey. But the succession of disasters that followed, all in fact of my own doing, were begun with the decision by Universal to drop the option for the series when the young female lead they had planned for the part of my habitual damsel in distress went into drug rehab for the second time and told the papers that the head of the studio was a lecher and a cokehead.

At the Madison Library I followed the progress on microfiche film of a young woman from Malibu to hell. She'd apparently never had a guardian angel. More the opposite, in the person of her profligate father, Matt Flynn. And very quickly, I knew more than I wanted to.

Maggie Flynn had been nominated for an academy award when she was fourteen years old, for playing a sixteen year old girl who had been abused by her retired soldier father —still a shocking theme for Hollywood at the time, and one that only added to the darkness of Matt Flynn's shadow over her life. She had been in two dozen films over the next twenty years, though the frequency diminished and the last was in 1985. Matt Flynn had been a very big television star from the 1950s and 1960s playing first a cowboy and then a down and out detective. He had died of a drug overdose in 1987, thought to be a suicide. Her mother, Abby Abernathy, a sometime actress, had died years before that in a car accident in 1957. The car had been driven by Maggie's father. In the years after, her step-mother Cheri Bing, a model, evidently had constant problems due to her own drug issues.

Despite the photo likeness, and allowing for age, it was nearly impossible for me to believe the two Maggies were one and the same person. She actually looked a lot worse when she was younger.

I wondered briefly if she had remembered I was the author of the book, *Berlin Liberty*, which was also the title of the movie that she'd once been contracted for. I decided the answer was a no. She must have been so drug addled at the time that the memory of it had been lost. I decided my next best move was to not say anything about what I knew and to let her tell me what she wanted to in time, if that time ever came.

I had succumbed completely to Margaret's idea of leaving the house as much as it was, or at least as much as circumstances would allow. My task was to find ways to preserve it as best I could. Besides, it was the expedient thing to do. I was getting pretty low on cash.

For a bed I'd been using my sleeping bag atop a slab of foam picked up at Walmart, but I'd had enough if that. I'm a light sleeper. Every lump beneath or bump in the night had me up on my feet and staring dumbly out the parlor window at the moonlit ghost of a road in front. The emptiness of the room magnified every sound. My own tread on the floor made a noise like a Junior High School drum majorette in a hurry. The chipmunks started their racket at dawn—before dawn—when the light outside was still blue and the smell of some spring flower I had yet to identify was wafting in through every pour of the structure around me. I'd moved my usual waking time to an hour earlier, but this was not enough.

My Ford pickup was still a youngster. It was only nine or ten years old at the time, but had less than a hundred thousand miles on her because there just wasn't that far to go for anything you wanted from Brooklyn. Everything is right there. Most of the mileage, in fact, had been picked up on several cross-country camping adventures with my son.

With the roof secure, I drove down to the warehouse in New York during the first week in May. I rented a U-Haul trailer at the warehouse on Flatbush Avenue and packed up all my worldly possessions.. Not that I have that much in the way of furniture. My reading chair. My writing desk—really just an old oak bedroom door that I salvaged one time from the curb on Garfield Place and refinished very nicely right down to the black pressed metal and glass knob. (I had always assumed it was a bedroom door for my own reasons). I set this up in the middle of the room on two short file cabinets with the knob away from me and this stayed put very securely beneath the twenty-pound weight of my Swiss-built Hermes typewriter. But it gave me a kick to see the reaction of people when they saw that I'd left the doorknob on. I could reliably get a groan when I told them it was what I used to open up my stories, and besides, a lonely guy needs a knob to fondle.

My bed frame has drawers beneath. My previous apartment in Brooklyn, though it cost more than three times as much, was half the size of this little house and I'd built the bed there myself from a kit to fit a room that was little more than a closet. Admittedly, t looked like something built from a kit. But it worked fine. Other than the shelves and books, bed frame and desk, the next largest component of my belongings were just the plain stuff of living. Clothes. Kitchen utensils. Towels. The like. The kitchen utensils were heavier by volume than any of the other boxes because I like to cook in iron pots and pans just like my own grandmother did and my plates are all what they call 'stoneware' for a reason.

The shelves and books were another matter. There were exactly twelve shelf units (I made those too, but I didn't need a kit), and just over three thousand books in 156 boxes. These were the remains of a painful triage performed some months before. The shelving units are all three feet wide and eight feet tall. I had never measured the ceilings in the house and I worried all the way to Brooklyn and back that they were too high and I'd have to trim them.

It was evening when I was home again and backed the trailer into the yard. A cold daylong rain had turned to night. In my rear view mirror I saw eyes staring back from the door. A second look and I realized that it was Fred, staring back at me in his usual protective pose. The door opened and out came Margaret. She had a flashlight in her hand. In keeping with my previous resolve, I decided not to ask what she was doing there.

I just hopped out and said hi. Fred's tail began to quiver and then wag at the sound of my voice. His head lowered just a little.

She said, "The power's off. There was some wind earlier. I didn't see a light so I brought over a camp light and left it inside."

I said, "Thanks." and then the second thought, "But that means my ice cream will be melting."

"You better eat it fast."

"There's too much. Have some with me."

"I should be getting back."

"Just a little. Strawberry. I have some chocolate syrup too."

She propped that hand up on her waist. "You have a box of oatmeal, and the heel from a loaf of bread, four cans of beans, a can of coffee, a half-empty six pack of beer, a container of Hershey's chocolate syrup and that ice cream."

"You've been looking."

"I was curious."

"Have some ice cream with me then."

"You mean before you eat your bread and beans."

"I ate some pizza on the road."

She relented for the moment, "Okay."

But a cloud of mosquitoes or black flies or both quickly followed me into the light of kitchen from the open door and I suggested we sit in the truck to eat it instead. At that point she took a rain check and headed back. This was probably for the best because there would have been little room for Fred on the seat between us and I was not sure where the bowls were in the boxes I still had to unload.

I slept better that night knowing that I had an inch to spare on the ceilings. Except for the part of it I slurped alone from the container, the ice cream was a loss.

4.

There was no lock on the door. This was the first place I had ever lived without a lock on the door. There was a bolt inside if I was home, but when I left, everything I owned would be available to anyone passing. I thought about this a lot during the month I worked on the roof. By May I had forgotten about it completely.

My next project was the garden. I wanted fresh tomatoes, lettuce and carrots. That was my key objective, but I was going to try a little of everything. Even corn and pumpkins. I had never grown anything on my own before, and I was too much aware of this essential inadequacy. My characters were most often city dwellers.

The minus factor about using the level area that had once been below the barn floor was that it was hard. But not as hard as the stony soil beyond. The plus was the untold generations of horse and cow manure imbedded there. I bought a shovel and a rake and a hoe. I quickly unearthed everything from rusty nails to old horseshoes. I kept the horseshoes and used the tarp from my truck to drag the bad crap away and then dug out more soil at the tree line and dragged that back again until I had the entire area that I'd loosened, a rectangle of about thirty by forty feet, at least six inches deep in black earth. Including what worms I found under the leaves in the woods. This procedure was all well described in a book I'd taken out at the local library and I followed the advice fairly closely. It was harder work than I had imagined it to be and I was feeling fairly proud of myself for getting it done as quickly as I did. And again, I will admit here an ulterior motive. I wanted to impress Margaret. I had to suppress the urge to run up the hill to fetch her and show off my handiwork. But she did not come by that week.

The next time I saw Margaret was at the supermarket in Conway. She saw me first because I was studying an array of cereal boxes at the time and she came over and took notes on what was in my cart while I was distracted.

"You'll need dishwashing liquid. That's a lot of grease to break up."

The sound of her voice shocked me just a little. Surveying the bacon and the sausages and the hamburger, I had no retort.

"It's on my list."

"And those muffins are overpriced."

"I like English muffins with my hamburgers."

"The store brand is just as good. Or make your own. The oven works."

There was an opportunity in that. I could probably bake just fine. The *Betty Crocker Cookbook* would have the plans all laid out in simple sign language. But if I told her I couldn't bake I was fairly certain she would not offer to teach me. I quickly opted for the opposite strategy.

"You're right. I should make my own bread. I'll pick up some flour."

"Do you know how?"

"Sure."

She let a moment pass on that lie. She was reading me like a comic book.

"You'll want to get the all-purpose type. Get a container of baking soda and one of baking powder. A couple aisles over they have sifters, rolling pins and the like. Shortening. Don't forget the shortening. Look at the recipe on the bag of King Arthur flour to see what else you need. I see you already have the eggs and salt."

"Thank you."

And then she was gone again.

The third week in May, when I had spent several days planting seeds according to the instructions on the packets, Margaret drove over in a great big Chevy Suburban, pulling a trailer loaded with wire fencing. She backed that right down to my garden, got out with a nod as if she was only doing what was expected, and rolled the fencing bundles out onto the grass.

I watched quietly.

She said, "You're going to need this. It won't keep everything out. The deer can go right over the top if they have the mind to. But it will stop the rabbits and the ground hogs and most of the other critters that'll eat your crop before it has a chance to grow. I was going to replace the fence on my chicken run but I'll hold off on that. When you get the chance, go down to the Home Depot and buy me some replacements."

She tossed several bundles of metal stakes out as well.

I said, "Thanks."

She said, "Run some string across the top of the stakes from side to side and tie pieces of fabric on that. It'll keep the dumber birds away."

Then she nodded and left.

My Grandpa Buck was a self-avowed primordial son-of-a-bitch. But none of his grandchildren believed him.

While in the Merchant Marines, he had survived the torpedoing of his ship in the First World War and later gone into business for himself, succeeded and failed several times, married once, helped raise four children, and never retired. He finally died at his desk filling out stock orders for his stationery store in Brooklyn when he was 84. And that was the way I wanted to leave the premises too. Maybe not in a stationery store, but retiring seemed to me a fool's wish—the vacant dream of someone who has not really been living their life in the first place. What was it you were going to do when you retired that you should not have done before when you were young enough to enjoy it? Paris? London? Rome? Daniel 'Buck'

McNeill had seen all of that and more at least once in his journeys around the world in tramp steamers as 'a kid,' But every August of his adult married life he and Grandma Doris were off on another trek, with one, two, three, and then four kids in tow. He told me once that if he couldn't afford to do that when he wanted, then he knew he was doing something wrong. That seemed like a very neat philosophy. It basically meant I'd been doing something wrong for most of my own life. But I did agree with him on the first point. I would never likely be able to retire.

Where the 'son-of-a-bitch' came into the picture for Grandpa was that he spent every dime he made. He had no intention of dying with more in his pocket than was needed to tie up loose ends. Their house on Sterling Place in Brooklyn had been mortgaged to the hilt. He'd already bought the plot next the grandma's family spot up near Boston and paid the insurance for the burial. My grandmother had made it to that place the year before he did. In other words, I inherited nothing from him but a contrary disposition.

My father is still very much alive in Florida and doing all he can to follow in my grandfather's footsteps on this account, though he has a shorter hurdle to accomplish the deed. He was bankrupted when he was seventy-eight, during the stock market collapse of 1987. For most of his career he dabbled in real estate and wrote some very successful travel books with my mother. Actually she does the writing. He does the photography. And she still goes by her maiden name of Cass Green. Before that, back when he still lived in Brooklyn and before the twenty years they spent raising their three kids in Queens, he was a crime photographer for the *New York Mirror*. I've seen some of his work from that time. Gruesome. That was during the 1930's and was where he met my mother when she was working as a reporter for the same newspaper. Now they still get by selling a little real estate down in Sarasota and producing the occasional travel article. But they don't travel quite as much as they used to.

The problem with being raised as I was in the suburbs of New York by such an unremittingly and unrepentantly middle-class family is that the values are in your genes. Bourgeois is what you are and what you will ever be. No excuses. Your poorer friends always suspect that you will not understand their fears. Your Marxist buddies will make their remarks at your expense and then freely complain to you if their trust fund check is late in the mail. Your nouveau riche acquaintances will keep you at arm's length, always afraid you might want to borrow some of their money. And those you know who are born rich are always too different to get close to. So you hang out with others of your own sort and soon get tired of talking about the same nostalgia, about wanting to get away to the same places, about paying all of the same taxes and suffering all of the same ills and misfortunes.

My endeavor in New Hampshire was to somehow break that cycle without demanding the rest of the world to be ripped asunder by revolution or plagued with catastrophe to accomplish my goal. My parents had certainly lived a good life and earned the right to enjoy the last sip of that. I just didn't want that for myself.

My problem is, and always has been, that I have never been sure just what kind of adventure I wanted out of life instead. Writing that out in my stories is perhaps the closest I would get.

5.

I was pretty sure that Margaret had meant for me to use the electric oven for my baking, but I was determined to use the wood stove. It was clear inside. I pulled the damper and the flame from a piece of discarded manuscript fluttered nicely. But the Betty Crocker cookbook had nothing about cooking with a wood stove so I made my dough according to Betty's recipe and then took a walk.

Unfortunately, or perhaps fortunately, Margaret wasn't home.

I went over the field then to see Marie Ferrell instead. But she wasn't home either. Back up the road again. I found three cars nosed in on the gravel at the Greiders' and Georgina in her kitchen with Ellen Macomber and Marie Ferrell, all drinking coffee and laughing loud enough to be heard before I could actually see the house in the trees.

They could see me when I knocked on the screen at the back door and they all went quiet and looked a little sheepish for a minute as I stepped in.

Ellen immediately said, "What did you hear?"

"You mean your laughing?"

Marie said, "Cackling I'll bet you thought it was. We were talking about you."

"What did I do?"

"Nothing, that we know of. That's the point. We all agree, you are a very sneaky customer."

"How so?"

Georgina had to get in on their conceit and waved Ellen off before the entire thing was obvious.

"We all had it figured that you'd have made your move on Maggie within a week. Two weeks tops. Sleeping in your little bag there on the floor. Too cute and oh so lonely. But you are the smart one after all. She would have kicked you right out if you had."

They paused to let me incriminate myself. So I did.

"I just figured we should get to know each other a little first. See what we had in common. I'm a little old-fashioned that way."

Ellen said, "I thought your type were all dead, or married, or both."

This was a conversation I wanted to curtail. I gave a laugh at that and thought it might be enough of a defense and then asked them all at once.

"Does anyone here know how to cook on a woodstove?"

They looked at each other with jaws open.

Ellen spoke up, "I guess I'm the former hippie in this bunch. What are you making?"

"I wanted to bake some bread."

Another momentary silence. Then she looked at me with a totally blank face. "You just forget about Maggie. You can marry me. I'll make you happier than any man has a right to be."

Georgina and Marie both thought this was hysterical.

Ellen drove me back to the house and wrote out her instructions on a pad of her company paper. (I noted that she underlined the phone number at the top.) Then she poked at my dough and said that it was ready. I put some cardboard from the empty boxes and some kindling in the stove. She spotted the baking stone lying loose in the hearth at the back and handed that to me because I was not using pans. I had an idea about something I'd eaten once in Brooklyn.

I asked, "How do I know when it's hot enough?"

"Sprinkle a little water on the stone. It'll speak to you. If you do it often enough, you'll learn the language."

Before the dough was in the oven, she took the opportunity to walk completely around the inside of the house and then came back.

"That's a lot of books you have there."

"I need them for my work . . . Actually need some more. I don't have the right ones."

"Have you talked to Jean at the library?"

"Several times."

"Impose on her. She likes to be useful. She has the time. People don't read like they used to. She'll find you anything you need."

"I will."

"And if you need anything else, you just let me know."

Her voice dropped with that last statement. I laughed to let her understand I thought she was joking.

When she left, she was still shaking her head.

This much was unfair, of course. Remember, my efforts were wholly self-serving, and not only because I was going to get something to eat out of it.

6.

I'd gotten the right consistency with my vaguely rounded loaves within a week. They had the rustic look of something on the cover of a cooking magazine and again I was feeling rather full of myself. When I carried one up the hill to Margaret, I caught her while she was shoveling chicken shit out of the hen house and I left my offering in a paper sack out on the table on her deck and went back to my own responsibilities.

That evening she showed up with Fred at my door, carrying a small sack of her own. Her hair was in a scarf and she had on one of her thick sweaters against the chill that was settling.

She at least gave me a partial smile. "Was that a loaf of bread you left me?"

"You didn't see it?"

"Fred saw it first. He seemed to like it."

Fred was all ears and total innocence. I invited her in.

This was the first time she'd come into the house since I had set up my shelves and gotten the books in place and all the rest. She stood at the door to the parlor and wandered with her eyes.

"Isaac would be surprised at all this. He wasn't a reader."

"I wondered about that. I was trying to imagine him out here by himself in the evenings for all those years before he married. I imagined him reading."

"Oh, he might have. He had a Bible, and a copy of *Pilgrims Progress*. They were both pretty worn, so perhaps I am being too hard on him."

I took the chance opening.

"What do you read?"

She squinted at me. I was growing fond of that squint. It was a put on look that was meant to be seen as unserious so I could be sure then that I hadn't done or said anything myself to be worried over.

"I'll tell you, if you won't laugh . . . I read children's books."

"Only children's books?"

"Yes. Any age, so long as they were meant for the young. Not recent ones though. Nothing much that was written after I grew up."

"Which means you probably haven't read any of my stuff."

She answered quickly, the thought perhaps already fixed in her mind. "No. I've determined not to. I don't want to know. . . . I'm sorry if that's rude. But I've read your mother's books —the kid's books about living in New York. I love your father's pictures in those too. I just wish New York was still that innocent."

I should have been surprised, but somehow I wasn't. The funny thing about it was, the children's books were the ones I've paid the least attention to. But at an early age I had begun to explore the world in my parents' travel books.

I made an excuse, "You're better off staying away from my stuff then. You might be disappointed and kick me out if you did."

She shook her head. "No! Not that. Because I believe writers are a lot like actors. They try to please the audience. They go for the big laugh or the tear. They put on a face for the public. They give their readers what they think is wanted. But it's never them that you know. It's only misdirection. No matter how true they try to be. It's always what they want you to see instead."

This was the longest string of words Margaret had spoken to me up to that moment. If it hadn't been so absolutely on target I might have come up with some defense. I couldn't. But now I understood something else. She knew I was aware she'd once been Maggie Flynn.

Foolishly, I turned that illumination away from myself in order to reveal the petty knowledge I'd gained. "Do you read those books now because you never had enough of a childhood of your own?"

Immediately the friendly squint was lost in a moment of bewilderment. For the first time since I'd met her, for a brief instant, she did not appear to be the strongest woman I had ever known. She looked like a girl. I didn't give her a chance to answer.

"Sorry. I shouldn't have said that. It's none of my business. Let me get you another loaf of bread. If you don't like that, you can at least give it to Fred."

I had another loaf of bread in the kitchen. As it was, I'd eaten most of my mistakes that week and had about enough of it. I was gone and back again in just a minute, but the door had already closed behind her. The paper sack she'd carried, filled with a dozen eggs, was on the mantel.

I was getting to know her schedule. Just as I do myself, she awakens before dawn. When the leaves of summer had not yet filled in I could see the smoke rising above the brim of the hill from her chimney into that first light, white or yellow or reddened by whatever weather had passed in the night. On Sundays she was home and I could usually catch her doing something around the house. On Mondays she was gone. I didn't know where. She took her eggs to a market in Madison on Tuesdays. She went to the grocery store in Conway on Wednesdays, when the extra 10% sale was on. On Thursdays she carried the fresh flowers from her four greenhouses to a shop near Wolfeboro and fresh herbs to a restaurant there. She wasn't Catholic but she always ate fish on Fridays. She said it was freshest then, and she was right. Everyday she attended to the chickens and her other chores early and found time to walk with Fred later in the day when she returned.

I was ready with a fresh loaf when she came up the road the next afternoon. I met her there.

An apology was clear in her eyes. "Sorry about leaving so abruptly. I just had to go."

I waved that off and handed her the sack.

She said, "Thank you. I'll keep Fred away from this if I can." She squinted briefly and then didn't and simply looked at me square on with those big green eyes and I was pretty much done in and could not say another thing. She said, "And to answer your question from yesterday—yes. But it's a little more obvious even than that. My mother died when I was seven. I had trouble reading before, I think because she would read everything to me. I liked that. By pretending I couldn't read, she would spend more time with me. Very basic stuff. Every psychologist I've ever spoken to discovers that in no time and thinks they have the key to revelations and that everything else will follow suit. Like everything else will follow in a neat little line. But I don't think it's all so neat as that. I think it has more to do with lost innocence. I cannot remember ever feeling such innocence myself as what I find in children's books. Flat out. Open-faced. I wish I'd been able to know some of that—that simple confidence in the good when I was younger. And even when my mother was reading those books to me, my mind was telling me that those characters were different. I would never be like that. I always knew the wolf was at the door."

There was nothing glib to say and nothing wise that I knew of. I thought she probably understood her situation better than I ever could. Then she waved her goodbye and went on with her walk.

7.

By accident, I'd discovered the bookshop in Sandwich that Margaret liked to visit each week. The owner was a fairly nosy woman who was intent on talking to me about everything that interested her as soon as she found out I was a writer. Trying to be polite only encouraged her. I had mistakenly said that I was renting the old Abernathy house on my first visit. She proceeded to tell me what she knew about 'Maggie,' which was nearly nothing but took a quarter-hour.

The day after I'd given Margaret the loaf of bread, I went back to the bookshop to look at the children's books but there was nothing on the shelf that I knew anything about that I liked. I was, however, made aware of two obvious facts I hadn't considered. One was that, unlike Margaret, I had not read much that qualified as children's literature since I was 'grown up.' I'd only given my son the things I'd liked as a boy. The other was the simple fact that I was a guy and probably read things years ago that she would not have. For some odd reason, most of what was written in that genre was directed at either girls or boys but seldom both.

The day afterward, having seen that they did not have a copy for sale, I brought one of my own books with me to the shop instead, already wrapped, and asked the woman there if she would give it to Miss Abernathy whenever she came in. I bought a copy of another book that I was interested in to make the request less onerous when the woman broke her usual line of conversation about herself and showed some hesitation.

"Why don't you give it to her yourself?"

"It's a surprise."

My next visit to Jean at the library was to ask her if she could find any good books about tramp steamer travel during my grandfather's time and order them through interlibrary loan. Grandpa had gone around the world in one vessel or another, and I could not remember any of the ship names. I knew that one of these ships had actually changed its registration in the short distance between the Azores and Lisbon. He suspected it of smuggling, though he had never learned the facts.

Jean is a small woman who stands up very straight and has her hair piled just a little higher on her head for the desired effect. I figured her to be somewhere in her thirties—with no wedding ring, a too quick smile, and reserved in the way that shy people often are. She was obviously more used to dealing with the demands of children. Quite fairly, a request from an adult was given exactly the same sort of attention and an equal tone of voice.

"Are you sure of the author's name? Are you sure of the title? Are you sure of the spelling? When do you think it was published?"

When I asked for 'anything' she might be able to find on tramp steamers she was flummoxed. She stared blindly into space, then turned, and went silently back to her office. I waited under the fair assumption that she would return, and after a few minutes she had found a particularly thick subject-index containing the category I wanted. She stared into the midst of that for a moment after licking a finger and flipping pages, and then turned the volume around to me on the desktop with no more questions asked.

I had the sense that she was pleased with herself for this discovery and I said, "Thanks," but she did not manage to say another word and went back to filing three by five cards in a loose drawer from an old wood case.

I was now in possession of all the wisdom of the ages, so long as I could further categorize my interest. Over the following months I looked into that same book a hundred times. Jean began pulling the inter-library loan slips from her drawer as soon as I walked in the door.

But soon after that first inquiry about steamships, a neatly collected line of my own books suddenly appeared on display at the front desk beneath a sign saying "local author." A dozen of them, at least. All I could do was give her a nod and a smile. I was not particularly proud of them at that moment, but it was a nice gesture.

Jean also knew of Margaret's interest in children's books.

This had come up in a different way. I'd started going through that section of the library to get an idea of those titles I knew very little about. Jean kept an eye on me and on my second visit to that alcove of the room, while I was sitting on the linoleum because the chairs were too small, and I was about three feet away from a tyke with a runny nose and bad habits, Jean came over. She handed a tissue to the kid before turning to me.

"What is the age of the child you are looking for?"

"Forty-nine."

Her reaction gained her an extra inch.

"Are they disabled?"

"Not yet. I just never read most children's books when I was a kid. I thought it was about time."

This got her to flush. She has very black hair and very white skin and the flush was brilliant and splotchy.

"I'm sorry. It's for you, then. I see."

"I really don't know what I read when I was very young. Holling C. Holling. Robert Lawson. That sort of thing. But I was reading *Tom Sawyer* by the time I was eight and I never looked back. I thought it was about time I learned a little something more."

"You have a child?"

"No. My son is grown and out on his own. He reads thrillers and true adventure books. Not much else."

"Are you thinking of writing one yourself?"

I was dumbstruck. I had never thought of the idea and now suddenly it seemed like the very best idea I'd ever heard. And just like that I said, "Yes."

"About a tramp steamer?"

"Yes. But not exactly. Something about my grandfather who was in the Merchant Marine."

"How wonderful! I hope you do. People don't have enough real adventures anymore. Too much TV."

"I agree with that."

The flush had gone to a quieter pink and filled her entire face when she turned to her desk again but half-way there she turned back.

"I'll tell you this. The person who knows the most about children's books of anyone around here is Margaret Abernathy. She loves them. She still reads them."

I had to be forthright then.

"She owns the house I live in."

Her eyes went wide but the pink faded.

"Old Isaac's place?"

"Yes."

She turned again to her desk as if to escape and it seemed to me that the pink had faded all away.

I told Margaret about the idea that afternoon when I joined her for her walk with Fred. This was an example of my being over-anxious, of course. I should have kept it to myself. I might have surprised her with the book and won her with a single gesture.

The fact was, I'd previously explained the need for buying a shotgun. This necessity made the ridges of the frown on her forehead curl downward in neat brackets at the ends.

Now when I told her I had decided to write the story as a kid's book, her first response was, "That will be unique. A children's story with shotguns."

I was humorless on the subject.

"It's not about shotguns. My grandfather once used a shotgun to hold off pirates in the Indian Ocean and again later to save my grandmother's life—and his own."

"Maybe so. But it's not a subject that's in demand nowadays, I think. I can't imagine librarians like Jean ordering such a thing. Fifty years ago, maybe. Back when people still read Robert Louis Stevenson. Not today."

She was right, of course. I could hold back the parts that involved pirates and outlaws and shotguns and temper my story to the sort of events that a child of our own day might better comprehend. But not without misgiving. I'd been asked to alter stories before to meet one editorial demand or another. I wasn't sure I should start this one while already assuming the worst. It seemed obvious to me that the constant resorting to fantasy in children's stories today was the result of just this sort of filing away the sharper edges of good and evil, and the removal of risk and consequences. Were the children of Robert Louis Stevenson's day so much stronger, or smarter?

<h1 style="text-align:center">8.</h1>

Summer came on in a rush. The summer people arrived and the local markets became busy and the roads loud at all hours. Old Isaac's house had often been rented during the summers before and a young couple showed up one morning when I was writing and knocked on the door. The fellow reminded me of myself about twenty years ago. His wife was not as good looking as my ex-wife was, but somehow seemed more appealing in her manner. They already had three kids. All five of them were standing there at the front door when I opened it. All with bright smiles.

The fellow spoke up immediately. "Hi. My name is Bob Decker. I was just wondering if you had bought the place? We've stayed here once before and we loved it but the realtor told us it was taken this year and she made it sound like that would be a permanent thing."

"I hope so."

Frowns grabbed at the faces of the children. His wife chimed in, "We just love it here. So peaceful."

I said, "I'm sorry. But maybe you should check in about it next year. You never know."

This seemed to be the most polite way I could put them off.

The girl in the family, a twelve-year old if I guessed correctly, decided it was her turn.

"My daddy wants to buy it."

Her father put up a hand in defense.

"Not this year, of course. No! But it's just the kind of second home we've always wanted. I was thinking of talking to Miss Abernathy about it."

I shrugged, "I don't think it's for sale." And then, as an afterthought I said too much. "But frankly, I'd buy it myself if it was."

All smiles were gone as they filed out the walkway to their car on the road. But the girl could not resist jumping from stone to stone as she brought up the rear.

I did not see Margaret on her walk that afternoon, but she was at my door early that evening.

She skipped the 'hello.' No hint of a smile.

"I hear you were talking to the Deckers."

"They showed up this morning."

"Bob said you told him you wanted to buy the house."

There is something more fierce than any expression on Margaret's face. That would be no expression at all, I think because her features seem to be made so well to reveal her thoughts.

I said, "Sorry about that. I shouldn't have. I only said it because he told me he wanted to buy it. I wanted to put him off."

"It's not for sale."

"And unfortunately, I couldn't afford to buy it if it was."

After a beat of consideration she seemed to accept that and took an extra breath. I could see that she'd worked herself up into being very angry.

"I know you've put some effort into the place and I appreciate that, but you should know now that this house will never be for sale. Not as long as I live."

"I'm glad of that. And I hope you live for a very long time."

She nodded enough to make it clear again that she now understood the situation I'd been in. The thought passed my mind that she had been stewing over this slight all day. Now her shoulders seemed to drop an inch as she relaxed. Even the green of her eyes lightened considerably. Fred stood his ground just behind her, mouth closed. He had not moved a quiver and had clearly heard the tone in voice. He sat back now and licked his chops as if he might be interested in another loaf of bread.

She took a breath, "Thank you for the book. That was a surprise. Jean seemed a bit puzzled by it all. But how did you know I'd never read *Kidnapped*?"

"Just a guess. It's a boy's book."

"But I read boys books too."

"I'll bet you do. I just wanted to get you something that I'd liked myself when I was a kid. That's what sprung to mind. When I was nine years old, I used to pray that I'd be kidnapped. I read it again a few years ago and was amazed it was still so good."

"You were a silly boy."

"I was. Still am."

"Thank you again. I was up all night with it. It's wonderful."

"I'm glad it was the right thing."

Behind her I could see that the roses had begun to bloom all over the rock wall in thick clusters and that they were blood crimson and lovely there in the amber of the evening light, like an old painting with the image subdued by age. I slipped out the doorway past her and cut a baker's dozen of them as a peace offering. I only had my little pocketknife and pricked my fingers pretty well on the small thorns, but I kept that to myself. She watched all this without saying a thing as I came past her again with the clutch of them, to wrap the prickly stems in some pages of wadded manuscript that were in the wastebasket close by so that she could handle them better herself, and presented this bouquet with an exaggerated bow.

"Is it a little too cheeky if I give you your own flowers as my apology?"

Her face again appeared expressionless to me. Truly blank. But at least she took them.

The beach at Silver Lake opened up, but it was crowded immediately with the summer folk on any warm day. Looking for a good alternative, one afternoon I asked Harold Jenks where it was that he used to swim when he was a boy.

"Boy, hell. Still go over ta the Swift River when I get all chaffed up. But you want a swim. The best swimmin' hole around here is Norris Pond. It's an old quarry and deepens off right quick. Sally and I used to put on our birthday suits and go in over there on any ol' hot day. Then the Norris dairy got to hurting for some cash and sold off the back part of it to a fellow from New York and he put up half a dozen cottages. We still used to go over with the kids, but it wasn't near as peaceful, and we had to start wearing bathing suits. Kinda spoilt it. But still a lot better that Silver Lake any day."

I knew the Swift River pretty well. I wanted to see the pond. He directed me to the old logging road that would get me back to a "big rock." This turned out to be a glacial boulder nearly the size of Isaac's house. From there the trail led directly into the shore of the lake. The dairy was long gone now and the pastures there overgrown with second growth, making it all look less appealing from the road, but at least the Norris land had been put in a conservancy trust. Further 'development' had been stopped. The 'New York' fellow's cottages squatted serenely in the shadows at the far side on that late afternoon. I went in without my bathing suit, just to say I had.

This visit became a regular midday routine as July came on.

9.

On July Fourth, at noon, there was an explosion in front of the house. Then I heard Fred's bark. I was out the door immediately. Smoke still curled in the air beneath the big maple. Margaret stood on the road, hands on her hips.

"I thought that might wake you up."

"I wasn't sleeping."

"It looked pretty quiet in there."

"Writing doesn't make a lot of noise."

"So that's your excuse. But I thought you said you liked fireworks?"

She held a bag up in her hand. "You want to make some noise?"

She put on a mischievous face. By the curl at the corners of her mouth she'd become a sprite.

I said, "You've got things out of order. First you go for a swim. Then you eat hot dogs and ice cream. Then you go for a swim again to see if you can get cramps like your mother warned you about. Then you eat a hamburger and go swimming again. And by then it's getting onto dusk and you do the fireworks."

"Is that it? I guess I just never did it like that before."

"I'll be happy to show you then. Go get your bathing suit."

She set the paper bag down by the wall and ran back up the road like a very large little girl, hair flying behind, arms pumping. Fred, seeing something he was unfamiliar with, followed her, leaping.

I followed her in a few moments in my pickup. At the top of her drive I met her practically dancing with anticipation. She had her bathing suit gripped in one hand and her towel in the other. I already had my trunks on.

"Where's Fred?"

"In the house. He gets too excited with the kids at the beach."

"But we aren't going to Silver Lake. We're going to Norris Pond."

"How do you know about that?"

"Harold."

"Harold is a wonder. But, there's no place to change there?"

"No."

"You'll just have to turn your back then."

She seemed a little giddy.

I had to ask as she climbed in, "What's happened?"

She just said, "What do you mean? It's gorgeous fabulous wonderous summer day."

"Wouldn't fabulous be enough? Did you sell a bunch of sweaters?"

"It's summer!"

"Did the hens lay a whole lot of eggs?"

"Like crazy, as usual."

"Did you sell all your flowers?"

"It's only roses right now. And herbs. Everybody has roses."

"Even I have roses."

"But you have the very best roses."

This was a wholly different Margaret, and yet the same. Every word out of her mouth was in her voice but in a brand new tone and said at a pace that would have matched the way my son often spoke to me when he called.

At the lake she was out the door and into the trees before I turned the motor off. I yelled after her that I would wait a minute and let her change, and then started to follow too quickly in the hope of maybe seeing something I shouldn't, and suddenly feeling some of the excitement, before I remembered the towels behind the seat of the truck and went back for those. She was already in the water before I got there. And very clearly she was naked.

It was not a difficult decision in that moment. I was no longer thinking all that clearly. I slipped off my trunks to a rather loud giggle from my singular audience and went in after her. The houses on the far shore seemed quiet and, I hoped, uninterested.

There in the water was where I first kissed her, and for the second time. And the fourth and the twelfth as well. I wasn't really counting. I was out of my mind.

10.

Idylls are necessarily brief, or they are not idylls at all.

For the rest of July and the entirety of August we saw each other every day. Her home, with all its glass and open spaces, and the 'great' room running nearly end to end on the south side, felt larger, but she liked it better to come down to Isaac's house in the late afternoons and seldom left until dawn to do her chores. It took me a week before I could manage to write another decent sentence.

Most of those first days were taken with one discovery after another. I suppose she found out things about me as well that might have pleased her, or not, but I thought my own existence was fairly plain for her to see. Her life alone on the hill however, though seemingly more visible from the distance, had been the greater mystery. I'd never been inside her house until that day, the Fourth of July, for instance. Wrought with curiosity, I'd peeked in the broad windows from the deck on several occasions when she was not home, but she usually had the sun blinds closed and the darkened shapes within only revealed a certain neatness and order. The smaller windows set high on the span of the northern exposure were nearly seven feet off the ground and offered little more to see.

Let me describe the house.

It is at the very top of the hill, built in a former pasture and surrounded by fields with no natural shade from the trees. The summit of land there is solid rock only partially covered with a thin veneer of soil so that there is no basement to the structure. The house is elevated above this and built on a flat carriage of heavy laminated wood beams, some spanning as much as twenty-four feet. These supports float horizontally like a dock amidst six poured concrete outer piers. At first appearance as I walked closer, the entire house reminded me of a strange anachronistic ship that must have the leeway between those pilings to accommodate the rise and fall of mysterious tides. That base carries the house above the surface of the earth, opening a space of about two feet at the closest point to the ground and over eight feet at it's highest beneath the outreach of the deck. The deck, and indeed the entire face of the house, opens to the south. From the road to Isaac's house, what you see above is only the span of the gray back wall facing the north with its narrow horizontal windows and the oddly arching white roof. From below, the roof line changes its shape depending on the day and the time of day.

There are, in fact, only two outer walls and these curve together at the ends, again like the bow and stern of a ship. This ocean reference is announced more clearly at the south side by a three-part upper canopy actually unconnected to the house beneath, but to the piers and held there between by attached spars, much like a series of white triangular 'jib sails' that look to have been blown loose at a bottom edge and are now far more horizontal than vertical. Those sails and jibs are in fact connected by ropes which allow them to be shifted for the need, pivoting from the piers and offering all the shade necessary to both house and deck on hotter days and even deflect much of the wind and weather from the actual fixed arch of white roof beneath. In bad weather the spars are brought together by a pulley at each end and set back against the piers.

The deck on that south side spans east to west, curving outward beyond the enclosed house and piers with no other visible means of support than the beams beneath which connect to the undercarriage of the whole structure. Thin oak rails at the extremity of the deck are also painted grey and easily forgotten by the eye.

A center 'mast' at the peak of the arching roof has a multipurpose. It's thicker and taller than the other piers that rise at the sides but not noticeably so. The visible uppermost portion is the chimney top. Below the roofline there is support at this center mast for a water cistern which is supplied by the windmill nearer the well and closer to the greenhouses below.

At its base this central mast is planted into the rock at the very highest point of the hill.

The main entry to the house from the drive is from the western end where several broad and open concrete steps rise to the deck and there meet the front door and an entry that fills the 'bow.' The nearly identical 'back door,' which is in the stern to the east, is the one I used more often to head away down the grassy slope of the hill to Isaac's house each day. All of this was very dramatic but had not been especially beautiful to me from the distance, and seeming out of place so far from the sea. Eccentric for its own sake I thought, until I lived there and realized the sense of floating above the earth that it offered. The exterior walls were smooth vertical shiplap cedar planking stained gray and in the right light on a rainy day the house nearly disappears.

In total, despite first appearances, her home is relatively small inside: a bedroom, a great room, a kitchen and a bath. But all of these are fairly large in themselves. The dining table is in the open extension of the south-facing great room at the western end. The kitchen occupies its quarter on the northwest wall. The bedroom is to the northeast. Between the bedroom and kitchen there is a laundry and water heater in the bathroom, entered through a short hall that is just behind the center hearth and beneath the cistern. In this respect, the whole plan roughly reflected Isaac's house in the positioning of the rooms, and is not much larger.

The great room occupies fully half the interior floorspace, wrapping the southern exposure nearly end to end, connecting both entries and looks out upon the dropping elevation at that side of the hill with floor to ceiling windows which form an arc of natural light facing the deck. The hearth is stone only at its base, but otherwise a modern contraption of welded iron and glass that is a Swedish reinvention of the woodstove with a black metal flue rising directly above it to the vaulted ceiling. This fireplace squats at the very center of a middle wall, which is glass again, and also runs from bow to stern.

When blinds are raised, the center glass wall affords a full view, through the great room for both kitchen and bedroom at either side of the hearth, but more importantly, it allows the light from the larger windows on the south to reach all the way to the enclosure of the back wall on the North. Unlike Isaac's house, all the interior ceilings are high, arching in sections defined by the rib-like beams that curve upward and correspond to the concrete piers outside, and this again offers the visual note of the interior ribs of a boat hull, but turned upside down.

I'd remarked casually on the house several times before first entering there because it was so obviously unusual and Margaret told me it had been built by a construction firm in Conway. Little else. And in that it did not at first appeal to me from the distance, I didn't press for anything more. I was well enchanted by my own cottage.

Now I learned the surprising fact of the matter. The house was built by the Farley Brothers Construction, true enough. But it had been designed by Margaret.

That knowledge was enough to place a considerable awe upon a mind already inebriated by love. But like the door that I used to write upon, once opened, the story beyond had dimensions I could not have guessed at before venturing there.

The shelving that held her collection of children's books was off-white and low, and punctuated the base of the middle wall of glass to either side of the hearth. The simple shiplap pine of the interior walls, here also set vertically in the manner of the exterior, were painted an off-white. This was the color of new vellum I told her. "Of hand-made paper," she said, well aware of her choice. The solid vertical space of those walls is decorated only by watercolors and drawings, unframed and pinned in place by simple thumbtacks, these pictures could catch the eye as if done right on the surface itself. They were not all of the same quality. Many appeared to be quite professional and focused and others simple and naïve. I especially liked the drawings done of singular things: a fence post, the apple trees in winter (before I trimmed them) with their short trunks stooped and limbs touching the snow with age, and the stonewall, still breached as I had first found it, and with a haunting sense of what would come in time for the wooden house behind. There were many drawings of Isaac's house, inside and out. The massive hearth had been sketched in charcoal several times. None of the work was signed but I had no doubt about the artist.

However, I saw at once that one of these pictures was completely unlike the others. This was a plain sheet of white, eight-and-a-half by eleven paper which had clearly been waded up, perhaps to throw away. Confused by the vague image, I brought my nose within six inches in order to see what the illustration there might be.

I could tell from the reverse impression that there was typing on the other side of the sheet, facing the wall. The faint and spotty impression, presented off-center and in a single but uneven maroon-like color, was made more ambiguous by water stains with several steaks as if struck by rain. It became clear to me only with some study. It was the palm of a hand. Portions of all five fingers were there. It took a moment longer then for my brain to comprehend that the hand was mine; that the color was the smear of blood, and that the water which had splashed that crude impression must be tears.

What had I done?

I had given her roses.

But what had I truly done? That was the question begging at a weakened mind.

I had been enchanted by a sorceress. I had fallen in love not with a common Dorothy but with the Good Witch of the North.

11.

I had to know then how a Hollywood brat becomes an artist. Having already skinned my shins before on her otherwise invisible sharp edges, I tried my questions in small increments. What it amounted to was this: that her father had tried in his own way to keep her from the excesses that he knew were ruining him. Matt Flynn had a sailboat for some years, before it was lost to debts. He used that to take his wife and daughter out whenever he could, and just the two of them after her mother's death, coasting from Baja to Monterey Bay. And most importantly, sensing some other nature in his girl, he had taken her to art classes from the time she was three or four. But she had always wanted to be an actor, like her father, and the art lessons had been pushed aside.

"The first day I came here to Isaac's house," she told me, "I hadn't drawn more than a doodle in twenty years. I was numb and it was cold and there was snow deep all about. Harold saw my feeble attempts at a fire by the color of the smoke from the chimney and came over with a load of good wood and an equal quantity of advice. I was lost, so I simply did everything he said. One thing was that I should stay busy. Never sit on my hands. If I was going to daydream, do it when I was getting something done. There is no time to waste. Life is short enough without cutting at the middle.

"I'd actually picked up some paper at the Aubuchon one day. Just something to plan a few fixes. The drawing quickly got out of hand, you might say."

Her own future home had been designed as if in a daydream the second week after she'd arrived to live at Isaac's house. She had used the better part of the life insurance left to her from her father, and it was dedicated to him.

Foolishly, concerned with her meager income from sweaters and flowers and eggs, I suggested, "You could sell your art work."

She had frowned deeply at me then, but at least offered a tone of patience in her voice. "I don't do it for that. It's not for money. It's for me. I feel like I'm a part of what I see when I draw or paint."

I wanted to argue but I kept it to myself. And I learned at last the answer to my wondering about where she went on Mondays. She was going to an art class in Meredith. She was learning to use oils.

And for that brief moment, a sort of domestic bliss overcame us, I think. It is difficult to consider the petty problems of life when all else seems perfect. You throw the bills in the drawer and make love instead. You wallow in clover. (There is indeed nearly an acre of clover there below the deck. What else was there to do?) You make a cliché of everything you say and become too stupid to hear yourself, and you are quite happy for it.

You are always aware in life of your own mortality. If not, you are insane and dangerous to yourself and others. This is not a specter or a haunt, but a dimension and a prompt—a sense that there is something behind or beneath and an awareness of the passage of time. It simply is; and it is that awareness that reminds you to enjoy what you have while you can, for it, and you, will not last.

We took turns cooking. For a while, at least, the trick seemed to be an effort to surprise the other with something different each night. I lost that battle after a few weeks because I had run out of ideas I could wrangle from Betty Crocker using the produce of my garden combined with any reasonable effort.

Waiting for the bread dough to rise, and then the baking itself, had quickly brought me new discoveries. Most importantly, I learned to make biscuits. Building a good steady fire in the wood stove was an art in itself and though I was a mere craftsman at it, I understood it was a waste of wood and effort if I used it only for the bread. I brewed my coffee there on the top well. I cooked my eggs and bacon and grits there too. Another change then for me was to make the dough first thing in the near dark of morning and while that was 'resting,' as the book called it, I would bake some biscuits first. Alone in Isaac's house I could flesh out my notes for the day on the metal-topped-table in the kitchen before I started in to writing and eat a couple of the biscuits right there with my coffee and some blueberry jam. Marie Farrell made the jam from wild blueberries and it was the best that I had ever had. At noon I made a mid-day meal and when Margaret arrived I fired up some bacon, or sausage, or ham and some eggs as well as the grits and we ate together then before our walk. She'd never had grits before, but I'd grown to love them when I was stationed at Ft. Belvoir. With sufficient butter, she came around.

But in mid-August something odd happened. Shortly after she left one morning she called down on the phone to say someone had been in her house the night before. She was upset. I went up there immediately and helped her look around for anything missing. Fred moved frenetically from one end of the house to the other, putting his nose on anything he could, but we found nothing moved or taken. That night and for the weeks that followed, I stayed with her there.

I knew she did not like guns, so I kept the shotgun in the truck beneath the seat, wrapped in a black plastic garbage bag. Thinking about it now, I wonder how rational I was. It would have done me little good out there in an emergency and might even have been a tool for someone else.

12.

On a Sunday night, the last week in August, we had a visitor. Fred had already alerted us to something going on outside, with both ears raised and mouth tight. In anxious anticipation, he finally barked. Someone knocked on the door immediately as if in response.

It was Margaret who opened it. From the side I could see a neatly dressed black man standing there and he immediately looked back at me before speaking to Margaret. He was of medium height, in a polo shirt and slacks. By the look of his shirt, he was very fit. And his shoes were shined. That was an odd thing to notice but you simply don't see a lot of shined shoes in the neighborhood. Not even boots. Nor black men. The African-American population of Carroll County must be less than 1%.

He said, "I'm sorry to bother you, but my car's broken down. Down on 113. Not broken exactly. Stalled. It's happened before. It just quits. I saw your light up here and was hoping I could use your phone to call a garage. I have a car phone but I can't get a thing on it."

He got all of that out without pause. Margaret studied him rather carefully the way she does. I spoke first. A reflex action I guess.

"Sunday, after nine. There aren't any garages open until you get down around Wolfeboro or over in Center Harbor. Maybe up in Conway."

"I can call in the morning, I guess. Is there a place to stay that's close?"

I said, "You might be lucky. There are two bed and breakfast places this side of Silver Lake. They both probably have a vacancy on a Sunday. A lot of weekend visitors go home. We can call them for you."

Margaret said, "Come in." The reluctance in her voice was clear. Fred growled. The fellow remained by the door as she closed it.

He was clean shaven, hair cut short to near military length, well spoken and clearly ill at ease being there. I figured him to be in his late thirties. I felt for him a little. I've broken down myself in difficult circumstances. Because Margaret did not seem to want to say anything else to him, I did. I reiterated all of this a day later, so the facts are still clear.

We exchanged names. He said his was Robert Smith. I asked, "Where're you from?"

"Greenwich, Connecticut. Just up looking for a place to spend Labor Day."

"Alone?"

"Well. Yeah. For now. I might get lucky. Who knows?"

He had the manner of someone who found it fairly easy to make his own luck.

I said, "Silver Lake is nice."

"Nah. I was up in through Crawford Notch and North Conway earlier. A little too rustic for me. I was told there was some kind of music thing going on in Wolfeboro. That sounds more like my speed."

Margaret called down to The Moon Rest Inn while we spoke.

She interrupted, "They have a room for $65. Is that good?"

"It's fine. How far a walk is it?"

I spoke up, "I'll drive you. It's right next to the Sunoco station. They can get your car running again in the morning when they open."

His eyes kept going back Margaret.

"I hope so. It's an old Jag. No one ever seems to have the right parts."

I said, "They'll be able to help you. They seem to be able to fix anything."

The fellow's eyes were now fixed on Margaret. He said, "Do I know you from someplace?"

She shook her head a little too quickly. "I don't think so. I don't think we've met."

"Right. Well . . ." He stepped aside as I opened the door and then followed me out. When he was in my pickup he was quiet for only a moment.

"Your wife looks very familiar to me. I don't know why. She must look like somebody."

I thought a little misdirection was in order, "I'm the one who usually gets that. People tell me I look like George Clooney."

He actually laughed before answering. "Clooney! You gotta be kidding. I've met Clooney. You don't look anything like him. And he's younger, a lot younger."

I was a little hurt by the added information. I suspected he meant it that way. But there was other information in his answer.

I asked, "You've spent time in Hollywood?"

In the dark of the cab I could not watch his face but he hesitated just long enough to make me think he was not giving me a straight answer.

"I spent some time there, a while back."

"Nice. I'd like to live in Southern California someday."

"Too much traffic. No fun anymore. Just the traffic."

In the dark beyond my headlights, the hunter green Jaguar parked to the side of the road lost its color. He hopped out and grabbed a leather duffle from the back seat, before slamming the door.

"Damn car. I had a Mercedes 300 before this one. That was nice. But this drives better. It's a pain in the ass though. There's a crack somewhere, I think. Everything is electronic these days. You get a crack in a circuit board and they can't find it. Pain in the ass."

With the truck door open he put the bag on the seat and unzipped it to reach in.

It was just then that a State Trooper car slowed as it passed us. I waved.

He repeated the words, "Pain in the ass," for a third time, zipped the bag again and climbed in. He was silent then, and we were at The Moon Rest in under five minutes. As he got out and said, "thanks for the lift," and reached over to shake my hand. I have no idea what he thought of me, but I thought his hand was soft. For a man as muscular as he clearly was, he was not used to doing much in the way of manual labor.

Back at the house Margaret was in a funk. She admitted she had lied.

"I know his face. I don't know who he is, but I know his face. He certainly knew me. Right from the moment I opened the door, he knew me. Acting like he wasn't sure was . . . Acting. He's an actor, maybe. I think I knew him in Hollywood. I don't remember his name."

After noon the next day I drove down to the Moon Rest to see how our visitor had gotten along. But he was long gone. His car was evidently fixed earlier that morning and he had left immediately.

I walked around to the Sunoco to see just when that was. I think I was also going to make sure of his name. The mechanic there said no one had asked for him to look at a Jag. He never liked looking at Jags anyway.

13.

As I mentioned before, fewer than 1% of the population of Carroll County are African American. That next afternoon I had reason to think the statistic might need adjustment.

I was hoeing in my garden a little late because the sun had just fallen behind the near trees and that offered a slight but needed relief from the heat. I removed half a dozen very ripe tomatoes that I'd neglected the day before and pulled a sack of green beans that were a little young but looked too good to leave behind. A car pulled up on the road at the front, one of those small white rental cars you get at airports, and out of it came a large and overweight black man wearing baggy brown slacks, and a white shirt soiled at the gibbous rounding of the front by the fresh drippings from a chocolate ice cream cone. He came down the slope toward me in no apparent hurry. He seemed not to appreciate the fact of the heat, sweating profusely, and breathing in a labored fashion that might even have been for some affect. Perhaps a play for pity. As he got closer I judged that the shirt had probably needed changing the day before in any event.

Nor was he in any rush to say hello, so I kept hacking at the ground in my ongoing effort to keep it loose like the book said. I'd long since discovered another drawback to having my garden set in the depression of the old barn foundation. Water ran in but did not run out as easily. The remainder dried up there and hardened the soil to a brick-like consistency wherever I'd failed to keep up with the matter.

The heaving fellow with the baggy slacks and dirty shirt appeared content to watch me so I kept working. My thought was that he would grow impatient and finally speak but he didn't. He just watched. He sized up the house. He surveyed the land around us with his eyes and looked squarely into the faces of Harold's cows, all twelve of which were just across the wire in the open field hoping I was going to toss something else their way that I'd pulled loose from the broken soil.

My own curiosity got the better of me.

"What can I do for you?"

"You are James McNeill?"

The thought ran through my head that he was a process server. Had my ex-wife found some hidden asset she hadn't tapped years before? Then I thought of my son. Had he hurt himself? I knew he'd been jumping out of airplanes. Then it flashed across my mind that the fellow was a cop and he was there to tell me my father's driving had finally accomplished what nature could not.

The last guess was almost half right.

"My name is Bill Reed. William R. Reed, when you check up on me. I used to work for the Los Angeles Police Department. Detective. Investigator. I'm officially retired now."

He reached out a sweaty hand that was easily larger than my own. Not soft. Reminded me of my father's.

"Hello. Well, you found me. I did indeed write the script for *Parson's Way*. I did it under duress but I knew someone would find me someday and arrest me for that."

There was no chuckle at my effort. He spent a glance out at the cows again instead. "Yeah. Right. Maybe so. But I was actually here to see Maggie Flynn. I hear she goes by the family name Margaret Abernathy up this way. The lady down the street tells me you and Miss Flynn are good friends." He hesitated. He wanted me to know he was fully aware of our relationship—at least as aware as he could be. "She's not at her home and I was hoping to find her here."

I figured, given his past profession and my previous encounters with the law, that I was best off simply giving him the information he wanted before asking anything. "Not right now. She's over in Meredith today. This is flower day. She grows flowers and takes them to a florist there."

"Right. And chickens, I hear. Do you know when she will be back?"

"Anytime. Soon. . . . How about now!"

Just then, Margaret's big Suburban pulled in beneath the shade of the sugar maple.

Mr. Reed waited in place, turning around to see, and introduced himself to her when she came down. He suggested that they should go back to her house to talk. She stood her ground, as she does. Unmoved from the moment she knew who he was.

"No. Jim can know. Whatever it is." She turned to me. "Maybe you should know a little more about me anyway."

Bill Reed turned at me as well then, with sad and weary eyes. I felt like he wanted to see something then that I was not sure I had to show him. Then he set one leg a little further behind himself for steadier support against the slope, looked directly at Margaret, and started in on his purpose.

"I am sorry to tell you that your stepmother is dead."

My eyes were immediately on Margaret. She showed nothing, but brushed some hair away from her face. She did not speak.

Bill Reed nodded at that as if she had. "She might have killed herself. The medical examiner won't have a report until," he shrugged his shoulders, "maybe next week. I don't have any friends in the New York police department so—"

Margaret asked, "She was in New York? Was she living there?"

Reed said, "She's been there for eight or nine years. She opened some sort of boutique. Fashion and jewelry. I saw that. Small little place. In SoHo. Evidently she did pretty well with it. But she was always short of cash. I think she was still playing with the cocaine."

He waited then for Margaret to add something more about that perhaps. But it was the quiet Margaret again, listening.

Reed looked at me, possibly thinking that I might not know. "Cheri Bing was Miss Flynn's step-mother."

I asked, "How do you think she died?"

He winced slightly as if at an uncomfortable fact. "I think she was murdered."

Margaret said, "When?"

"Three days ago. In her shop. After hours . . . You knew her as well as anyone. Or at least you did. Was she the type of person who would kill herself?"

Margaret was staring at the ground. "No."

Mr. Reed took a heavy breath, pulled a white handkerchief from one pocket and wiped his forehead and face. The handkerchief did not look much cleaner than his shirt.

"No. I don't think so either. But you know, we all make mistakes. She might have taken an overdose. Maybe. She had a couple of needle marks . . . But, tell me, do you think she would have taken heroin?"

"No. She was a health nut. She thought cocaine was good for you. Heroin was poison."

He nodded in an exaggerated motion that moved his entire upper body. "Right. I remember her saying something of the sort one time to me. Just the kind of foolishness you remember. And that's what I told the New York police." Then he nodded again as if in consideration of what else he should say. "I told them that, and about the fact that I'd made another very bad mistake a couple of weeks ago. Anyway, that's why I'm here."

Mr. Reed had our complete attention now, but I could not help but look again at Margaret's face. Her first lack of expression had altered just slightly. She was shaken.

I said, "What happened then. A couple weeks ago."

Mr. Reed took another audible breath, this one heavier than the last.

"I'd gotten it into my head to close some of the cases that were never properly finished up on my watch. So, I decided to look into Matt Flynn's death again—this time with some of what I've learned since then. And then I talked about some of that with a former colleague who knew most of the details. . . . I shouldn't have done that." He choked on his last words. "I have to apologize. It's been a rough year for me too, I guess. That's not an excuse, mind you. Just the fact. And those things have slowed me down quite a bit . . . My wife died last year. I just wasn't ready for that. I thought she'd outlive me for sure. Then she went and had a heart attack and that was done. And here I was just retired. It's usually the guy that retires and then drops dead. But no. It killed my wife, instead. I guess when she suddenly had to put up with me every day. It was too much."

Margaret said, "I'm sorry. That sort of loss takes a long time. But what exactly was the mistake you mentioned?"

He shook his head. "No. No. You see, my first mistake was that I decided that I was never going to go on all those trips we used to talk about. Not by myself. I really didn't give a hoot about all that anyway. It was just for Ethel. She wanted to see the Taj Mahal. That's just another tomb to me. And you know, I finally saw Grant's Tomb the other day. I was in New York and I figured I might as well go see that. I don't think it would have impressed Ethel in the least and it did not impress me. What impressed me was the memorial at Pearl. What impressed me was all those rows of white crosses at Colleville-sur-Mer in Normandy."

Having seen it myself, I said, "You are right about that."

Bill Reed licked his lips as if he had more to say on this point and was not sure of his words quite yet.

Margaret asked, "But why would someone kill Cheri?"

Reed studied her for a moment, staring her directly in the face before answering.

"Do you remember me?"

"I don't think so."

He rocked back on his leg and patted his stomach. "Age does that. I've gained a little weight. And I had a nice little pencil mustache back in those days, but it turned gray and I was not about to dye it.

Margaret suddenly nodded. "Yes! You were the police detective who was investigating my father's death."

'Righto."

"I only met you once, I think. You were with another fellow."

"Lt. Anderson. Yeah." Mr. Reed clenched his jaw against an inner jolt of anger. "He's a Captain now. And I should not have spoken with him. But I did . . . And now, well that's done too. . . . Gotta live with that. And I know you left Hollywood right after your father's death to get away from all that and came here . . . As you know, his death was ruled a drug overdose. And you may remember that you once insisted to me that your father never used heroin. And the coroner then just up and ruled it a possible suicide because there was no evidence he had used heroin previous to that one time."

She said, "He was a drunk. He was always a drunk. But he never took drugs. It was Cheri who took drugs."

"And she only used cocaine. That was all we ever had on her. With all the arrests. But she was getting that money to buy the cocaine from someplace. Somebody. Your father surely did not have it. Not then. He was already broke. As you know. And then Miss Bing left town all of a sudden, right after you did. And that was that. Case closed."

I said, "Only you don't think so."

"No. I don't think so."

Bill Reed wiped his face again. I finally suggested we go into Isaac's house. I had half a gallon of ice tea and some fresh lemons. He sighed loudly at that suggestion, clearly relieved at the thought of it, and followed us up to the kitchen. His previous dramatics were now clear to me—an effort to get the offer of some hospitality.

14.

It was Margaret who first put two and two together.

Mr. Reed and Margaret were sitting at my little metal-topped table while I leaned against the counter after I pouring the tea.

She said, "There was a fellow here just the evening before last."

Mr. Reed gave that a long straight-faced stare and waited for her to add something else. It was clear she was rethinking what she had not considered before. And I was beginning to realize Mr. Reed was given to a certain theatrical presentation. Perhaps that was a result of being so close to Hollywood for too long.

He finally said, "A black fella. About six inches shorter than me. Handsome devil. Short hair. Muscular?"

I said, "Yes."

Reed looked at me and then back at Margaret. "Did you think you might have known him?"

"Yes! I know for certain now that I did. He used to come to visit Cheri about once a month. He was leaner then. He'd show up at the pool and take a swim and chat and then leave. She said he was just a friend. But I wasn't sure of it until you started talking about all this."

Mr. Reed nodded his head with a rocking of his body and a complaint from the chair, "His name is usually Robert Smith these days. At one time it was Terrell Wood."

Margaret said, "That was it! Terrell."

Bill Reed raised his glass and emptied it to the bottom.

"I don't think either one is the real thing. At least not all of it. Maybe it was Terrell Smith before that. But he has I.D. for both. I think the oldest record we have on him is for the Wood character." Mr. Reed licked his lips again but I did not take the hint. "When you knew him before, he was just a legman. Not much better than a mule. He was just out of college then. He'd done very well for himself at UCLA carrying the drugs from his underboss, Jorge Gee, in Mexico, to the addicts they had on the line as 'vendors,' for them to sell directly to the customers. Cheri was one of those. She was right there in Hollywood. In the middle of it. She was known there. And I've spoken to people she used to supply.

I asked the obvious, "Why didn't you just arrest him."

"Because he was smart. He never had it on him. I don't even think he was ever a user himself. Maybe when he was in the Army. The discharge was unclear about that. We don't know. But he was always clean when we picked him up. His only record is for breaking a fella's nose, and once for carrying a concealed weapon. That's it! All we had otherwise was the word of a few Hollywood types—" He nodded to Margaret, "if you'll excuse the expression. Nothing good enough for a conviction."

Margaret shrugged. "You were right. That's why I left. I was in need of a steady dose of reality."

I said, "But what's a legman doing here?"

Bill Reed kept his eyes on Margaret. "Mr. Smith moved up the ladder after your father's death. Did real well for himself. When he was in the Army he wanted to go into the Special Forces. They rejected him. So he quit that but starting taking martial arts classes and the like anyway. I think he wanted to see himself as some sort of Rambo. A bad Rambo. He seemed to have found his calling. Now he's simply called the 'Repo Man.'"

I said, "Those repo guys work for mortgage companies —lease companies—don't they."

"Yeah. No. Mr. Smith doesn't do that. He's just a sort of a grim repo." He hesitated at his joke but it went over our heads. "He repossesses the lives of people who try to escape— who think they've escaped. The ones who still owe money. He enjoys it. A regular sociopath, our Mr. Smith."

"Did he kill Cheri?"

'That's what I think. I'm a long way from any proof of that. He was in New York two days ago. He was in the proximity. But opportunity is only one count, an important one, but it can be hard to prove. We know he had motive and means."

I asked, "But why would he come here looking for Margaret?"

Mr. Reed rocked back once in my secondhand chair until it squeaked with pain. "Because, he thinks Miss Flynn took the money that was missing when Cheri skipped out of L.A. ten years ago. There was a goodly sum of money and drugs that went missing. Her clients were fairly heavy consumers and paid the price. Given her own situation, moneywise, it must have been hard for Miss Bing to see all that cash passing through her hands."

Margaret could only ask, "But why? Why would he think I had anything to do with that?"

Bill Reed paused to give his answer some added dramatic heft. His voice was deliberate and calm. "Well. If I had to guess, it would be because she told him you took it, in an effort to save her own skin. I believe she'd done exactly that same thing ten years before when Terrell Wood came looking for the money she'd collected for the drugs she was distributing to her various friends in Hollywoodland back in 1987. Only her clients were pretty quick to complain that they did not get their usual allotments. And I think she told Mr. Smith back then that your father had taken both the money and the drugs. I do know that some of your father's friends had told him that she was dealing, and he'd promised he was going to stop her from doing it."

Mr. Reed held his glass up without even looking at me. He'd been waiting for me to notice it was empty. I got my wits and finally poured it full again.

Understanding at last what had happened, Margaret sat still, her mouth open with the realization. Mr. Reed took a large swallow and continued. "For whatever reason—probably because Mr. Wood was sleeping with your step-mother at the time—he had believed Cheri that first time when she told him Matt Flynn had taken everything. And that's the reason I believe Mr. Smith killed your father instead."

After a silence, while Margaret tried to comprehend everything from a moment of her life that must have seemed a total chaos in her mind, I smartly said, "But that was a long time ago."

Bill Reed nodded with his whole upper body, again making the chair squeal. I was thinking that the furniture in his house must be rather sturdy.

He says, "But neither the money or the drugs was ever found. We know that or they would have stopped looking. And we know that there was a lot of scrambling around. There was a lot a noise going on then. I think Jorge Gee told Mr. Wood that if he wanted to keep working he would have to go out and collect every dime again from Cheri's clients. They could write off the drugs, but they wouldn't take a loss on the cash. People could get the wrong idea if they let a thing like that slide . . . And we now know that Cheri Bing showed up in New York with about a quarter million dollars in 1989. That and a new name. But I tracked her down. You can use these new computers to track anything, you know. Credit cards. Bank deposits. Car rentals. I tracked her first to Memphis . . . Now, I like Memphis. I like the food around about there especially. Dry ribs. Pecan pie. Good God Almighty!" He hit the side of his head with the palm of his hand hard enough to hear the slap. "My father was born just south of there in a shack with mud chinking in the walls. And you know the air there still smells like home to me—anyway, that's where Cheri picked her new name. That and a new social security number. Bought them for an exchange of some drugs, I think. That's a transaction I could not trace so well. But she hadn't bothered to change her address while she was playing that game, so I found her again. That was one mistake that she made. Then she moved on to New York. I found her there too. And then I made my second mistake. Like I said. I told my old pal Captain Anderson about it."

15.

And there was one more matter. Margaret was pregnant.

She was 46 years old. She would be 47 when the baby was born. I would be 50. Somehow, that didn't matter to either of us. I think it must have been hours later when we let the reality of the fact sink it. I was the one who was a little giddy this time. But I was certain she was happy.

I know an editor down in New York who has six kids. The last one was born when she was well into her forties. So, I called her. She said her doctor was the best in the world. So that was the one we wanted. I got an appointment and Margaret and I drove down together. They did a dozen tests. A few more. Modern medical science told us that Margaret was healthy and the baby would likely be fine.

The real problem was that I wanted to get married. Immediately, if not sooner. I had the one bad experience behind me, but the rest of what I knew about that proposition was all for the good. Margaret had nothing of the sort to rely on. She wanted the baby, but she was not sure about marriage.

This might seem to be a little ahead of the story, but it is important because Margaret already knew and I knew it next and it immediately influenced our behavior.

At the table there in Isaac's kitchen, Bill Reed looked up at me and said, "Do you have a gun?"

"A shotgun and a twenty-two."

He looked at Margaret. "How about you?"

"No."

"Well, I'd keep those guys pretty near at hand if you know how to use them—and I assume you do. I imagine you two'll be close anyway, but I wouldn't let Miss Flynn get very far without you being there."

Margaret asked, "For how long?"

"I don't know. Mr. Smith did not come all this way to say hello. I believe he's around someplace. He'll do something. And I should go now and talk to the State Police about that." He arose from the table then with a prolonged grunt and a push on the metal table top with the flat of his hands. "The knees are no good. When the knees go, everything else sorta collapses."

With directions from me about the best route to the State Police, he fit himself into his little car and was gone.

Margaret was still at the table when I came back in.

She said, "Sit down."

It was a definitive sounding statement. I sat down. But I wrongly anticipated what she was going to say.

"I'll be careful with the guns. The shotgun is a bear, but I think I have the hang of it."

"It's not the guns . . . I bought a steak."

"That's great! I'll grill it!"

"No! I bought it to celebrate. I have something to tell you. But, now it's spoiled." The words barely got out of her throat. In an instant her face was suddenly transfigured.

I had never seen her cry before. I had to practically lift her out of her chair because it is very difficult to hug someone when they are sitting down.

All I could find to say was, "It'll be fine. Everything will be fine. I'm sorry about your step-mother but I'm here now and everything will be okay. The son of a bitch has probably gone anyway. He probably saw the situation and decided it wasn't worth the trouble. He's gone."

Margaret shook her head against my shoulder, wiping her face on my shirt as she did.

"That's not it. If he comes back I want to kill the son of a bitch myself. He killed my father!"

She said this while hugging me pretty tight, and me feeling the pity of the ages at the same time as I just as suddenly wanted to make love to her. It was about impossible for me to hold her and not feel that way, but with her crying, all that feeling was magnified beyond any sort of reservation.

"What is it then?"

"I'm pregnant!"

As absolutely as a woman can totally destroy a guy by crying, she can completely stun him with those particular words. I had heard them once before in my life. I think I felt just about the same both times. And the most interesting thing about that is, when my first wife told me, she was crying too, but for the exact opposite reason—she had never wanted a kid in the first place.

Bill Reed found us later on, up the hill on Margaret's deck, with the steak on the grill and Fred being very obedient as he slobbered on himself and patiently waited. Fred's singular interest was so absolute that he practically ignored our visitor and Mr. Reed sat heavily into one of the Adirondack chairs and sighed with satisfaction as he appraised the view over the treetops to the blue-green of the hills beyond.

"This is the sweet spot, isn't it?"

"The best. Do you want some steak? Fred will eat anything we don't manage to anyway."

He reached a hand out and scratched the dog's neck. "I wouldn't want to deprive Fred." Fred ignored him.

"Fred is not deprived, I can tell you that . . . Did the State Police have anything to say."

"More than I expected. Did you see a police car the other night when you gave Mr. Smith a lift?"

"Yes."

"Well, they'd already run those plates. A Jaguar abandoned beside the road on a Sunday night is not so common up here to be ignored. That car was a rental. Some place in Boston rents Jags. Can you imagine? And he used another name entirely. Robert Evans. They are trying to track that credit card now."

"What are the police going to do?"

"They can't do anything. He hasn't done anything wrong. That's the same reason we couldn't arrest him in L.A. He's very careful. Like I said, never has any drugs on him. Never even had a gun except once."

"But you think he's still around here now?"

"I do. The State Police will keep an eye out, but they can't sit down here and babysit. They don't have the crew for it. Labor Day weekend. Like the sergeant said, they'll have their hands full down at Winnipesaukee. He told me every year some genius gets drunk and tries to set a midnight speed record on his jet ski. Then they have to go fish the body out sometime after at three in the morning when his buddies notice he's missing. That sort of thing."

"What are you going to do?"

"I thought I'd hang around a day or to. I'm on my own budget though. I can't afford to stay for long."

Margaret said, "You could sleep here."

Mr. Reed nodded at that without a pause and smiled. "I was hoping you'd ask. If that would be okay?"

Margaret had been in the kitchen making a salad. She was standing now at the screen.

"This couch in the living room turns into a bed. It's pretty good. But the sun comes right in every morning at dawn. You won't be able to sleep much longer than that. I was going to stay down at Jim's tonight, anyway.

"That would be mighty fine. That would be just right."

16.

I had no idea of the actual time when I heard the first shot. Fred was down at Isaac's with us and he tried to go through the front door first without opening it. That alone would have been enough to wake me up. Then there was another shot. The sound was not that close but I was fairly certain of the direction. I got on my pants and boots, told Margaret to call the State Police and then bolt the door and go into the cellar with the twenty-two. Fred went by me when I opened the door to leave and was gone into the dark.

The moon was down and the sky hazy, but there was enough starlight to see my way as I went up across the open field toward Margaret's house. There were no more shots. I was probably fairly conspicuous in my headlong dash and should have been more careful but before that thought sank in, I saw a large figure standing still at the top of the drive. I let him know it was me coming on.

Bill answered, "He was here."

"Did he have a gun?"

"I don't know. What you heard was me."

He held up a revolver in his hand that I had not seen before.

"Did you hit him?"

"Don't know that either. He was moving pretty good. It surprised the shit out of him to find me there in the living room. Practically squealed. Don't know how he got in but he was quiet about that. Or else I'm losing my ears along with everything else."

At that moment we heard Fred somewhere down the road in a fight. His growl was unmistakable and then just as quickly there was silence. Bill Reed and I were already running in that direction.

I found Bob and Marie Ferrell both out on the road near their house when I got to where Fred lay panting on the gravel at the side. Marie was talking to the dog in tones I did not like.

Blood glistened from the pavement. Just then at the bottom of the road the lights of a car came on and the wheels spun and scattered gravel.

Bill shouted, coming up from behind me. "Call the police quick!"

Margaret said, "I've already done it," as she came up behind him, in feet bare and wearing only her bathrobe. The twenty-two rifle fell to the ground with a clatter as she bent over Fred. His ears moved to her voice. In the flashlight it was clear that his wound was from beneath. Perhaps from a knife. She said, "Call the vet. Wake Molly up, damn it!"

We lifted Fred into the back seat of Marie's car. Margaret, still dressed only in her robe, went with her to the vets. The State Police came up, first one car and then another, light's twirling as Marie and Margaret were driving down.

It was Bob Ferrell who made the first observation concerning the blood.

"I don't think that's all from Fred." It was clear that Bill had hit something.

The State Police found that Margaret had left the window in the laundry room open when she had washed Bill's shirt and other things that evening. They walked the stretch of field between the house and the road several times until it was nearly dawn while I went back to Isaac's and got a few more clothes on myself and some things for Margaret and drove to the vet's.

Fred was alive. I knew that the moment I opened the door. Margaret smiled at me when I came in.

We got back to the house about seven o'clock, both of us totally played out, Bill Reed was in the chair on the deck, his bulky figure gilt by the early light and a mug of coffee in his fist. He turned to us, clearly expecting the worst, and Margaret told him that the Vet thought Fred would be okay.

Bill said, "Well then, it's a better day after all. You were right about that sun. When I die, this is what I want heaven to be like. Right here. Right now."

The report came in later that the Jaguar had been returned to the dealer in Boston the day before. Our Mr. Smith had been smart enough to get himself another car before coming back to finish his job. That was the reason the State Police had not been able to stop him in his retreat.

A question I had was what Smith had intended to do when he entered the house with a dog there and me as well. He might have assumed I would have a gun. The dog might bark. I could have shot him. We could not know the answers but Bill had a thought.

"He has shot people before without the sound of it being reported. He might have a silencer on his weapon. We know he had a knife. I expect he always moves fast. He would have been in and out of the house in less than five minutes. And you were never trained for close combat. You would likely have never known what hit you. . . . What is it you said you did in the army?"

"Intelligence."

"Right. Well, my intelligence assumes he had a plan of some sort. It just didn't include me. But now he knows I was there. He might even have recognized me. I said something before I fired. I've spoken to him before. And he had some sort of mask on so he had himself covered, so to speak."

Bill stayed one more day. A 'vacation day' he called it, spent walking over most of the hill from Isaac's house on down to Harold's barn, looking at everything he found of interest. Harold keeps turkeys and Bill Reed later told me with a straight face that he had been adept at their language for some time and greatly enjoyed the conversation. I liked his sense of humor.

I couldn't write under the circumstances and spent time splitting some logs I had dumped in the driveway the week before in preparation for a cold weather. Not having the back of an Abe Lincoln, I was using an electric log splitter I'd rented at Home Depot and Bill found the device fascinating and split several sections himself before moving on. The machine worked fine but it was still more effort than I had the energy for. Before mid-afternoon I took the chance for a doze. That was when Margaret took the opportunity to go shopping alone. This was an act of defiance against me having to be with her. But she was fine.

246

17.

Bill Reed was an interesting fellow. I imagine being a police officer for nearly thirty years would alone be a cause of that, but there was more. He was a 100% California boy. Specifically Southern California. He had grown up in the suburbs of L.A. near Long Beach. Served as a Master-At-Arms in the U.S. Navy out of Long Beach Naval Station. Had gone to college at USC. He had lived in the same three-bedroom house in Inglewood for most of his time on the force. I know he had a small boat and a trailer which he hooked up to a big second-hand Ford Crown Victoria and used that for fishing at Lake Tahoe once a year. Or had done, previous to his wife's death. He had three children, two girls and a boy. The oldest girl was presently a Senior Chief Petty Officer and finally thinking about getting married. His youngest daughter was already married and had three kids and lived in Santa Barbara. His son worked for a computer company in San Jose. But all that wasn't the interesting part. Not to him, at least. What he thought most interesting about himself was the fact that he was, " the best French Chef in Southern California. Bar none."

This was a sort of self-assumed pride I did not often encounter and it needed immediate challenging. I should have guessed from his weight problems that he was at least half right. It appeared that his one recreation during the year since his wife's death had been cooking. "She never liked to cook. She liked things that came in packages and cans. You can call that a fault, given her other abilities, but it caused me to learn."

The second evening he was with us he went down to my little garden and pulled an assortment of everything I had, added a collection of fresh mint and herbs that Margaret grew near her back door, and made us the best meal either Margaret or I had ever had using store-bought chicken when Margaret refused to sacrifice one of her own to the cause. Fred was not yet home from the animal hospital so he was not driven to further madness by the smell of it.

A phone call from California came shortly after we had finished with the main course and he presented us with a pastry dessert using strawberries, almonds and a custard cream on a shortcake and added to that the word that Mr. Smith had just been seen back in L.A. on his old stomping grounds. Apparently, he had injured himself but it was not clear how.

I had the pleasure of doing the dishes while Bill and Margaret sat on the deck and chatted about the future.

Getting married again was an upheaval. Likely more for Margaret, but she did not complain as much as I did. Neither of us was religious, nor did we have any interest in having our arrangement officiated over by a government factotum. My parents were nominal Catholics, as Margaret's father had been. But the Abernathy family had been Congregationalists. In honor of Isaac we talked to the Congregational Minister in Conway and made the arrangement for October. The upheaval was in the matter of reconsidering everything in your life from the status of 'mine' to 'ours.' Reweighing all your priorities in terms of what is best for the both of you—or for the three of you, as the case was. Or simply reconstructing your habits so that you could find your toothbrush when you wanted it.

Bachelorhood is an inferior state of being in every respect. Suddenly you see the pettiness of it and wonder how you managed to get by. When you decide to get married you are in fact 'married' long before the legal settlement. It's a state of mind. Once accepted, it is done. You can't be a little bit pregnant or a little bit hitched. It's just that very sense of being which you feel bereft of after a divorce. And I image that was part of the feeling of loss felt by Bill Reed following his wife's death. It was my estimate that the modern attitude toward marriage as a mere convenience to clothe your periodic nakedness was very much responsible for a lot of the mischief in society at large.

I had lived as a bachelor for about as long as Margaret had lived in New Hampshire. This fact seemed somehow very important to my assessment of our situation, but despite my facility with words, I was unable to put my pen on the actual reason why these two disparate facts were equivalent.

One change was immediate. I officially moved up the hill to Margaret's house and only used Isaac's each morning for my writing. For her part, Margaret set up a studio space in the dining room there to use in the afternoons, and on the better days would work on the rebuilt side porch, which was still roofless, in order to catch the later sun. She expressed no interest in a 'northern light.' And perhaps with some encouragement from me, or at least by my example, she began to work down there for hours. She was surprised she had never thought of it before.

When Fred came back he was not particularly happy with this arrangement and I was sure his moping around then for a week or so had more to do with my still being around than his recovery from a stab wound which had missed his heart by a quarter inch.

Bill's advice to me concerning marriage had been quite fatherly. "Learn how to bend your tongue back in your throat without gagging. That'll keep you from arguing. She's going to be right anyway. Get used to it."

He left the next morning after our grand meal, following coffee and a final 'sit-down' on the deck. He said he would keep in touch and try to keep an eye on Mr. Smith.

That was the last we saw of him.

In October—one great and glorious October day when I had actually thought of Bill Reed that same morning, sitting in the Adirondack chair and gazing out over the splendor of autumn with a mug of coffee in his hand—I received a call from the State Police. They had been trying to contact Bill on a follow-up. Their news was that Bill Reed had been found dead at his house in Inglewood. An apparent heart attack.

Like beauty, all that color was not enough. Not for warmth, certainly. It was a balmy day, but we both were properly chilled by the news.

Margaret asked simply, "What are we going to do?"

I had said only what I could, "Whatever we have to."

18.

When we had driven to New York to see the doctor for Margaret, I detoured over to Brooklyn and opened the safe deposit box I had at the bank. The reason was not only for the pistols. There was a ring there. It was my grandmother's engagement ring. I had been saving it for my son, but I had an interim purpose for it now.

That ring is a story in itself. Legendary in the small way of family tales. My grandfather, Daniel 'Buck' McNeill, had bought it at a hock shop in Hong Kong with his last U.S. gold piece—evidently all the pay he had left from one job or another

—and before he had even met my grandmother, simply because he thought it was the kind of ring he should have just in case. He met her that very year. She had worn it until my father had brought my mother home to meet his parents. They had sized that situation up correctly and my grandmother had taken the ring off her finger and given it to Dad then and there. He had immediately presented it to my mother right in front of them. When I came home at last with Sandra and introduced her to my parents, mom had removed the ring again and passed it to me. Sandra tried it on. She even wore it for a while, but then put it away as too old fashioned. During the divorce, I had asked for it back and she had refused. It was my son, Dan, then twelve years old, who had heard that argument and after I left, had told her he wanted it. I am not sure exactly what he said to her but she gave it to him. He then gave it back to me.

I told this story to Margaret in the truck as we drove and had her slobbering like Fred, but with tears. It was only the second time I had seen her cry. Then I gave her the ring.

Margaret agreed to learn how to shoot a pistol. This did not require the persuasion I thought it might. The reality of our situation had sunken in. We practiced at the range I'd set up in the field just below the garden. She preferred the 9mm Smith and Wesson and got fairly good with it in less than a week.

The joke there was that she hit the bull's eye the very first time she pulled the trigger. I never did, no matter how I compensated. And after hitting the target where she wanted, she always said, "Puckoo," and blew the imaginary smoke from the end of barrel. I told her I only knew one other person who ever used that made-up word for the sound of a gun firing. My mother.

Between that, the .32 Colt Police Special, a few rounds with the shotgun and the twenty-two, we burned almost two hundred dollars in ammunition before Thanksgiving.

The apples were ripe by late September and we had a barbeque in the yard close by the trees and invited anyone who hadn't already had enough of their own to come. Everyone in the neighborhood had apple trees. But everyone came none-the-less. For the barbeque.

Our marriage was witnessed by my son, Dan, who wrangled himself a week's leave of duty and was Best Man, and by my parents who flew up from Florida for the occasion. They were clearly very happy for both of us. Dad took more pictures than I thought we would ever have the patience to look at. Dan had to get back, but my parents stayed in Isaac's house for the week. Harold Jenks also attended, as well as Bob and Marie Ferrell, Terry Bills and Georgina Greider, and Ellen Macomber (who was Bridesmaid and several times repeated the fact to all assembled that it was she who had brought us together) and by Fred who had received a special dispensation from the Reverend to attend.

Nevertheless, the event felt dampened by the news about Bill, and I know I looked at Margaret several times that day and saw the same thought in her mind.

My father's wedding gift to us was the price of a trip to Italy, by steamship. In fact, it was possibly one of the last of its kind and operated by a Polish company which had resurrected a ship built prior to the Second World War and, I thought brilliantly, had named it the *Joseph Conrad*. The Ferrells took Fred in custody while we were gone.

19.

The excitement of our return was short-lived. Fred was in full health again and after a month of being unrestricted while in the care of the Ferrells, was difficult to command on the first day or two. As good a trip as it was, our emotions had been tied to getting back, and this was spoiled almost immediately by the evidence once again that someone had been in the house while we were gone.

This time his visit was less subtle. He clearly wanted us to know he had been there—as if the intention was to spoil any happiness we felt. He had made himself a pot of coffee and eaten some canned tuna fish and left the tin on the table. And he had slept in our bed.

I called the State Police and they came and took fingerprints where they could but Mr. Smith had worn gloves, as he always did.

The conjecture of Sergeant Geddes, who had spoken with Bill Reed several times before and was well aware of the case, was that Mr. Smith had come to get the job done at last and, finding us gone, had reacted with anger. There was petulance in his leaving evidence of his visit. But there was nothing they could really do. The Sergeant's prediction was that Mr. Smith would return yet again. Given the perverse temperament of the man, he might even choose a holiday like Thanksgiving or Christmas. The Sergeant said he would pass the word on to the L.A. Police and perhaps they would be able to keep some sort of watch. At least enough for a heads up that he had left the area again.

Sergeant Geddes was oddly enthusiastic about our prospects. He was young, under thirty, and was not yet worn down by the process, I suppose. Unmarried, he also appeared to have more time to spend. He was ex-military, as so many of the cops I have met were, and still kept his hair cut short and worked out daily at a local gym. Importantly for me, he was willing to conjecture aloud about Mr. Smith from the profile of whatever evidence he had, and this prompted me instead to form a model of the Sergeant that first week we were back, with the hope of using him in a story someday when a good plot thickened. It was difficult, in fact, not to suppose the sort of relationship that a young fellow like Geddes might have had with an older partner such as a Bill Reed. The problem there was only in avoiding the caricatures in every half-baked Hollywood buddy movie I had ever seen.

With several other police still checking around the premises, the Sergeant took the time to bring us up-to-date.

"You should know that the medical examiner in L.A. has determined that Bill Reed did not die of a natural heart attack. It was chemically induced."

It was Margaret who said, "Damn!"

I had little to add to that sadness.

His thoughts about Mr. Smith were instructive.

The man was obviously smart. "Quick" he called him. But just as clearly plagued by the character flaws that dominated his life—and his kind. He fed off the faults of others, "like a maggot in a wound." I thought that characterization was apt. Sergeant Geddes had read the L.A. Police report. Geddes had even researched a little about the drug cartel of which Mr. Smith's boss, Mr. Jorge Gee, was a ranking member.

Sergeant Geddes advised us, "The common sense belief among these people was that everyone was corrupt, and that there was no innocent party in any transaction to be concerned over. Advantages must always be taken. Anyone who left money or opportunity on the table was a fool. Emotions were not to be trusted, and those who displayed that weakness were to be avoided or eliminated. Anger was the sole exception. Anger could be channeled. And Mr. Smith is always angry."

The Sergeant sat in the same chair on the deck that had once been occupied by Bill Reed and made his predictions and added to that some of the motivations that might matter.

Geddes speculated, "Cheri Bing had betrayed Robert Smith. He should not have allowed that to happen, but once it did, it was his responsibility to take care of the matter. But he had let emotion blind him to necessity. He probably liked her. Worse, she was likely the sole witness that tied him to the murder of Matt Flynn. As for Margaret, it didn't matter any longer whether Smith believed she'd taken the drugs or the money. He'd failed to take care of business. It was a loose end. As long as she was alive—now, as long as both of you are alive—you're a link to his past actions and things he might still be held accountable for—either by the police or by the cartel. And the cartel could care less, you understand, unless it caused unwanted friction in their bailiwick.

"I think what Bill Reed told you will still be true. And I think Smith lingered here while you were gone to make a statement. But he wouldn't do that again. He'll plan his moves differently the next time and be here and gone before any trooper can respond to an alarm. He hasn't survived this long in a nasty business by being careless."

This was not encouraging.

"Why do you think we can survive it then?"

"Because you know it. And we know it. You know what he'll do when the time comes. You can prepare for it."

"How?"

"Think it through. You write stories? What would you do in his place?"

This is actually a thought I had considered multiple times—pretty much on any night when there was an odd sound to awaken me. Margaret would always be awake then as well.

Taking the part of Mr. Smith, I said, "For one thing I wouldn't be caught again on foot. I wouldn't walk up that road. I would just drive right in."

"Bingo to that! That's what I'm talking about. Now, if you know that, there are ways to react. If he thinks you'll be expecting him to be sneaking around again, he'll think you won't be prepared for him to drive right up to the house. But that's the only way he can be done and outta here in minutes. Right?"

"Right."

"What else?"

"He'll cut the lines."

"Well, he's probably seen you have a generator that'll come on if he cuts the power, and he might even cut that line as well, but certainly the phone lines—you gotta figure those are dead. He could accomplish that much anywhere along about three miles of road. As for the generator, he could even turn that off with a finger. Listen. We are going to give you a panic button for this. A radio alarm. It's like an SOS. And it has its own battery, so it'll work, one way or the other."

"But the house is completely exposed. If the door is locked, he can just shoot out the glass."

"That's right. He came in the laundry window before because it was an open invitation. That won't happen again, I'm sure—but a lock won't slow him more than a few seconds, if that."

"What do we do then? We can't live like we're under assault every night of our lives."

"You won't. This will be over, one way or the other, pretty soon. It's dragged on long enough. Because of the murder of Bill Reed, the L. A. Police have reopened the investigation on Matt Flynn. That's even in the papers out there. That's the friction I was talking about. Whoever's supplying the precious young things of Hollywood with their dope is now in the spotlight. And remember, Jorge Gee has climbed the ladder in the last ten years as well. He likes being on top, I'm sure. Mr. Smith will be in here to take care of business sooner than later, or he'll be out of a job more permanently." He paused on that to make sure we understood. "What I need you and your wife to do, when the time comes, is to stay alive—just long enough for the Troopers to get here. Maybe ten minutes. What we need you to do is just slow him down."

Given a certain reasonable paranoia, I began to carry the 32 Police Special with me all the time. Following on Sergeant Geddes' conjecture, there was no certainty that Mr. Smith would come at night. He might hit us in broad daylight. We could not assume any less. I bought a couple of nice black fabric Velcro holsters

Margaret was less consistent about carrying her 9mm. This was a psychological hurdle from too many years spent in the politics of Hollywood to get over quickly.

I kept the shotgun beneath my side of the bed. Margaret had offered the after-thought that ours had turned into a 'shotgun wedding' anyway. It seemed a proper use of the idea.

20.

There was a lot of cleaning up to do. My garden, which had already seen more than one early frost, was as dry as the grass in the field. We had harvested most of the apples from the trees by the first of October. The remains now littered the ground beneath in a dark rubble. They could be left. The pumpkins were still good and I took those into Isaac's kitchen. The last tomatoes had gone soft and rotten. The green peppers hung wilted and blackened from their stems, in scrotal sacks. I had told Harold and the others to take what they wanted while we were away, but I'd over-planted and the crop we had was more than anyone needed. I dug over a hundred white and red potatoes out of their mounds and filled two bushel-baskets that I set in the cellar at Isaac's house along the apple hoard.

I put my limited carpentry skills to use on a trap door in the bedroom, and this was another matter for negotiation

Margaret asked, "Who are you trying to trap?"

"It's for us to escape."

"Then why do they call it a trap door? Why not an escape door? Like a fire escape?"

"What would you suggest? Escape hatch? Everyone needs an escape hatch."

"How about a decamp? Or a skedaddle?"

I agreed then to calling it a 'skedaddle,' but promptly forgot.

I cut our escape hatch right into the wood floor between two beams, using a reciprocal saw borrowed from Terry Bills. I put it close by the bedroom wall on the northeast side. The windows there are high and narrow and were likely, I thought, to offer the least interest to our intruder. I framed it so that it was not visible unless it was being looked for, but we kept a rug there as well.

Supposing we were to make an escape, I began to consider a possible means of getting away. It was no good imagining Margaret running hell bent and pregnant down that slope. Given that the slope of the hill down toward Isaac's house offered the most convenient objective as well as accounting for the snow that would soon be there, the first thing that came to mind was a sled.

Finding a proper sled was my next project. A kid sized Flexible Flyer was not going to do the trick in deep snow. Margaret had a sledge that was good enough for hauling wood and chicken crap but had to be pulled and would not steer. I began to check catalogs. I asked around. The best thing I found was a nice old-fashioned wooden deal with curved ash runners and a good seat, perfectly fine for a child of six or eight, but not sufficient for two adults, a supernumerary, and a dog. But the design of it was good. If Margaret could design a house, I could at least do as much for a sleigh.

Terry Bills, being the better carpenter, helped me to execute the plan. Broad hardwood runners. Ash again. I brought those to a woodshop to have them steamed and bent upward at the ends in a very pretty curve. The seat would fit the four of us in a pinch, one in front of the other. A basic metal leaf spring was used between the runners and the seat. Two bolted rudders were attached to a pull bar for slowing down. After the first snow I tested it a few dozen times along with all the neighbors to make sure it worked. There was a general sense of satisfaction in being middle-aged and still able to have such fun.

With the onslaught of a snowy winter I set up a very simple alarm each evening in the form of a fishing line across the plowed driveway. This was attached to a cluster of Christmas bells. They made a considerable racket. The battery connected panic button was placed right on the wall above the bed and had a very small red light that glowed disturbingly in the dark to remind us it was working. Awakened by any noise at all, my eyes went to it immediately.

It was my thought that Margaret was still the primary target. This caused me the greatest concern each morning when I knew she would be headed down to the hen house, which was so much closer to the main road, and from there would be an easier target. She carried her pistol high on her waist then in a black cloth holster riding above the swell at her tummy. But whenever I said or did the wrong thing now, she stuck her hand out at me with two fingers together like the barrel of a gun and said, "puckoo," and then raised them to her lips and blew a kiss across the ends as if she would take care of the problem. The sound of that, though very cute, was not convincing to my ears.

In general we tried to keep to our normal schedules. I wrote in the mornings and did my chores in the afternoons. She finished her chores early and worked at her painting later. The one change for her was to take her walk with Fred at midday along with me, immediately following her work in the greenhouses. Each day I looked forward to the sound of her boots on the front walk.

21.

The greenhouses are on the southeast slope about a hundred yards below the house, in a wide-open field that captures nearly as much light as the house itself and shadowed only by a windmill that is less than thirty feet high with small blades that spin almost continuously depending on the breeze. The inspiration for those greenhouses had been yet another story. Margaret had no intention of gardening at first. She had never grown more than a houseplant in California. But necessity is still the mother of invention.

Margaret had served as her own contractor after getting several outrageous quotes from professionals, and as a result of misestimations had a quantity of low UV glass as well as concrete leftover from building the house. The manufacturer would not take the glass back. But in another of her sudden inspirations, she had traded this excess off to a local builder for a quantity of regular glass and this she then used along with the concrete for her two original greenhouse structures—which had since increased in number to four.

Each of these are low in profile, with gravel floors dropping about three feet below grade and roofed with a series of lean-to panels rising to about eight feet at the back, and hinged there. The back wall of each structure, as well as a front lip, is blackened concrete. A silvered fabric shade is pulled down from the upper ridge to block out the sun on individual panels. Each structure is no more than eight feet across with a narrow aisle up the backside. The plants are cultivated in broad containers which are at least two feet deep. She admitted to me, not being a business woman and never having played one on TV, that she had grossly over-spent on everything, not realizing that it would be years before the structures could reasonably pay for themselves.

The henhouse was another matter. Margaret thought from the start that she might raise chickens and looked into the matter the winter she arrived. She had read of people doing such things. She had even read a book, *The Egg and I*, about a woman doing the same thing and the debacle that followed, which had not in the least discouraged her. Someone else had advertised in the paper the following autumn that they were retiring and selling off their equipment. Margaret had bought it all, including the long henhouse itself, which was broken down into sections, and had it moved to its present location nearer the trees, just below the house on the southwest side.

I also learned some more facts of the matter, perhaps relating to why Mr. Smith thought Margaret might have in fact taken the money and drugs from her stepmother. Matt Flynn, through a life insurance policy bought during the days when he was a television star, had left Margaret a million dollars, tax-free.

With her existence in Hollywood shaken by her father's death, Margaret had awakened one morning clearly remembering her mother and their last time together on a trip to New Hampshire for the summer when she had just turned eight. This visit had occurred when her grandmother died, and she had met old Isaac only that once. She had slept in the attic where her mother had years before. She had played in the fields with her grandfather's ancient dog Theo. She had fed the chickens her grandfather still kept in a henhouse, a structure long gone when Margaret later returned. She remembered, "cupping the warm eggs in her hands and smelling them for the odors of the mother hens." She had warmed herself on crisp mornings at the iron stove and sipped warm milk laced with coffee. She had long remembered the place as the refuge her mother had sought at a difficult time. The car accident which had killed her mother had happened the following autumn.

Margaret had purchased the land from her aunt and uncle, both still alive and living happily in Florida. She was told the old house was not worth saving, but she was determined to stay and so she built her own. She had new wells dug, and new septic systems. Blasting into the rock at the top of the hill deeply enough for the water and waste pipes as well as the pilings and then building the house along with the rest of it, she had managed to run through all of her money in just three years. As of the moment I met her, Margaret was living hand to mouth. Far better than most, it was true, but with no reserve.

Her best luck had come with growing herbs. The market for that was increasing and she had cut back some on flowers and learned the values of anise and horehound, basil and oregano, catnip and thyme.

One chilly morning when my writing had run into a ditch, I wandered up to be with her in the moist calm of a greenhouse. I understood perfectly why these were her favorite moments of the day. The profound quiet alone was sufficient. The fragrances of things she had just picked filled the soft air.

She told me, "Dill makes the air fresher. And basil also keeps the flies away."

I said, smartly, "There are no flies on me, so basil can bug off. But horehound sounds interesting."

"Sore throats. And did you know that catnip discourages mosquitoes."

"No. I have never met a discouraged mosquito. Not one that was alive."

She pouted, "You aren't taking it seriously. These are remedies that go back in history to ancient times."

I said, "It's all fine with me. I'll just throw some salt over my shoulder and get back to work."

"You can use the salt to kill fleas."

"I would rather use it to keep the devil away for now."

And he stayed away, for a time, at least.

22.

Harold raises several dozen turkeys each year. These he gave names and in the quiet of an evening you could often hear them being called to the pen where the raccoons and foxes and coyotes couldn't get to them. The call was distinctive. Harold's own take on a turkey call. Over the course of the months Harold acquired a fair knowledge of their personalities. For instance, he could always predict which of them would be the last to scoot through the gate, or the first to come in for the corn. I had never known that a turkey had a personality. Just giblets.

Harold's daughter Connie, a woman who is relatively short and reminds you immediately of   all the woman in the framed photographs in the parlor at the house, but perhaps a little more stout, comes over from Sandwich to visit on Saturdays and did a little housework and drives her father to the supermarket in Conway. She was not as talkative as her father, and has a wrier sense of humor, but I got her to tell me about a few things. There was really not a lot to do in taking care of her Dad, she said, mostly just laundry and vacuuming, because the 'Old Man' spent most of his time outdoors and nothing much in the house had changed since her mother's death. He used to play cards with Isaac, mostly penny poker, and go hunting in season, but now he just tended to spend his time fixing things. Despite her promises, he was worried someone would take him off and put him in a 'home' if he let the place run down. I soon found a little irony in that.

One Saturday morning Connie walked up to the Isaac's house to ask if I was interested in getting a turkey for Thanksgiving. I wasn't sure if it was a question.

I was surprised. "He eats them? I thought he just raised them. Like the cows."

She thought I was kidding. She said, "He only eats the ones that argue. Do you want one?"

"Do I get to pick?"

"No. You get George."

"Why George?"

"Because he's the biggest pain in the ass."

"He argues more than the others?"

"They all argue. But George is the only one who doesn't know his ass from his elbow. Maggie usually gets a turkey, but I figured to ask you first this time. You were closer and maybe you had different plans."

"How does Maggie manage to eat a whole turkey?"

"With a fork, I expect."

"By herself?"

"She has friends. You may have been the center of attention lately, but she has friends."

"She hasn't mentioned anyone."

"Don't worry about that. She will. Meantime, tell Maggie that Dad'll hold onto George for you."

George was enormous. I had gotten a peek at him striding up to the pen one evening and that made waiting for Margaret to tell me about her friends just a little too difficult.

On our walk that day I said, "I hear we're having George for Thanksgiving."

Margaret frowned at me. "Who's George?"

"A very large turkey."

"Oh." She got the point. "We were busy. I forgot to tell you."

"We're having guests for Thanksgiving?"

"A few."

On Thanksgiving Day at three o'clock the entire ambulatory population at Mountain Air Elder Care not otherwise spoken for by their own families, a total of eleven including a nurse who also did the driving, arrived in a bright yellow school bus. They brought their own function table and folding chairs. The party, which amazingly included not one but two banjo players, did not break up until nine. Everyone had heard about enough of the banjos by that hour.

I was given the job of cooking the turkey and had to call my father in Florida for a few tips. His first piece of advice was not to try cooking George in the woodstove at Isaac's. I concurred. But I did bring up apples and potatoes and turnips from Isaac's basement. The rest was easy.

The gist of the situation was this. The autumn after Margaret had finished building her house and the greenhouses, she already had lots of flowers and no customers for them, so she started taking them around to give to various clinics and health care facilities and the like. At several of those places she got to talking to the residents who were most appreciative. When Thanksgiving had come and she realized she would be alone in her brand new house with no one to enjoy it with her, she had been struck with better idea.

The variety of the characters present at the tables, which were set end to end in the great room with Margaret and I across from each other at the middle, was exaggerated by the fact that they had each planned a short poem for the occasion. Something they did every year. Arising from their chairs in some predetermined order they delivered their verse with a delightful flourish of hands and inflection. Some of these were sweet and traditional. Others were a stretching of the envelope of rhyme. Included were some limericks with obvious potential for double meanings. And several were prayers. Humorous or not, they were all affecting.

A small woman with short and curly white hair who had helped with the others on the steps coming in, quickly set about distributing the plates and silverware they had carried with them, and later on had officiated over the kitchen duties, turned out to be the oldest of the group at ninety-six. Despite her physical abilities, she was also the quietest.

I pushed into a space on the couch beside her.

"Your name is Milly?"

"Millicent."

"Whereabouts did you live before?"

"My son's house."

"Before that."

"Down the road."

"Is the house still there?"

"They widened the road in around there."

I was afraid to ask about her children, or her husband. I had already stumbled on that point while speaking with someone else. The mere mention of family unbidden could open a box of memories and regrets, often centered on an untimely death or divorce, or the recounting a prolonged illness. One of the banjo players had started to cry when I was speaking to him briefly before dinner.

So I asked, "Did you know Isaac?"

She said, "Too well."

How should I respond to an answer like that? The gaunt fellow, wearing a red tie and one of Margaret's pink carnations as a boutonniere, who was sitting next to me at the other side chipped in.

"Old Isaac was what you call a free spirit."

Clearly there was nothing I could fairly inquire about there. Not at a Thanksgiving party.

Then Milly spoke back at the other fellow's answer.

"Not so much. No like they say. It was more the girls who had their eyes on him. He was a handsome fellow. What was a fellow to do?"

"Were you one of those?"

She sighed, "Yes . . . But he was too old for me. My mother said."

"How old were you then?"

"Old enough."

I figured there might be a little color to be had out of that.

I said, "Did you know Margaret's grandmother too?"

"I knew Naomi quite well."

"What did you think of her?"

"I think that once he met Her, poor Isaac never had a chance."

Milly got up then to break the conversation and moved off to the kitchen.

The event was a good preoccupation for the mind under the circumstances. I did not recall Sergeant Geddes's warning about Mr. Smith's likely perversities until our guests were gone, and the sudden quiet then made being alone there on the hill on that cold and breezy November night a little more chilling. I blamed the fact that I did not sleep well afterward on having put too much butter in the stuffing.

23.

My grandfather, Dan McNeill had been born on a rocky bit of New Hampshire soil somewhere near Exeter, a place he referred to as the 'Apple Farm,' where he had eaten apples for breakfast, lunch, and dinner; had been weaned on apple sauce and first been drunk on apple jack. This last incident, and his subsequent destruction of a wagon, was the cause of his leaving home, never to return, as well as his life-long vow to never eat another apple. This is also where he acquired the nick name, 'Buck,' as in the reaction of an unbroken horse to a saddle.

That place of his birth has long since been swallowed by urban sprawl creeping north out of Massachusetts, and the specific location difficult to discern amidst tract houses and trailer parks. There is not an apple tree visible there to mark any corner of the farm. Given his disdain for apples, I'm not sure he would be unhappy to know it.

He had run away from home when he was 16. My thrill in life at that age was my first kiss. Grandpa 'Buck' worked his first steamer out of Boston the year William McKinley became President. Though for a time he had no shotgun of his own, early on he had learned to use his father's, hunting ducks and pheasant in the tidal basin of the Squamscott River. In passing, if you listened to his stories, you came to understand that he was an excellent shot, but that was between the lines, so to speak. He never bragged. "A boast is a sign of weakness," he often said. "Beware!" and "You'll know your advantage with the other fellow when he puts up a brag to hide behind."

It seemed to me that Mr. Smith's camping out in our home and sleeping in our bed was a sort of brag. If he could do that he could do anything, he was saying. "Be afraid." This gave me my own thoughts on the matter.

My grandfather had his shotgun 'taken down' and stored away in his sea trunk at the time pirates attacked the ship he was working on in 1906. This mistake had cost two lives.

This was ninety years before I'd found my own way back to his home state for good. And there was something else for me to consider in the passage of that time as well. Something about whole lifetimes come and gone.

But the story he told me was that those raiders of that seemingly distant past had disguised themselves as traders, coming to the ship on small boats visibly laden with fruits and melons and dates. The ship had just been through a slow passage across rough seas from Goa, and the captain, an American unused to the ways of Indian Ocean traffic, had slowed to get some fresh fruits for his crew. The pirates had taken the opportunity to storm the ship from both sides at once.

On that day, Grandpa "practically fell" his way below decks to his sleeping quarters where he bunked amidst six or seven others, had assembled the gun there, loaded it, and stuffed a box of cartridges "in his pants." By the time he had returned above, the Captain was dead and another man beheaded as punishment and example for the others to cooperate. Grandpa had shot the man with the bloody sword first, and then the one who appeared to be the leader.

He had killed seven men in all that day. And he told the story to me long after, while sitting on a sunny porch on Long Island just after a little league game in which we had brawled, and he had said that what we had done on the playing field was a sad display of poor sportsmanship. "You might as well quit that game if the measure of yourselves is not playing well but knocking heads. It's not a game at all."

"We should have killed them."

"You should choose your words more carefully. Killing is no game."

My contrary nature already in gear I said, "How do you know? Have you ever killed anyone?"

"Sadly."

"Tell me!"

"It's not the stuff of idle conversation. Another time, perhaps."

"You're going home tomorrow. Please."

He said, "Not now," again.

But I was a smart aleck kid. I had my ways to get what I wanted.

"Dad said you once killed a boatload of pirates with a shotgun."

He nodded at me then as if to say the outcome of this contest was inevitable. He was already used to my persistence.

"There were seven. Likely that made seven widows and a dozen orphans. Bad enough."

"But they were pirates!"

"Foolish men persuaded by greed and their own stupidity."

"They were bad guys!"

"They were indeed that, because they had a poor idea about the value of human life. Be still now. I'll tell you all of it so you will know and not ask again."

And he did, not as a boast but as a caution.

At the end he said, "Always be ready to defend yourself in strange company. Know which way you'll go before you have the need."

I related this to Margaret all at once with as much detail as I remembered.

In return she said, "My grandfather lived his entire life right here on this land. He hardly ever left, or wanted to."

"Thank goodness," was all I could answer.

Margaret had her own interest in the story now.

"You said your Grandpa Buck saved your grandmother as well."

"He did, sort of. That was some years later . . . Her father, Parker Dean, was a 'Harvard Lawyer.' At least that's how he was always described in the family, though he had not passed the bar until after he had gone to California. That much is on the framed certificate which I've actually seen. For some years he had wandered around in the West after graduating from Harvard in 1878. Family lore is that he had even been a cowboy for a time. In any case, he married a rancher's daughter, named Bertha, somewhere near Sacramento, settled down and raised a family.

"My great grandmother always called him Parker in her letters, but Dr. 'Dean' was the way he was known to others, I suppose because of his degree. By 1908 or so, my grandfather had already been smitten by Dr. Dean's daughter for several years, though they had been forbidden to see each other. We have a few of those letters as well. Buck was uneducated and uncouth. Doris Dean was a beauty and likely a debutante. But this denial of their relationship had, of course, closed the matter for them. They saw each other every chance they got. Dr. Dean evidently had an opportunity to move into Sacramento and take over a practice and probable judgeship there. Which he did. However, he quickly fell afoul of local custom.

"The housekeeper he had hired, a Chinese woman, had fallen in love with a local brewer, who was white, and she asked Dr. Dean to marry them. Which he did, of course. But there were anti-miscegenation laws on the books in California then and for long after. Dr. Dean appealed to the higher court to strike the law down. But they upheld it, instead. In defiance, he had by then married another couple—a Chinese man and a Caucasian woman. All hell broke loose after that.

"The law firm was dissolved when the partners resigned. Dr. Dean was ostracized. Another judge annulled the marriages. The second couple had fled, but police came to arrest the housemaid and her husband. Dr. Dean stood at the door with his gun in hand. A mob formed.

"It was about this time that Buck McNeill was there once again on one of his periodic visitations. "Like a bee to the flower," he said of his courtship. He had been staying at a local hotel, and was well informed of the imminent confrontation. When the time came, he was at the house, standing beside his future father-in-law."

"Did he kill anyone then?"

"No. They threw stink bombs but grandpa threw them back. Dr. Dean negotiated a temporary truce with the police and they were allowed to put their things in order and leave town, but not before grandpa managed to put a round of buckshot through the 'O' in a placard that said, 'Chinese Out!' to prove to the mob that he meant business. Though that sounds like embellishment to me, he never mentioned that detail himself."

24.

Isaac Abernathy was literate, but seldom wrote much more than his name on one legal document or another. He did, however, write Christmas cards.

This surprising fact was revealed to me on Christmas Eve when Margaret opened a flour tin and showed me the few that remained.

Some of these had been returned by the United States Army during the war, and were addressed to Margaret's Uncle Jack, who was then in Europe. Another to Jack had failed to find him during a sojourn he'd made to California, perhaps to visit his sister there. Margaret's mother had received one at that address as well, and that too was returned. Perhaps she had moved. Another was sent the Margaret's Aunt Cornelia.

These cards, the envelopes stamped repeatedly at various stops on their way, had not been kept by Isaac himself, but by his wife. It was one of her own hair ribbons that bound them and they had been found amidst her grandmother's clothes in a bedroom trunk.

Each was a simple note wishing them well and good tidings for the season, but the real magic of them was in their decoration. They were each illustrated by a simple picture of the farm, each one different, first drawn in pencil, and then colored not with paint, but by the juice of some fruit or another—a cranberry, a blueberry, a raspberry, the green of a squash perhaps, or the black char from the hearth.

I was impressed as much I think by their creation as I was by the new thoughts I had already gained about the one who had saved them.

Allowing for the deterioration of time, and the loss of chinking and flashing around the chimney at its meeting with the roof, I think that the attic must have once been the warmest place in the house. Certainly it had been plastered for a reason. That was not an extravagance to be wasted. I understood at last that making the children sleep up there at night was not an act of meanness then at all.

But Margaret did not know much about her grandmother, Naomi Grant. She had been a quiet woman, strict in her ways, a hard worker, and by reputation, difficult. Margaret's Aunt Cornelia had often referred to her as merciless. Making them sleep in the attic was symbolic of this. And one more thing. She had red hair. The only one of the family other than Margaret to have that singular characteristic.

Curiosity brought me down to the Madison Town Hall and then to the Library again, and though I found her family name repeatedly, there was no mention of Naomi Grant in particular. It was Jean who first noticed that there was a mention of an Ossipee Mountains clan of the same name.

I found more at the library is Center Ossipee. This was in early December and the thought had already occurred to me that a small biography of the woman might be a nice present to give to Margaret. But just having made the decision, I was suddenly faced with an annotation on a school record for 1912. Naomi Grant, the only one by that name I'd found, was listed there as an adopted child.

There were no adoption records to be had except in Manchester. I didn't want to be away from Margaret for such a period of time. My jaunts had previously been timed to her own scheduled rounds and she was seldom gone on those for more than a few hours. The only course was to lie and say I needed other records there for my writing and ask her to go with me. Thankfully, that required only one trip. I had expected there to be some secrecy about the matter. Perhaps Naomi Grant had been born out of wedlock to an unnamed mother and thus put up for adoption. But instead it was yet another tragedy. Her birth mother, Amelia Grant Cobb had died young. Her father, Horace Cobb had given her up for adoption in 1917 and she had been taken back into her mother's family instead. Horace Cobb was nowhere else to be found, but his hair color was noted there and it was listed as red.

Thus, Naomi Grant was an original red headed step child.

At the Ossipee Library I found more about that branch of the Grant family. They were carpenters. Builders. They were responsible for many of the houses in the neighborhood for over a hundred years. And likely as not, they had built the very house Isaac Abernathy had been born in.

And more. Jean uncovered a firsthand account by one William Merrow, a New York theatre man with local family connections, of a hunting expedition into the Ossipee Mountains in 1932. This had been guided by one Isaac Abernathy, "a local fellow with a reputation as the best deer hunter in New Hampshire."

Brilliant! I had neglected to quiz a primary source. And this brought me all the way back again to Harold. Harold was, as he liked to remind you, young enough to be Isaac's son. But he had been around in those days. "Just a kid, but it was a small place then and you knew everyone to know."

It was Harold who told me, "Isaac went out every year and shot himself a deer. He said he liked the taste'a beef better, or he would have shot more. Thing was, he didn't ever shoot the first deer he saw. He waited. My Pop swore he would never go hunting with Isaac Abernathy again because of it. Isaac would go up in those mountains and spend a week if he had to. Then he'd find just the right one for himself and take it."

I asked, "Do you know if he met his wife there?"

"Why sure. She was one of those Grants who lived up near to Dan Hole. The deer in thereabouts used to be something. Stags as old as a man, they said."

"Did you know her family?"

"No. They were a private people. Scots. They would harvest their own timber, kiln it, mill it, and then build you a house out of it. They were an independent lot."

"Did you ever hear any stories about their courtship?"

"Courtship! You didn't know Isaac! He was not a man for courting. That's why it took him so long to find a wife. And when he found her, wouldn't you know it, she was no better.

"Can you tell me anything more about her."

"Just that she always helped out at sugarin' time and knew how to birth a calf. She's the one first started raising chicks for the eggs around here. She had a way with them. But Naomi was not to be fooled with. Just like her Granddaughter."

On Christmas Eve I gave Margaret my short account of the life of her Grandmother. I had embellished where I had room to speculate, using the appropriate qualifiers like 'might' and 'could,' but for the most part it was a simple history. Isaac Abernathy had been out hunting for several days when he first saw Naomi Grant. The first thing he saw was her hair. It was the first thing he could have seen in that autumn wood with the leaves all down and the snow already boot deep.

25.

New Year's Eve was cloudy. Warmer than it should be on that day, with fog arising from the snow in mysterious drifts. Anxiousness had been common over the months since Bill Reed's death and this had exposed an anger at our circumstance that I felt keenly about my small paradise lost. As if this whole matter were just about us, or me. The look of the fog was enough to put an edge on that. It was dark early and I knew I was alone in the house, with Margaret just outside doing something or another, and the quiet was depressing.

Suddenly there was an explosion. Gun in hand, I ran to the deck. Unnatural colors flushed in the mist above.

Margaret's voice was calm. "Is it time yet?"

She stood on the snowfield just below, where clover would bob its white flowers in a summer breeze, and looked up at me with complete insouciance.

I asked reflexively, "What time?"

"For the fireworks!"

I had forgotten entirely about the long neglected bag from July 4th in the closet.

"You like to do that when I'm least expecting it, don't you?"

She smiled her imp smile. It easily brought back that day in when everything had changed for us.

I said, "I think we should wait until midnight!"

She gave her head a tilt to express her doubt. "Alright. If you won't fall asleep on me."

"But I love to fall asleep on you."

She rubbed her hand at the middle of her coat front where it was already well extended.

"But you can't now."

"Well then, you both can fall asleep on me"

"After the fireworks."

"After midnight."

"I'll make dinner now. I won't fall asleep."

With smoke from that bit of business still lingering, a car came roaring up the drive, moving at an alarming clip.

I only had the presence of mind to say, "Come in, quick!" But as she moved, the blue strobe from the top-bar ignited and we saw that it was police.

Sergeant Geddes climbed out of his car very deliberately and walked slowly up to the deck.

I apologized for the false alarm cause by the fireworks.

He called in a report and stood with me then at the rail on the deck and stared out at the thickness of the dark.

"You ought to know that Mr. Smith has not been seen in a while. Maybe Jorge Gee got tired of waiting. Or maybe Mr. Smith has been away on other business. He has a house in Malibu, right in there with all the Hollywood types. But no one has seen him."

"What's your guess?"

"My guess is he's still in business. If his boss got rid of him he'd want everyone to know. There's no good in getting rid of someone quietly in that business. It's all show and tell. He's probably just off making someone else's life miserable."

"Is there anything I can do?"

"Just stay on you toes." He winced at his words. "You know, I don't even know what that expression really means. My sister took ballet. Is it from that? When I play basketball with the other guys, the coach is always saying that. So I told him it was a ballet term. Got a good laugh."

Sergeant Geddes had asked me about my writing once before. I think he assumed I would know.

"I think it just means to be light on your feet."

"Be light on your feet then. Keep your mind on thinking of ways Smith could get to you and not get caught doing it."

We were well chastised for our own game. But this incident gave me another thought. If the lines were cut, fireworks were a possible signal for the fact. At the very least, they might be a good diversion.

And because I had written a fair amount about him earlier that day, I made an apple pie in honor of my grandfather that evening instead.

26.

A month later, it was the sound of Christmas again that awakened me from my dream. The small metal bells sounded more like falling ice in the still hard cold of night.

My hand hit the panic button atop Margaret's.

Then I pulled the wire to the battery connected to the fireworks.

Mr. Smith had a truck. From the sound of the motor it was likely a 350 diesel, and rode high. He drove this right up to the smaller bedroom windows on the North side. Fred barked in a near continuous cry as several tear gas canisters burst through the double glass above our heads. The spray of shards bit at us as we moved, and the canisters popped on the bed and on the floor while I foolishly pulled at the trap door while my big toe was in the way blocking my efforts. We had both strapped on our Velcro gun belts first thing over our pajamas, just as we had rehearsed, like a couple ultra cool cowboys. Margaret's belt hung just below her breasts and atop her belly and was a sight to see, even in the near dark.

Momentarily hearing nothing, I tugged on the wire to my contraption once more. The object now was not to breathe, but the gush of cold air from beneath the house, joined with the close smell and grunt of the diesel, was doubly frightening and made breathing an involuntary reaction. Margaret gasped and grabbed Fred's collar for support and I went down first onto the gravel beneath to help her through and pulled the shotgun down after her from where it lay beneath the bed. The truck had remained idling there close at that side, but I was certain Mr. Smith had not.

There was no time for more clothes. In the dark, even our slippers had eluded us. My bare feet numbed quickly. Crouching low beneath the beams, we scrambled onto the snow. I heard glass shatter on the deck. At least we knew he was now on the floor above. With my free hand I hooked the cord of the sled from where it lay just under the house edge and set Margaret down at the middle, she pulled Fred onto her lap against his will, and I put the shotgun between them and started to push.

The thought crossed my mind right there that perhaps I should turn and take Mr. Smith's truck instead for the getaway. I don't believe I stopped to consider this for even a second. I am certain had I done that, and even if the door was unlocked, or I had broken the window glass, we would have lost our chance and once in the cab we'd have been sitting ducks. But such thoughts linger.

Amidst the grinding sound of the runners across the breaking crust of snow and my own gasping breath, I actually heard the first bullet that passed by my head. The first of the fireworks exploded immediately after that. And then another bullet, and then I looked behind us for the first time. The dark figure of Mr. Smith stood at the nearest corner of the deck, maybe sixty yards away, taking aim across the end of the rail. He was wearing what I assumed was a gas mask and the obvious bulk of a ballistic vest. The falling embers of the fireworks glared behind him. The third of those went off, shooting up and out toward the main road. I thought certainly he might have some night vision goggles as well and could see us clearly there on the snow with that additional illumination and I turned the sled with a sudden jerk from our course down hill in the open, toward the trees of the woodlot, if only to make his work a little harder. The sled veered and nearly flipped, but stopped instead. A third bullet passed. The minor clap of the firing in the silent night made the sound of it seem somehow less dangerous.

Stricken with my stupidity then I looked to the sky and suddenly saw what was there and said aloud, "Look up!" The stars were thick and clear and spread in clouds of light. I was sure that we would soon be dead and I wanted Margaret to see that at least. "We can see forever!"

And she repeated, "To the end of time."

It was only the foolishness of an instant. I could hear Smith moving across the snow crust behind us. Margaret tried to stand and I held her down and began to push again. Another bullet passed.

As we gained some speed then on the steeper portion of slope, I attempted to climb on the back of the rails but missed the moment and was forced to follow, stumbling behind instead. Near halfway down I heard the motor of the truck growling and the crying spin of tires as Smith first steered onto the snow and then backed it away and headed down the drive.

Would he leave?

No. It was a race now.

The driveway led off to a lower part of the hill at the far side, but he was traveling at a speed that would make up quickly for his loss. The numbness of the cold and the hard edged crust on my feet was now replaced by a jarring pain. Several times in my gallop, breaking through the surface, my feet went too far and sent me into a headlong tumble.

My odd thought, how was I to stay on my toes in this?

Margaret was at the bottom already, and climbed off the sled and crossed the fence. Her light blue nightgown fluttered and pulled against the rounding of her body and I could not reject the thought of an angel in the night. Like a bad dream that might not be refused before you awaken. But my own progress felt unnaturally slow. My legs had suddenly stiffened. There at last, she handed me the shotgun as I clambered over the top rail. Fred struggled against her grip on his collar, but she held tight. In the starlight I could see the looming shape of the truck at the top of the rise but the sound alone in the dark was enough to move us. We went immediately into the house.

We had not practiced this part so well. I bolted the door but then my bare feet slipped on the shedding snow and my own blood as I crossed the polished wood in the dining room and I fell again. I reached Margaret at the kitchen door, kissed her too briefly there, and helped her down into the dark on the cellar stairs, keeping a hold on her hand until she had gone beyond my reach. She pulled Fred along behind her, moaning. At the last second, I fit myself into the dark space of the hearth behind the kitchen stove. This was not done for any strategic advantage. I was simply afraid of falling on top of Margaret in the dark. A window had broken, likely on the door to the small porch. Mr. Smith was almost instantly in the house.

I could hear him stride across the dining room floor, perhaps even seeing the gleam trail of blood from my ice-shredded feet through his visor. I could not control my breath at first and I heard Margaret cautioning Fred in the cellar below. She would be close behind the base of the chimney now, crouching in the old stone cistern there. Smith stopped at the kitchen door. Listening, I think. I knew we must be heard. But he could only guess at what would come at him when he entered the threshold there and some basic instinct perhaps had halted him.

A second passed. Perhaps even two. Time enough for several thoughts. I wondered if he fully comprehended that the police would be coming, or that he had only moments left, and waiting would certainly lose him any advantage of escape. He must. He must not care.

He stepped through into the kitchen. I fired.

The distance to the portion of his body I hit was no more than three feet. The glancing force of it from the side punched him back into the dining room and I heard him fall there in a clatter. And then a strained breath. And just as quickly he scramble up to his feet again and lunged low through the door. I fired a second time. This shot missed him entirely, but destroyed the pantry window across the room. He fired back toward me immediately from the kitchen floor. This was a continuous spray of bullets, striking the iron of the stove in a ringing cacophony and I knew that one or more of those hit my legs from beneath and others stung my back in ricochet. I fell from my crouch. The pain was not terrible. I simply could not stand. Thankfully, he must have heard my fall though, he could not see me there for the moment. I gripped my pistol and held my breath and hoped he would peek around the edge to see.

Instead he stood, opened the door to the cellar and went down.

Our unrehearsed plan was that if he came down the cellar stairs Margaret should shoot as he came, before he could locate her position, but just as soon as she could locate his by hearing him on the steps in the dark. Not to wait. And she was ready. The 9mm fired through its load in a near continuous barrage in mere seconds. I suppose most of that missed him or whatever protective armor he wore was enough to save him from those lighter rounds. Now I was most worried for Margaret's safety instead because of the deflection of the bullets against the stone foundation. That was another matter we had not properly considered beforehand.

And I could immediately smell the apples that were hit.

I knew that Smith's night-vision goggles would not serve him quite well in the near total black of the cellar, though he would probably have some sort of red light with him. When he turned that on, he would see her well enough. Only then did I recall Fred's eyes looking back at me from my door on the night when I had first moved in.

I wiggled my body to get past the legs of the stove. I hoped that the sound of this would be at least a momentary distraction for him. As a final thought I reached and grabbed an iron frying pan from the surface above me, extending this ahead of myself. He saw the rounded shadow of that I think, in the meager framing of light in the doorway, and fired upward just then from the bottom of the stair. His bullet struck the pan like a church bell. I saw his position, and fired down.

Margret had let Fred loose only when her ammunition was gone. Fred saw the flash of Smith's weapon as well. Enough at least to see the raising of the man's arm as he craned his neck around to fire at me.

But he was already dead. I had aimed at the opening of his vest at the throat and hit him in the eye instead.

27.

The shinbone in my right leg was fractured. The anklebone on my left was badly chipped. Those were Mr. Smith's only real hits. I would not be taking any long walks for a couple of months. And I only had forty-eight stitches in all. Besides the wounds on my legs, there were twelve on my back and the ones on my butt. These were primarily from bits of stone and metal I had acquired while in the hearth behind the stove. Many of them left small tattoos from the ancient char that I could now show off like tiny badges when I am at the beach—or in bed, if anyone cares to see.

I thought I should have had more stitches. At least a hundred. But the doctor called the lacerations on my feet and shins from the snow crust and ice 'superficial.' It was my 'lay opinion' not being a doctor but having written about several of them through the years and having done an extensive day's worth of research as well as being prone to such judgments while lying down, as I was (and would necessarily be for the next six to eight weeks), that 'superficial' was a category of wound which did not adequately cover the degree of pain or itching.

Margaret agreed with me. She didn't have a scratch, but was very sympathetic. At least so long as I would be available for duty the first week in April. And she did manage to find a long smooth bamboo strip she could slip down beneath the casts. And she is very good at sponge baths.

For a time, at least until the real thing came along, she also got to calling me her "baby," or "a baby, as in "Don't be a baby." Same thing.

Between my complaints and the sponge baths, I sat on a foam pillow which would not be as likely to disturb the three or four wounds on my ass, and wrote another book. At least this one was spoken for. I had a fairly sizable advance in hand, which was a necessary help with the medical bills. And that had come about unexpectedly after a reporter for the *Union Leader* had figured out who Margaret Abernathy had been, and why we had been attacked, and then connected the dots from Robert Smith to Bill Reed and Jorge Gee. The only good in that report was a confirmation that it was Cheri who had stolen the money and drugs, which very publicly cleared Margaret of this transgression against the pride of Mr. Gee, when the story was picked up by the Associated Press and then republished everywhere else.

finis

About the author

It is hard to be serious about so unserious a subject as oneself. Though I now live in New Hampshire, I was born in New York City and raised there, with intermissions in South Carolina. I have had a fair number of mundane jobs through the years, from mowing lawns to shoveling snow and house painting—all of it good material for stories. But my favorite of those occupations was being a hotel night clerk, which is the background to a failed novel that I will continue to work until I get it right.

For higher education I attended an experimental college in the hills of Vermont (it was all the rage at the time). And for an all too brief period of about ten years I was an editor, publisher, and chief window-washer for several publications produced under the aegis of Avenue Victor Hugo, the new & used bookshop I conducted on Newbury Street in Boston for most of my life and yet maintain a semblance of here in Lee, out of habit as much as necessity.

Hound was my first published novel, issued by Small Beer Press, along with its sequel *Slepyng Hound to Wake*. As part of my revolt against establishment publishing, its sales psychosis, and the whole 'query' system of our day that reduces literature to the artificial product of writing workshops and a politically correct zeitgeist, I have since published *The Dark Heart of Night*, a story set in the New York City of 1937, *The knight's tale*, a story of the future, *John Finn*, a mystery, and *A Republic of Books*, a story of novel ideas, all of them now available in soft cover, along with the two novellas, *I am William McGuire* and *If Blood Were Orange*, published here with a few other favorite stories. *Biedermeier*, a mystery of identity, both mistaken and true, and *I imagine my salvation*, which I call a 'Menckenesque,' will also be available soon.

I hope to be publishing a few other things, and continue to sell used books both on-line and through the bookshop at our barn in Lee, so long as 'the centre' holds.

It is noteworthy that my dear family has been, for the most part, quite tolerant of all this.